BUCKLE UP

L. Lee Stout

ANAPHORA LITERARY PRESS

QUANAH, TEXAS

Anaphora Literary Press
1108 W 3rd Street
Quanah, TX 79252
https://anaphoraliterary.com

Book design by Anna Faktorovich, Ph.D.

Printed in the United States of America, United Kingdom and in Australia on acid-free paper.

Published in 2018 by Anaphora Literary Press

Buckle Up
L. Lee Stout—1st edition.

Library of Congress Control Number: 2018955589

Library Cataloging Information
Stout, L. Lee, 1967-, author.
    Buckle up / L. Lee Stout
    214 p. ; 9 in.
    ISBN 978-1-68114-472-6 (softcover : alk. paper)
    ISBN 978-1-68114-473-3 (hardcover : alk. paper)
    ISBN 978-1-68114-474-0 (e-book)
1. Fiction—Sports. 2. Self-Help—Motivational & Inspirational.
3. Sports & Recreation—Coaching—Football.
PN3311-3503: Literature: Prose fiction
813: American fiction in English

This Book is dedicated to Mimi and Ben. Your love and support make all things possible.

PROLOGUE

Savannah

He braked the older KIA SUV to a hurried stop next to a late model Honda Accord. The scorching Georgia sun was descending behind the deserted coffee shop. A burly man dressed in a starched white shirt, sleeves rolled at the wrist, leaned against the rear of the Accord pulling his last draw from a Marlboro. He could have used his sunglasses against the last blazing rays of the sun but they were buried in the litter in his messy vehicle.

Early in September, outside Savannah, a stifling humidity, challenging even for the locals made it feel like July. His shirt was taking a beating from the perspiration and his forehead could have used a towel. A tie and jacket lay crumpled in the back seat. A thin briefcase sat atop the passenger seat. Assorted paper bags from fast food chains covered the floor. His wife had begged him to take better care of himself and he adhered to her wishes-- until the stress hit.

A thin man emerged from the SUV and hurried toward him.

"Let's go inside and grab a cup," the burly man said. He crushed the cigarette butt with his foot and followed him inside the restaurant. There were no patrons. The restaurant saw busier times in the early morning hours and after the bars had closed. A young girl hurried over to their table to take their order. She recognized both of them from the local high school she had recently dropped out of in exchange for night classes and a GED.

"I'm Nancy and I will be taking care of you. What can I get you?"

"Just coffee, black please," the larger man said.

"Same here."

The Chairman of the School Board locked eyes with the principal of his largest South Georgia High School. This meeting had been arranged through a call, was not on any calendar or traceable through an email.

They sat in silence until she was out of earshot. "Ok, Dan," the slim man said, "why the secrecy?"

Dan Jamison let the words sink in. He knew this would be one of his hardest conversations he had ever had.

He lowered his voice and looked directly at the Principal. "Paul, we have a problem with your Head Football Coach. I am afraid we are going to have to release him immediately."

The words hit Paul Edmonson like a Louisville Slugger, right to the gut. His jaw went slack. The football season less than two weeks old with the Southeast Georgia school competing in the mighty 6 A bracket, the shock would be lasting.

The young waitress returned with the ceramic cups only half full. "I have another pot brewing; I'll get 'em out as soon as I can."

Edmonson did not really hear her. He held the cup in two hands and stared at the coffee then raised his head to look into the eyes of his mentor.

"What are you saying, Dan? I am stunned. What in the hell happened? Coach won eleven games last year. We were one play from State. My God the program was featured on ESPN! Help me understand!"

Dan Jamison took a furtive glance around. The waitress was at the coffee station. He had seen a manager earlier at a small desk shuffling papers, but was now gone. He chose his words carefully. "There is going to be an investigation, it could get ugly. It is going to depend on how hard the board and the State Athletic Association want to pursue it. I would like to get out ahead of this. Say to everyone that we caught this in an internal investigation and took appropriate action."

Edmonson let the information sink in. He gazed at the darkening parking lot waiting for the one street lamp to start its warm up and serve as a rallying place for the oversize flying insects. "I don't understand," he said. "Is this a moral violation in the contract? Does this involve a player or a student?" The questions were machine gun rapid.

Edmonson continued. "I know Coach is single and he likes to enjoy a cocktail. Hell, you and I have both closed down River Street bars with him. Did he get arrested, DUI? What in is going on?"

"There is a hotshot, fresh out of school, reporter over at the NBC affiliate. He has information on an illegal recruit from last year. No one lived in the district. The parent records were all fabricated. The rumor is that Coach and a prominent booster were paying for everything. Kid had a big role on the team last year. Needless to say, when this breaks the other coaches are going to be smelling blood. This kid single handily accounted for at least four wins outright last year."

Edmonson breathed heavily, a veiled sign of relief. He knew the player. He actually suspected something was amiss when he first saw the transcripts. He didn't allow himself to go down the road of analyzing the situation. He concentrated on what it would take to help his friend. Jamison sensed it and decided to not allow this meeting to end with any false hope.

"You or I cannot save him. He is a high school coach and yes this will seriously hurt his career, but, I share this with you in absolute secrecy." He paused for effect and looked deep into the principal's eyes. "I cannot have this come to light and affect this booster. The impact on him and his family would be devastating. Coach is going to have to fall on his sword for this one and that is it. We can discuss interim coaches after the dust settles."

Edmonson knew it was now or never. He briefly thought of the awkwardness of pulling the coach from his office or his home and telling him the devastating news. His anger started to surface. He also knew his job was always on the line and he better watch how he handled the next few minutes. He had a wife, and two kids who would be leaving for college soon. Being out of work in this Southeast Georgia town was not on his radar when he pulled into the restaurant.

The young waitress returned with a fresh pot for refills. Her face dropped when she didn't have more than a trace to pour in the two cups. Within seconds she was back at the station, her head buried in a tabloid magazine.

"Dan, think about what you are asking me to do. The kids love this coach. He has this team competing for a State title. He is one of the most respected coaches in his profession. We are talking irreparable damage to his career and he is a young man."

Jamison sat in silence. He concentrated on his coffee wishing he could light up in the restaurant. He was thinking about the many diners he had sat in enjoying his Marlboros with his coffee before the smoking ban had taken effect. Society was screaming for him to enjoy his peanut and jelly sandwich without the peanut butter.

Edmonson let his mind drift. He was thinking about the warm July weekend he and Coach enjoyed a late round of golf, wings and beer at a River Street sport bar. There were long discussions on career paths and next steps for each of them. They were both type A personalities who expected results from their subordinates.

That day had turned to night quickly and there was an Uber ride home that had to be explained to his wife while fighting a screaming headache the next morning. He smiled at the memory.

"So, you are saying, he must be relieved of his duties immediately?" Jamison nodded.

Edmonson thought about the last time he had seen him. He had made his way into the locker room during the pre-game pep talk before their last home game. He tried to blend in and not become noticed by the players or staff. The coach's fire and intensity always brought him back to yesteryear.

It was twenty plus years earlier when he wore the helmet and hung on every word from his head coach. The man talked of one play at a time with perfection in execution. He told the kids how hard they had worked and in spite of the other team having more they were going to win tonight. Damned if they didn't.

Edmonson stared at Jamison. Struggling with just how in the hell he was going to approach his friend with this news. He shook his head. Then he mumbled under his breath the last words from the coach to his team as they made their way to the field to start the game. "Buckle Up."

CHAPTER 1

Amist captured the sky with a never-ending cobweb. Puffy white clouds joined at the hip spitting a cold wetness penetrating the skin. The locals would have characterized it as just plain nasty for any other time. And any other time it was pizza and a DVR rental surrounded by the warmth and comfort of home. But it was Friday in late September and the two local high schools had squared off in a highly anticipated match-up.

The football paused for maybe a second or two in the North Georgia sky and then sailed in a customary end over end direction toward the chalked lines of the end zone. Players 31 and 27 dressed in white tops and crimson pants were the deep backs lined up on opposite ends. Both watched the flight of the ball ready to execute the plan shared with them at halftime. Nine thousand fans on hand waited with anxiety; now back in their seats from the twenty-minute break. The roar from the crowd displayed the enthusiasm. A barn burner of a second half was expected.

Matt Davis, Head Football Coach for the Dance County Patriots, made his way along the sideline. His team wore the traditional home uniforms. Red tops encased with blue numbers and off-white pants. He glanced for a second at the tied score between his men and the Greenwood Trojans. He had pushed them hard with his speech in the locker room at the break. Ten years earlier a chair may have flown across the room for emphasis. Profanity seemed to expire with age. Nevertheless, he always expected more from his team. The opposition had athletes but history would dictate a herculean effort needed tonight to match the depth that his county team had accumulated over the last decade. Despite of Greenwood dropping in classification six years earlier, the area still saw this is as an intense and long-standing rivalry. An unexpected upset last year of the Patriots brought a touch of doubt and increased intensity to the match-up tonight. The Patriots would still win the battle 4 to 1 for more fans in the seats.

At sixty-three years of age Davis was already the elder statesman to fellow high school coaches. He walked along the white chalked line with the swagger of a surgeon strolling down a hospital corridor. His sharp mind only handicapped by poor hearing. He kept the headsets at maximum volume. His second in command stood atop the media press box directly behind him. The chatter had been higher than normal and despite the fact that it was only the third game of the season, the stadium had a playoff feel that had almost become routine in this hamlet community tucked away in rural northern Georgia.

Coach Davis envisioned the opponent's strategy before the leg was extended from kicker Jay Ross. Hours of film study of the Trojans prepared him for the moment. He started a trot from his 45 following the ball in the air. At the 50, the piercing scream of the night came through his headset. "It's a reverse!" Davis yelled in unison with the voices ripping through the earpiece. "Reverse! They are running a reverse!" The players were on it. The offense fresh from the locker room rest screamed in unison, "Hand off!"

Dante Alexander anticipated the pending transaction between the two backs with discipline. He had lined up at end and had raced down the field almost untouched. An undersized sophomore up back attempted to slow his progress at the thirty yard line to no avail. Alexander was a senior for the home team Patriots and saw the majority of playing time as a linebacker for the defense. His coaches loved his athleticism so much that they didn't hesitate to give him a few snaps at offense. He loved the brute force involved in contact and was a very physical player that pushed the refs toward the yellow cloth each time he was near the football.

Alexander met the runner seconds after he cradled the ball and headed north toward the opponent's goal post. The loud pop screamed through the air as Alexander's helmet careened off the chest of the lean runner just under the shoulder pads. The runner's body was stood up by Alexander and planted on the back numbers of his jersey. He lay still for a moment then exhaled slowly as Alexander popped his body back upright to the roar of the crowd.

"That will cost you a cold one, Coach." Davis looked up at Sammy Parks perched atop the cramped press box. Parks had been with Davis for almost twenty years serving has his offensive coordinator and assistant head coach. Davis preferred the old school defense and allowed Parks the freedom to keep up with the latest offenses trickling down from the NFL and NCAA level. Davis believed in keeping it simple and keeping the opponent out of the end zone. If they couldn't score, they couldn't win. "I coach the defense, remember," Davis said.

The Trojans offense would sputter in the second half. The depth and strength of both sides of the interior line swung heavily in the Patriots' favor. The Trojan offense had four of seven drives going three plays and punt. The other possessions ended before they could cross the opponent fifty. Kyle Morgan, a senior quarterback for the Patriots had his way with the secondary on the first two possessions and the score was now 21-7. The crowd was enjoying it. Students huddled on the first row of stands rang loud bells during each of the offensive series for the Trojans. The roar added at least three offside penalties to the stat ledger. After another three and out, the Patriots moved the punt return to their thirty-four.

The All Region Quarterback assembled his troops on the twenty-five. "All right, we have them where we want them, do not take the foot off the gas." Morgan took the snap from junior center Ben Young. He faked a handoff to his tailback and lifted a beautiful spiral down the far sideline to Chris Ponder. The defensive back bit one step on the fake and that tenth of a second was all Ponder would need to scoot past. He caught the ball in full stride on the opponent's thirty and never looked back. Three cheerleaders did cartwheels down the length of the home sideline on the newly constructed track. An oversized flag with the Patriot crouched in a three-point stance was carried around the field by a student in quick sprint while the teams lined up for the ensuing kickoff. Seven thousand fans roared their approval with some of the Trojan fans making their way to the exits.

The game ended fifteen minutes later with the Patriots over the Trojans 28 to 7. Davis huddled his team at the midfield stripe. "Ben Young, lead us in prayer." The big lineman cleared his throat caught by surprise with the request.

"Our Father," he said slowly, cognitive of the opposing team players circled around the team. "Who art in Heaven, Hallowed be thy name," speaking now with confidence and authority. "Thy Kingdom come, thy will be done on earth as it is in heaven." Young looked toward the stands. He wanted to catch a glimpse of his parents. He was one of the few underclassman starters on offense. His game tonight would grade out later on film by the assistants in the high eighties. It was a very good performance for a young player. "Give us this day our daily bread and forgive us of our trespass, as we forgive those who trespass against us." Kyle Morgan looked across the field for his girlfriend Stephanie. In spite of the religion upon him, his thoughts turned toward her as he considered the night ahead. He caught a glimpse of her underneath the goal post, her long reddish hair shining beneath the stadium lights. "Lead us not into temptation but deliver us from evil." There was emphasis and edge to Young's voice as he finished the request from his coach. "For thine is the kingdom, the power and the glory, forever, amen."

The Trojan players huddled for the prayer slowly move away from the Patriot team. Davis stared at his team and cleared his throat. "I challenged you at halftime." He looked directly at Kyle Morgan. The attention was still on Stephanie but he was now captured by the voice of his head coach. "I told you that just going through the motions will get you nowhere." His head moved from left to right across the faces of his team. "You are going to have times in your life when just an effort is not good enough, where appearances and showing up just won't cut it." The coach paused for a moment, allowing his next few words sink in. "We can win the games we are supposed to win and lose to the teams we are not supposed to beat," he said. "That would be a good season for most teams."

Dante Alexander leaned forward. His right leg was cramping from sitting still. He stretched slightly while staring intently at the coach. "Well gentlemen, that effort won't be enough, not here and not under my watch. There will be a time in each of your lives when there will be that moment of doubt, that second of fear when you question how hard you can push. I can assure each of you that you have what it takes, but you are going to have to drive it." He continued, "I am looking for 57 men who are willing to take it to the next level, to lay everything they have on the practice field moving forward for next Friday night." Davis took a step back. He now smiled at his team. "I want to thank the coaches, very good game plan tonight, and I want to thank each of you. I am proud of you boys, proud of you stepping up in the second half, proud of the opportunity to walk off this field with you in victory." Davis backed away from the huddle. "Seniors, take us out!"

The players huddled close with their hands stretched toward the sky tightly holding their headgear. "One, Two, Three, PATRIOTS!"

CHAPTER 2

The restaurant sat next to a large twelve pump gas station. It was named the Waffle Stop though the highest selling item on the menu was the cheese eggs and raisin toast. The four-lane highway was once a major thoroughfare for the north south travelers. The time was long before the Interstates. The diner ran 24 / 7 and saw a steady stream of business throughout the day and night. Rose Wilkes was the unofficial manager on duty and had meals to locals and tourist passing through for the last fifteen years. She worked the four to midnight shifts out of preference and not by necessity. She lived on six acres with her husband off a rural road, ten miles north of the city. They were both early risers and did not shy away from hard work.

"You want a cup to go?" she asked the man in the starched blue and gray uniform. The shiny badge pinned to his shirt appeared tiny against his lean muscular frame as he approached from a back table.

Sergeant William Alexander looked at his watch and smiled back at Rose. "Sounds good, Rose." He laid six dollars beside his plate. The three eggs scrambled, without the cheese, he enjoyed with sliced tomato was priced just under four bucks and provided enough nourishment to avoid getting heavy eyed during the latter hours of his overnight watch.

Rose and her husband lived on a small plot of acreage willed down from her great grandmother. Her husband had recently turned sixty and had been with the Post Office for over thirty years before recently retiring. The two boys they had raised had enjoyed success on the football field and in the classroom at Dance County High. The youngest was finishing his college career at a FCS school in Florida and the oldest an officer's candidate in the US Marines. Alexander had known the family all of his life. He had a great deal of respect for the God fearing, simple and straightforward, life rules they went by.

"Your boy had a great game tonight," she said. "Ten tackles and a busted reverse to start the half," she added. He looked at the small AM radio perched in the corner realizing the source of her timely feedback. The antenna was just strong enough to pick up the AM station that carried the local football and basketball games for the high school. Rose followed both teams closely during her shift. She kept better stats in her head than some of the press assigned to cover the game.

Alexander smiled thinking of his son's performance and the double-digit tackles that he delivered. "He has to keep working, keep improving."

Rose was a little surprised with the response, but not much. She had raised two boys and new the importance of pushing them higher. "Honey, be careful out there," she said. She turned away and made her way to clean up the table. Alexander thanked her again and headed to his car.

The sleek and stylish Dodge Charger had all of the latest bells and whistles. The silver paint accented with the orange lettering identified to the good and bad people of Dance County that the mighty resource of the Georgia State Patrol was now on the scene. This was a Law and Order County where anything remotely associated with being illegal was dealt with swiftly. He paused for a moment admiring the shiny exterior in the moonlight. It was Friday night in Northern Georgia after a big win for the Patriots. He knew it would be fairly busy. There was always a chance for a celebration to last until the wee hours of the morning.

He had been blessed to see the game in person before his shift had started. His son Dante was attracting interest from several schools. He had played on the same field many years earlier. With his six-foot three frame and athletic tone, he too had attracted the scouts and the scholarship offers. A knee injury his third year ended his career. He didn't lose sight of the importance of education. Alexander was the first in his family to graduate from college.

He had seen the men wearing the stylish wind shirts identifying various colleges in the press box when he took his usual last row seat earlier in the evening. He had made eye contact with Sammy Parks and one of his young assistants at the far end of the booth. The older coach acknowledged his presence. The younger staff member gave him a thumbs up before the kickoff.

He had exited the stadium exchanging the usual pleasantries and compliments shortly after the team had huddled at midfield for the closing words from their coach and prayer with the students and family members. Time was of the essence. He made a quick stop at his modest three-bedroom ranch in the county seat, showered, and changed into his work attire. He liked the night shifts. They allowed him to visit practice and enjoy off season work outs with his son. He only needed four to five hours of sleep at daybreak to function. Dinner was breakfast to Alexander and always came before the shift started.

He pulled onto to the four-lane highway and headed south. He thought about the interstate and running radar. He decided to stay close at least until the post-game crowd had called it a night. The full moon lit up the roadway and he was a little surprised with the decreased amount of traffic on the state thoroughfare. He did a u turn before entering the Greenwood city limits. Their local PD had responded to a house alarm call and a trespass report earlier. For a Friday night, it was a pretty, quiet start for local law enforcement.

Alexander approached a red light and brought the Charger to a halt. He noticed a gray Saturn stopped with a green light to his right. He focused on the vehicle. After a minute, his instincts went from distracted driver to possible impaired. He turned the car and maneuvered it behind the vehicle. He waited only a few seconds before hitting the darkness with the sharp and piercing blue L.E.D lights.

He reached for his radio to signal to his dispatcher a suspicious vehicle. "Unit 73, 10-38 Hwy 25 and Roxboro Rd." Alexander aimed his spotlight at the driver's side window and exited his vehicle. There were two people inside the compact. There was no distance between the two. They seemed to be intertwined with arms and heads moving quickly slowly realizing what was occurring. The driver shifted to his left shaking his head. He rolled down his window and stared at the imposing figure holding the flashlight. "Good evening, Sergeant Alexander." A smile broke across the officer's face. He shook his head at the two startled passengers who had been caught red handed enjoying each other's company at the intersection.

"Hello, Coach Watters," he said. Alexander looked at the young woman. They had only been dating a few months. The coach was in his second year on the staff and had shared the press box with Coach Sammy Parks earlier in the evening. He did not know the young woman's name but had heard third party that the two had went to college together. She sat quietly in her seat. This would be her first brush with law enforcement outside of showing her license at a DUI roadblock several years earlier.

Alexander was not going to let them off that easy. He knew Watters ran a tight ship of discipline with the kids and he felt it might not be bad to share little taste of the same medicine. "You neglected to move the car through the intersection during the green light."

Watters thought he had Alexander at good evening. He paused for a second, contemplating reaching for the wallet and the expired out of state license he was too busy to deal with.

"Just what were you folks up to?"

The female passenger turned beet red. The top two buttons on her blouse were open as she nervously looked at the officer holding the bright light. The few minutes of passion on the roadway they had enjoyed was now being consumed with a very high price tag.

"I guess we were a little caught up in the win tonight." He smiled at Alexander. It was now time for the coach to leverage a little power back in his direction.

He pulled his one ace out of the deck. "Your boy played one of his best games, some of the college coaches were asking about him tonight."

Alexander turned toward his car and made sure traffic was not being impacted by the stop. He looked back at Watters and his date and shook his head. "Keep your attention on the road when behind the wheel, please." He turned the flashlight off and chuckled to himself as he turned away. "Y'all have a good night."

"Thank you, Sergeant," Watters said.

Alexander opened the door and slid behind the wheel. "Unit 73, clear."

CHAPTER 3

The locker room was quiet. Following a win on Friday night, the kids were anxious to change and reunite with friends and family. Coach Davis had banned music several years ago when the lyrics crossed the line on profanity and what he called common sense morality. The rule had cut down on the after game and post-practice loitering. Davis was a little surprised on the hasty retreat of his players. He always worried with high school kids hyped up after a big win. In a thirty plus year career he had lost a player to a tragic vehicle accident that still bothered him.

Davis sat behind a steel desk in an office located between the team weight room and locker area. A small banquet chair supported the large frame of Parks to the right of the desk. Davis shuffled the laminated game plan on his desktop. He eyeballed a practice schedule for the following week. "You going to bring them in on Sunday?" Parks waited patiently for his answer. His wife had been nagging him about a trip to the pumpkin farm with the grandkids this weekend. Davis looked up from his work pile at his close friend. He had been pretty consistent with having his players come to the school on Sunday afternoon and spend an hour watching the previous week's film.

Following the Sunday session, the players were required to run a mile and a half in less than twelve minutes. Make the time and you were good for the week on your running duties. If you did not make the cutoff you could count on running the same course Monday in full pads after a three-hour practice. "Coach, go ahead and send out an email letting them know they have Sunday off," Davis said. "We have a bye week soon and can bring them in next week." Parks smiled. He was looking forward to seeing his grandkids and strolling through the patch of enormous pumpkins. His wife would be very happy with the news.

"Where was Morgan's head the first half?" Davis was referring to the anemic offensive start and lack of points before the break.

Parks looked at his boss and shook his head. "He's seventeen,

Coach." Davis stared at small frame on his wall. The border was cheap plastic and would not have cost more than a couple of dollars at the local drug store. The color picture was a team from 1991 he had led to a Regional Championship.

"I sure didn't have to worry about the internet and everything that comes with it back twenty years ago."

Parks smiled back at the coach. He knew the coach was referring to an online article on the senior QB. Some of the players had made copies of the piece and taped them to the QB's locker.

Davis appreciated the recognition for his player and his team. He wished it would have come after a state title and not one third of the way into the season. "I'll talk to him Monday, he's in a good spot," Parks said. "We keep his head screwed on straight and Kyle has a real shot at a D 1 program."

Davis listened closely. He had the utmost respect for his Offensive Coordinator and closest friend. "We need to win now," Davis said sternly. "One or two losses and we miss the playoffs."

Parks nodded in agreement. "These new ranking systems look at everything that happens on the field from how good the opponent to touchdowns scored." Davis looked across the small office. "We can't have distractions. I want some extra time spent with Morgan and just the receivers," Davis said. "The routes were off in the first half and we missed some opportunities."

Parks shook his head in agreement.

"Most of the kids have the weight class together before lunch," said Davis. "I can pull Morgan and the three starters and get some throws in on Monday." Davis liked the initiative and Parks thinking outside the box. The approval nod gave Parks the green light for the extra work. Parks considered asking for more time on the offensive side for star player Alexander. The position debates had been lively and long. Parks blocked the question and thought for a moment and decides to leave it alone.

The picture of his wife caught his eye as he shuffled the papers again on his desk. There was a long stare and Parks noticed his boss's reaction. The conversation regarding her recent battle with cancer had remained pretty much off limits between the two men. Davis was old school and had a steel exterior. Parks wanted to give him a sounding board. Take the pressure of all the worry from his close friend. Davis seldom let him in when it came to family challenges. Parks decided to press. "How's Mary?"

Davis kept his eyes lowered. He pushed the worn desk chair back across the tile floor. A deep breath raced through his nose followed by a slow exhale. "She's down, Sam," he said. "That chemo is eating her from within."

His eyes watered and for a moment he looked away from his dear friend. "I'd trade places with her today," he said.

Parks eyeballed his coach with empathy and warmth. He wanted to tell his friend he would get through this and they would all be ok. Of all the injustices he could comprehend, nothing bothered him more than seeing Coach Davis and his wife of 39 years going through the hell only a devastating illness could bring. "Coach; is there anything Beth and I can do?"

A slight smile erupted. Davis acknowledged the gesture and thanked the coach again with his eyes. He reached down to the large desk in front of him and unlocked the third drawer. He pulled out a small canvas lunch cooler and placed it on his desk. He unzipped the top and handed Parks a cold beverage. He popped the can top and took a sip of the iced brew. His feet went from the floor to on the side of the desk. Not to be outdone, Parks threw an expensive cigar back at the feet of his boss. "Good job with the defense, Coach."

Davis smiled back. "Offense came around in the second half."

Parks appreciated the compliment. It was high praise from a man with sometimes unattainable standards. The coach raised the bar on players and coaches alike. Davis took another pull from the can. "To Friends."

CHAPTER 4

San Francisco

He made his way from the commuter train station then made a left headed north. The Port of San Francisco was to his right. His path separated by the expansive concrete building with four lanes of moderate vehicle traffic. The historic cable busses dissected the middle of the roadway. The wind whipped through his thick dark hair. He expected a little warmer weather when he abruptly purchased the plane ticket online only days earlier. His decision to travel three thousand miles came after a few restless hours in a recliner armed with a remote, iPad, and a fully stocked fridge of longneck bottled beer.

He wore a faded University of Georgia sweatshirt hoodie and long athletic shorts. His socks ended below the ankle. His shoes were department store issue Nike discounted with an internet coupon. At six one and one hundred ninety-five, he could have passed for a much younger man. Time never stands still. The recent three-day drinking binge made him feel ill and much older.

There were a few homeless people just past the art stands before reaching the Embarcadero. He had seen the faces during a few trips to Atlanta. He seen them in the small Georgia town he resided one hundred sixty plus miles to the south of Macon. They were male and female with all races represented. Hopelessness and despair did not discriminate. One held a sign announcing military service. He reached for a crumpled ball of dollar bills from his pocket and dropped it in the plastic jar held by the elderly gentleman.

He could have run and enjoyed a brief episode of exercise that the beer and recent poor diet had taken away. He thought he might be up to it. The late afternoon had allowed the spirits ingested on the plane ride west to run their course. He kept walking and saw the numbering of the piers increasing. At pier 23 he thought he recognized a restaurant featured on the cable food network. He had casually glanced at the program during a film session late on a Friday night after a disappointing playoff loss. The grading of his team superseded the interest in the flamboyant host hawking the diner's seafood offerings from a flat screen. The bar and subsequent cold draft beer would require crossing of four lanes and avoiding the frequent cable car crossing. He decided it could wait and travelled onward.

A small family made eye contact from across the busy crosswalk. A young girl in a stroller patiently smiled and pointed at a group of bikers headed toward the Bay Bridge. The young father held a tourist map and suggested to his wife they continue their journey onward. He looked at them while waiting for the crosswalk sign to approve his movement. He momentarily remembered the young family on the flight from back east the night before. He had been rewarded with an exit row aisle seat in coach for his west coast journey. The feeling of victory snatched away when the first piercing scream came from the one year old wearing pony tails sitting behind his seat. He would soon drown out the tantrum with a large headset and three bourbon shots on ice from a flirtatious flight attendant.

At Pier 39, he looked toward the cold gray waters of magnificent San Francisco Bay. He watched the sea lions move slowly across the wooden ties. There was momentary fascination by their ability to lay in the howling wind oblivious to the tourist pointing camera phones and gulls circling like South Georgia vultures overheard.

His lunch date in Sausalito, just across the Bay he was now staring across, was many years earlier. They had sat outside at a patio restaurant, enjoying chardonnay trucked in from Napa. She introduced him to sautéed calamari and made a futile run at educating him on wine pairings for the evening meal. She was twenty-two, had the social and business acumen well beyond years with the beauty and body of a homecoming queen. He had been mesmerized with her long dark hair and penetrating eyes that sparkled with a take down the room confidence. She had a passion and commitment to whatever task was in front of her.

They had held hands on the ferry ride back to their hotel. They were young and in love, oblivious to the once in a lifetime and breathtaking view of the Golden Gate Bridge before them. He stole a kiss in front of the other passengers with no regards for the public display of affection as the sun began to slowly set. He was not demonstrating the hardened signs of a grid iron warrior. She was far removed from her role as a conservative law student with academic performance that would make the Washington types jealous.

He worked through the fog bank of his jet lagged mind to remember if their trip had begun at the pier he was now standing. He would have given all and then some to recreate that moment in time, that weekend.

Convinced any additional sea lion action was completed he turned and continued his journey. The tourists were crowded around the street vendors hawking hot chowder in a sourdough bowl. The wind was taking its toll on the underdressed man from Georgia and the warmth of the soup would have been a treat. Pangs from his stomach erupted as he took in the aroma from the bakery. He was hungry and his blood sugar was dropping. He looked at the "discounted down" thirteen-dollar fleeces for sale in the mom and pop retail shops across the street to take his mind off the food and cold. "Tough it out," he mumbled. Nice to haves could wait he reminded himself as he crossed the street.

He walked into a convenience store and studied the shelves. A twenty something underweight clerk stood behind the counter. He figured the young man to be from Far East lands he had only seen on television or read about on the internet. "May I help you?" The language was perfect English with a tone and command that he would have love to have seen from his former American born players. The kid had that intelligence he could see in his eyes that begged the question from the coach, why are you here? The young man was polite but quickly becoming impatient. A line formed in seconds behind him. While the shops were plentiful in the wharf area, the tourist preferred the bottled water and chips to come from the nationally known chain he was now standing in. He looked at the shelf and saw the brown and white package. "Levi Garret, chew." The young man looked back with a blank stare. He did not want to cause any further delay. He pointed at it. "Chewing tobacco, brown pouch, left of the Pall Mall cigarettes" That was plenty of coaching for the young man. He picked it up, punched two keys on the register and asked for $8.37. He picked up the pouch and put it in his hoodie pocket. Perfect English, responded with a thank you, sir and moved his attention toward the next guest in line.

He stood across from the pier and contemplated his next move. A mime stood on the corner soliciting donations. The hat was low on cash, but a few donations were trickling in. On the other side of the intersection, a four-man band of guitar players harmonized a Crosby, Stills, Nash tune. They kept his attention with their expertise of the string instruments and vocal pitch. He did not see a cash jar but did see back packs and their path to this spot in time left him wondering as well.

His hotel was three blocks from the wharf and would require a few more minutes of activity. He thought briefly of his home and what seemed a million miles away. What would it take to make things right? The harshness of the cold wet air from the bay brought a last cleansing thought as he turned away. Life always boiled down to a series of decisions. The images of the last hour caught in his mind. The mime and what brought the act to the busy street corner. How four talented kids ended up singing a song from forty years ago with nothing but guitars and life possessions in a back-pack. He thought of the kid with the perfect English with a language comprehension that would probably beat out ninety-five percent of kids his age standing behind a cash register that would generate a slightly higher than minimum wage paycheck. He paused while the biggest question hung in the northern California air. He pulled the sticky brown leaf from the pouch in his pocket. He looked at the street sign instructing him to walk. He was now ready to ask himself. How did one of the top and most sought after high school football coaches in the great State of Georgia end up unemployed standing on a street corner twenty-seven hundred miles from home?

CHAPTER 5

Sergeant Alexander allowed the parked police unit to idle in the center median on the deserted interstate. He was in plain view of the oncoming traffic. His vehicle partially hidden behind towering pines for the cars headed south. He ran radar earlier in the evening and had written one ticket and a warning. The ticket could not be avoided as the Mustang he had pulled over was running 85 mph in a 65 -mph zone. The warning ticket went to one of the county high school students. It proved to be a gift for the young female for being on her best behavior and not interrupting him during his speech on the dangers of high speed at night.

Traffic was light, and this was a danger zone for many officers in a rural area. It would be easy to drift off and catch a quick cat nap. He listened closely to the radio. His thoughts turned toward his son.

Dante was a talented young man. Self-driven and self-motivated. He had done well in school and avoided many of the pitfalls of young teen aged men. He didn't drink nor smoke. His workouts were intense, independent, with little encouragement or reminders needed.

Alexander greatly loved his son and wished his upbringing could have been easier. He had separated from Dante's mother when the child was in elementary school. She did not push for custody. They had met in college and she never warmed to the idea of living in a small town in Georgia married to a state law enforcement officer.

Alexander had excelled on the college grid iron. He was on the radar for several NFL teams. There was a devastating ACL injury his junior year that would sideline those dreams. He didn't live angry. He took the news and moved forward finishing a four-year degree in criminal justice. He worked for the campus police for three years before moving home. He worked for a small municipal agency then moved on to the State Patrol.

Dante had grown up so fast. He would see his mother occasionally with a quick flight to DC from Atlanta. She came from an affluent family. She would remarry before Dante began middle school. Alexander knew this was painful for Dante as his mother never showed him the love he saw other kids receive at school or during the team events. She had made one of his games, complained to William throughout the visit on the trip from the airport and lack of hotels in the area. Both men took the complaining in stride and made the best of it. Dante had a tough exterior and Alexander worked hard taking on additional overtime to make sure he had everything he needed.

He knew Dante would be going to school soon. He knew he would miss him terribly. There was hope the state flagship school would offer. Alexander had seen the coaches at the practices and the games. He knew there would be much competition for those spots, but he believed in his kid. He knew he had the work ethic but more importantly he knew he had been blessed with athletic talent.

The crackling sound from the radio pierced the night. A traffic accident had occurred on a two-lane road three miles from the high school. This was Greenwood jurisdiction with three police units on patrol during the overnight hours. Alexander checked the north bound lane of the interstate. He turned the blue lights on and made his way toward the accident. The second transmission from the radio brought a heightened sense of urgency as he accelerated the vehicle to seventy miles per hour. "Greenwood PD on scene, we have one serious injury and one fatality," said the male voice. Alexander knew the young patrolman. His next transmission was not a surprise. "Greenwood PD requesting assistance from the Georgia State Patrol."

Alexander reached for the mic. "Unit 73 responding, ETA three minutes." The whooping sound of the siren travelled down the deserted highway.

He would think about colleges and his son later. His focus was wet pavement and maneuvering the police unit at a very high rate of speed and not becoming involved in an accident himself. The traffic continued to be light. He pushed the limits of the adherence with the asphalt and the tires. He passed a SUV on a long stretch of two lane highway. The driver quickly made his way to the shoulder. Alexander tried to visualize the scene before arrival. A serious injury would most likely require life flight. He thought about the geography and where they could put the helicopter down. He communicated with the young patrolman on the scene. His ETA was now one minute.

Alexander pulled the Charger on to the shoulder to pass three vehicles that had been stopped short of the scene. All available Greenwood PD cars were lined up on the right side of the roadway. The Greenwood Fire Department responded one of three engines and had taken up the left-hand side of the roadway. Alexander could see the ambulance in the distance screaming toward the scene. He still had not seen the accident vehicles. Two patrolmen had donned their orange vest and one was signaling the Charger with his flashlight. Alexander slowed the Charger and parked on the grass. The Greenwood patrolman pointed toward the tree line with his flashlight. Alexander looked to his left and saw the truck for the first time and momentarily froze in disbelief. He turned back to the roadway and watched the choreography in place. The ambulance was now parked with its rear doors open. The paramedics were lowering the gurney. Three firemen in full protective gear were standing next to the accident vehicle.

Officer Bill Yates started walking toward Alexander's unit. He knew the accident scene was now his. "Unit 73 at scene," he barked into the mic.

"What do we have, Yates?" He pulled his flashlight from his utility belt. Yates was visibly shaken, his face ashen.

Alexander knew when he saw the truck. The look on the young officer's face was confirmation. "It's bad, Sergeant." Alexander absorbed the words. "Single car accident, two victims, one fatal." Alexander started at the tailgate. Local plates. A lone bumper sticker read Dance County Patriots Football. He had seen the sticker every day for the last three years. Alexander took a deep breath of cool air through his nostrils. A relaxation technique he used to lower his increasing heart rate.

"Any witnesses?" Yates pointed his light toward the opposite roadway.

"Just one," he said. "He was following the truck and said a pack of deer had run across the roadway." Alexander looked at the young man sitting on the gravel. His head was buried in his hands. He was sobbing. "The truck swerved and hydroplaned," said Yates. "They never had a chance." Alexander thought he recognized the boy. He would talk to him soon enough.

He was standing still by Yates with the light pointed at the license plate. He started walking toward the pickup. A small hill next to a ravine had provided a slight lift of the vehicle in its projection toward the forest. The Ford pick-up had hit a large pine at what seemed a high speed. Not crazy excessive, but too fast for conditions. The investigation would come later. The truck was forty years old and was not afforded the modern safety features of vehicles today. Without seat belts, chances of survival were remote at best.

Alexander looked at Yates. He saw the young officer's eyes watering. He moved toward the front of the vehicle. The ground was muddy and the recently shined black shoes were taking a beating from the red Georgia clay. Two of the firemen appeared as statues on the driver's side of the vehicle. One turned and looked back at the trooper. Alexander acknowledged his presence with a nod. He moved between the two men. He shined the light into the cab of the truck. The next minute would feel like forever. Time stood still. His emotions were fighting him vigorously to surface. To show the world that this highly educated, highly experienced law enforcement officer was about to lose it. His mind raced back to the diner and his dinner just hours before. Would the eggs and tomatoes rocket up from his gut and now be a part of the clay at his feet. He turned off the light. Kept breathing through his nose. He looked at the sky then briefly closed his eyes and asked for God's immediate help.

He opened his eyes and looked back at the lifeless figure in front of him. Coach Matt Davis was dead.

CHAPTER 6

He rolled over in the hotel bed facing the alarm clock atop the wooden nightstand. There was a lamp that had seen its better days beside it. His vision began to clear, and he gently massaged his temples. He stared at the numbers and began the recollection process. There was the inventory that always came first. Watch and wallet were next to the clock. His cash was neatly tucked under the watch. That was a good sign. The phone would be a little more involved. Location? He saw it next to the television. His insecurity begged him to check the call log. Was there any embarrassing communication that took place last night? He felt a little surge of confidence that he had not let the alcohol take over, enough that he did not make a move toward the phone. He turned and stared at the ceiling. The next phase was all mental.

He started piecing together the chain of events that have now left him with a throbbing head and insatiable thirst. The walk taken earlier had led him back to his room and a quick shower and change of clothes. He knew once in the hotel he had to get some food in his system and he narrowed his choices to the food stands at the pier and a hotel bar he had spied when he arrived. He did a quick financial inventory and decided to pay the extra and go with the hotel fare.

The bar stool had become quite comfortable after four beers with an order of overcooked wings. He mostly kept to himself despite the questions from the thirty something attractive bar keep. She had beautiful long red hair with piercing olive colored eyes. She was being bold in her statements and policy set by her employer was not being followed. He now remembered his heart skipping a couple of beats when she touched his hand after she had moved him into conversation. He remembered the anxiety felt when she turned away from him and he stared at her. By midnight, a cell phone number would find its way on a napkin and under his sixth drink. Time accelerated and by his eighth beer he was feeling no pain and returning the flirtation.

Did he kiss her? He could not remember the walk from the bar

back to the hotel. He remembered her announcing last call while giving him a wink from her long eyelashes. He tried to picture the few
patrons left in the establishment. He vaguely remembered an older
man nursing a small glass of amber liquid at the end of the bar and a
young girl working her iPhone alone at a small table for two. He now
remembered, she had mentioned a studio apartment several blocks
away. He also remembered his juvenile reaction when she shared with
him how much she paid in rent. The beer was flowing. She may have
even bought him a shot. That would have been the kiss of death. He
could hang with anyone when drinking light beer, throw in the hard
stuff and he would be down for the count.

Now, the conversation was coming back to him. There was his ad-
mittance of a fiancée. The acknowledgement she was not ready to sacrifice a law career with a top five firm for a coach's wife. To suddenly
adapt a lifestyle for a young beautiful woman who was raised in the big
city would now be living in the rural areas of Georgia. Now having lot-
tery type dreams and life with a U-Haul attached versus immediately
reaping the rewards for well- planned decisions and instincts and plain
hard work. Sacrificing relationships with friends of means and dinners
in restaurants prepared by television chefs. All in the hope and prayers
for a Division 1 NCAA opportunity at a pay she was guaranteed before
she was thirty.

The coach turned in his bed and faced the drapes in the room.
The layout was standard hotel design. The no frills chain included two
double beds, a several year-old flat screen television. There was heavy
checkered carpet that had seen better days. This was simply a tired hotel chain holding steady with high occupancy rates. Location, location,
and location drove the popularity and the higher rates. Place the same
room off an interstate in Iowa and customers are disappointed.

The room included three pictures. Just enough to show the guest
they were in the heart of Fisherman's Wharf area in San Francisco. The
sea lions had returned in one of the prints. A second showed a beautiful
black and white local rendition of the Golden Gate Bridge. In happier
times and in his only previous visit, the Coach had run that bridge. A
simple jog that was very quick and surprisingly a distance not as long
as anticipated. He had been amazed at the beauty before him and all
that life had to offer. He had made love to her earlier that morning. He
remembered holding her and kissing her afterward. But that was a different time, an earlier time, and now he was struggling with his future

with a heightened concerned about his alcohol abuse.

He rolled out of the bed catching a glimpse of himself in the narrow mirror. He carried very little fat even with the alcohol and fried food choices. His biceps were still tight even though he had not worked out in the last few months. His face carried rough stubble that was pushing five days growth. He told himself that strict protein diet with zero sugar allowed him to imbibe in the adulteress spirits without the obligatory weight gain.

He thought back to the bartender. He now struggled to remember the come on she'd mustered when he signed the credit card receipt. He was lonely and drunk and was now very close to a one night stand many miles from home. He stared back at the mirror. He surveyed his thick hair and glassy eyes. He knew he needed to ignore the noise and drop to the stale carpet and bang out 50 push-ups. He knew exercise would give him that jolt, that feeling of accomplishment, and a sense of purpose that he desperately longed for but would not share with his closest confident. He turned toward the drapes. Pulled the fabric apart and stared at the street below. He saw tourists lined up and down the street. There were many making a hurried walk toward the ferries and the tours of the bay and Alcatraz. They were being hawked by noisy street vendors offering discounts to their products lining the entrances to their packed store fronts. He stared just for a moment and headed back to his bed.

Inventory, that is what he was taking. Thinking about the red hair and inviting stare from the lone bartender. How she took a couple of open ended questions and had him sharing intimate and personal details by the end of the night. He thought momentarily of looking for that napkin. The old Southern soul could not embrace a one night or momentary episode. Was she hustling him? That had happened very few times in his life and especially with the opposite sex. The coach didn't pull offers for male catalogue modeling but his attractiveness was noted. He struggled with his thoughts. Was it the booze still circulating his vessels that gnawed at him to take action and dial her number?

It had been so long since he had held a woman. Was it his fault? Sure, some of it was. Most of it was.

He tried to deter from the urges and think now about his professional life. He pushed the envelope when it came to his players. He connected with people. Said the right things at the right time and genuinely cared. His favorite lesson was they will never care how much you know until they know how much you care. His players knew the standards would be high to the point of unattainable but they also knew he loved them.

He knew how to work with the decision makers and he knew it always came back to wins and losses. There was always an establishment wherever the team originated. And that establishment wanted championships regardless if it was a youth league, a high school in South Georgia, or the Southeastern Conference. No one prepared like he did. He would outwork the best of them. His efforts were noticed early and his attention to detail made him very special. The script his life should be following had been detoured. He should be in his first or second year at a D II school in a head coach role or a position coach at a D I level.

But his fall came suddenly, without warning, and now he was here. Yearning for the touch of a past love, knowing a crack of a cold beer would temporarily relieve that pain he was feeling. A second drink this early would remove the inhibition protecting him from picking up that phone. Who would he call? Would it be the redhead from last night? Or would the call go to a forever love lost in the shark pit of Washington, DC? A plea for one more visit. A chance to see her again and reveal deep down inside he still loved her.

He looked toward the bathroom. He saw the small sink next to the door. He had iced down a six pack before he left for dinner the previous night. A twist of the bottle cap would be pleasant on the front end but bring challenging questions from his inner self. Demons. He knew he had them and now they were knocking on his door.

"The hell with it," he mumbled as he fished the television remote from the land of twisted low thread count sheets. He pointed it at the tube and brought to life a local morning news show. He tossed the remote back toward the bed and walked toward the bathroom. He fished the Budweiser from the bottom of the sink and flipped the bottle cap toward the window. He slowly exhaled then proceeded to finish half of the beer in one pull.

CHAPTER 7

Alexander walked toward the ambulance. He stared briefly at the senior paramedic working to establish an IV on Coach Parks inside the vehicle. He turned and looked for Yates. He saw him speaking with another Greenwood patrolman as he approached. He knew the importance of channeling the high emotions and keeping everyone to task. Time was of the essence.

"I just spoke with Rescue," barked Yates. "Life flight is three minutes out." Alexander nodded. He was witnessing a young officer take control of an accident scene and exhibit leadership to his peers. Losing focus during this enormous tragedy was not an option. "They are going to transport Coach Parks to Grady Hospital in Atlanta."

"What are his chances?" Yates looked sternly at Alexander

"Not good, 30/70, maybe 40/60 at best. He has severe internal injuries and needs the best trauma care and a prayer."

Alexander took one last survey of the scene. The coroner had arrived and was making his way down to the pickup. He looked for his one witness. The kid was visibly shaken and leaning on a patrol car. Alexander turned toward Yates. "Ok, you get over to Coach Parks' house now and share what has happened with Mrs. Parks. I don't want her to hear about this from anyone else." Alexander cleared his throat. "Put her in your car and get her to Atlanta as fast as you can. I will clear it with your supervisor." Alexander looked at the young officer's determined face. "Yates, we know the odds are stacked against him right now. Let's get his wife to him as quickly as possible. I'll let the Patrol Substation know. Travel I-75 South. Lights and siren if you need it."

Yates nodded in approval. The roar of the helicopter came suddenly above the trees. The large blades cutting through the rain drenched air. The pilot circled the highway three times before picking a spot close to the last police car. He skillfully touched the copter down in the street and the firemen began the task of moving the Coach from the ambulance to the helicopter. Yates' patrol car shot gravel into the air as it sped away from the scene. He hit the siren after he cleared the accident area. Yates walked toward the witness. This would be a difficult discussion. The witness was Chris Ponder. He was a star receiver for the Patriots, who'd had one of his best games just hours ago. Alexander walked up, turned his flashlight off and greeted the talented athlete.

"How are you doing tonight, son?"

Ponder stared at the man in uniform. He had kidded Dante about his Dad's line of work during a recent practice. "Your Dad ain't never going to catch me, not with my speed and my car's engine." Dante had heard banter from classmates like that since elementary school. He was immune to it. Ponder was in no joking mood tonight. He had moved from the tail of Yates' patrol car back to the wet pavement of the roadway. His eyes were red and puffy. He had been crying for some time. He had never in his life seen life taken away so instantly, so violently. The wreck would haunt him for many years. He immediately lied to Dante's Father with a childish sniffle. "I'm ok," he stuttered.

"What did you see, son?"

Ponder looked at the truck for just a second. He made a feeble attempt to clear his throat. "I was headed home, and I saw Coach's truck in front of me." I remember complaining to myself how Coach was driving so slow. I mean he's always on our asses about moving fast in practice yet he's driving this old truck like forty miles an hour." Alexander showed empathy for the child and nodded for him to continue. "We rounded the corner and these deer moved from the side into the road. There must have been six or seven of them. Coach swerved hard and all of a sudden he's headed toward the woods." Ponder paused as the scene he was about to describe brought back a moment of sheer terror. "I couldn't believe it. They hit the tree and the back end of the truck went high into the air." "There was smoke at first, I thought there was a fire. I slammed on the brakes and ran toward the truck. Coach Davis wasn't breathing and Coach Parks, he was hurt bad, I mean bad."

Alexander listed intently. "What happened next, son?"

"Once I saw there was no fire, I ran back to my car and called 911. The police were here in just a couple of minutes." Ponder looked at Alexander hoping the father figure before him would take back the previous scene and make it all better. "They're both dead aren't they?"

Alexander helped the boy to his feet. "Listen, son, what you saw here tonight, no one should have to see. I am very sorry to say we have lost Coach Davis, Coach Parks is in very serious condition and they are taking him to Atlanta." Alexander continued. "What we need to do now is pray for both these families." He turned toward Ponder's car. "Would you like for me to have one of the officers drive you home?"

Ponder consider the offer. This gifted athlete with the chiseled frame and striking presence had been reduced to a small child emotionally. "That's ok; I am going to call my mother."

Alexander told Ponder to not share the details of the accident with anyone outside of his family. "We have notifications to make, son," he said. Alexander shared with him a final good night and handed him his card with his phone number to call him if he could help in any way. Ponder nodded and made his way toward his car.

Alexander turned his attention to Mary Davis. He knew what was ahead of him. The shock of receiving news that a loved one, a spouse, had been tragically killed is devastating. He thought of her illness and knew the family was struggling with her cancer prognosis. He knew the same direction he had given Yates had to be followed. He gave some last-minute instructions to the Greenwood PD and made his way to his car.

It took six minutes to get to the Davis house. A dirt road approximately the length of three football fields separated the house from the main road. He knew the property well. His thoughts drifted to many years before when he made his way up the same road to share with his coach the news he had received a scholarship offer. He remembered how the Coach took on a different personality that day. The look he had in his eyes as if Alexander had given him the highest in career satisfaction. How the man known for tough talk and what seemed like unattainable standards reached out and gave one of his earliest star players a hug. It was a father son type moment that he had never forgotten.

Three lab retrievers ran toward the State Patrol vehicle and interrupted the soothing memory. Alexander killed the engine and sat momentarily in the car and thought about the life changing, never be the same again, words he was about to deliver. He whispered a prayer to himself and asked for God's support for Mary Davis.

He looked at the two cars in the driveway. He immediately recognized the older model Cadillac. The Coach and his wife always arrived in style to local events that requested a quick speech, or fundraisers for the school, and of course being church fixtures. Mary had been the primary driver of the Caddy. Coach Davis loved his truck. A second vehicle he did not immediately recognize. A new Camry with Tennessee plates was parked next to the Cadillac.

A porch light came on. Mary Davis's daughter appeared between the door and storm glass. He vaguely remembered her from one of the award banquets. He slowly raised his large frame from the seat and gingerly shut the front door and made his way to the house.

Susan Davis saw the large man in uniform and tried to keep her voice calm. Her mother had been watching the late news in the recliner while dozing in and out of sleep. Susan opened the glass door and took a few steps out on the porch careful to not slam the door behind her and startle her mother. Alexander approached and made his way up the steps to the door.

"Good evening, Ma'am, I'm Sergeant Alexander with the Georgia State Patrol."

"Yes, I believe I remember you from High School." Her voice was already shaking. She had struggled with what next to say as the veteran law enforcement officer stood before her. Victims of the family have that sixth sense. Never is it a social call when a police cruiser hits your driveway at this hour of night. Alexander took a deep breath. More air flowed through his nostrils.

"You are Susan Davis, correct?"

She nodded. "Yes, I am Coach's and Mary's daughter."

The veteran officer cleared his throat. "Ma'am, is Mrs. Davis here?"

"Yes, she was watching the news and dozing on the recliner."

Alexander paused for just a second. "Ma'am, I am extremely sorry for the news I am about to share with you. There was a single car accident tonight near the high school involving your father."

Susan's eyes widened as she pleaded with her facial expressions to not hear what was coming next. To hear that the man that had had such a profound impact on her and her family was ok. Alexander knew that there was no other way to deliver the next line but truthful and factual. "I'm sorry, Susan, your father, Coach Matt Davis, suffered fatal injuries in the accident."

Her shock and disbelief surfaced immediately. "No, No, No." She grabbed the storm door for support. She then buried her head into the fold in her arm as Alexander moved toward her. He gingerly patted her shoulder and let her absorb the news.

He loved his job any other moment. He hated his job right now. Being a part of a discussion like this never got easier even after too damn many of them. He waited a few minutes to help her compose herself. He then said quietly, "I need to share this with Mrs. Davis."

CHAPTER 8

Ben Young stared at his teammates walking underneath the goal post on the southern end of the practice field. For a moment he wished it was August and a hundred degrees. He wanted the undershirt already drenched with sweat and not dry like it was in the cool fall air. He wanted the sweat dripping from his brow and his mental state questioning if he could stand another three-hour practice in the heat. The simple wants for August timeline would mean no changes, his coaches would be there. His coaches would be alive.

He longed to see Coach Parks laughing it up with the linemen and joking about who was the stronger player. He prayed to see Davis standing at midfield with that damn clipboard analyzing every five-minute snapshot of practice crafted the night before. The team had seen the same clipboard thrown a hundred times when one of the players had missed an assignment. He had missed a block on punt return team in a game last November. The clipboard had missed his head by inches. The memory, the wish for a preseason already gone faded and the big lineman now shook his head in disbelief. A few of the players had long faces. Some didn't. Coach would have never begun a practice with that type of effort. Players were not supposed to walk through the goal post. His summer camp speech always began with his first rule for any practice or game. He could hear the graveled voice now. "Gentleman, when you leave that locker room you run toward the field and through the goal post." He fondly remembered Davis' eyes never leaving his players. "Good work habits, start to finish, our expectations, gentlemen." The first damn practice without him and things were already falling apart.

Young pulled the can of Copenhagen from the oversized and rolled down to his ankle athletic sock. He placed a pinch of the dark compressed particles between his teeth and lip. He stared at his quarterback chatting it up with a couple of receivers. He wondered what practice would be like. Dante Alexander tapped him from behind. "What's up, Young?"

Ben nodded back, "Hey, man, you alright?"

"Yeah, my Dad worked the wreck Friday night. He had to go to Coach's house and tell Ms. Davis." Ben listened closely to his good friend. "He then went down to Atlanta where Coach Parks was." Alexander paused, breathing deeply. "Coach died in the middle of the night." Ben focused his attention back on the goal post and the last of the players coming through the goal post. The non-starters strolled through lethargically. He shot a cold stare at the kids that never played and always seemed the first to check out. "This season, I just don't know what's going to happen." Ben turned back to the star player. He slapped him gently on the shoulder. Gave him the 'it all works out in the end look' then turned his attention toward the coaches.

At the opposite end of the field, Kyle Morgan threw the football in a tight spiral toward his favorite receiver. Chris Ponder snagged it with one hand and pulled it close to his body and held it for a few seconds. Before he returned the throw to the backup QB standing next to Morgan, he looked at the adults lined up along the iron fence circling the field. It was a Monday and the weather was clear. Not unusual for the some of the Dad's to come to practice after a big win. What made this different was the timing. Practice today was earlier, and the players had not officially stretched. The crowd was always late arriving. Coaches felt the arrivals were planned on purpose so that no one arrived before 5 and ran the risk of getting in trouble for leaving work early.

Morgan ran his fingers through his sandy blond hair. He had went along with his offensive line in preseason and allowed the cute stylist at the local Great Clips to perform a buzz cut. The hair grew back quickly. He thought about his weekend and how his parents shared the news regarding the coaches. There were scholarships at stake and the head ball coach rode him hard since his arrival on the big campus two years earlier. He tolerated all the coaches, never tried to get chummy, or build a relationship. A good soldier was he, did what he was told, threw in a few additional reps, and chased the after-hours wants of a teen with his girlfriend and affinity for a cold beverage. He feels a tinge of guilt not being more upset with the tragic deaths. His Baptist parents have instilled prayer and he mumbles a quick one. Internally, His ego grounds him knowing that this was one step in an athletic journey that began in elementary school.

It always came easy for Morgan, the girls, the grades, the friends. If he missed an assignment in school, a teacher was always around to deliver the fix. The school was rewarded. Division 1 Coaches were a fixture in the large rural public school and Kyle Morgan was a target.

The principal had called Coach Watters about the same time Alexander was parking his State Patrol Cruiser at Grady Hospital in the wee hours of the morning on Saturday. He would be the interim coach for a job that would ultimately see a national search begin in earnest. Watters had tried to show compassion and empathy, but his ego took over as he lobbied for the job at the end of the conversation. Principal Tim Lee was a Bostonian by birth. Sometimes his tact was found as abrasive in the small Southern community. Regardless, Lee was quickly put off by the tone coming from the young assistant. "Have the team at practice 30 minutes early on Monday." Lee told Watters that during the early morning hours. "I will address the team and we will do the best we can in moving forward from this horrible tragedy."

The shrill whistle reverberated through the practice field. Heads turned toward the midfield mark. Watters screamed for everyone to huddle up. He was flanked by two assistants, Coach Griffin and Coach Williams. Ben Young saw Principal Lee walking from the far end zone. He had a somber expression and picked up his pace to a slow trot as the team circled around the coaches. "Ok, men, listen up," Watters yelled. "Principal Lee will be addressing the team before practice."

Principal Lee looked at the players, much like a father when telling a young child the family pet was very sick and not going to make it. He cleared his throat and scanned the team with his eyes. Four players had decided they were not going to come back after hearing the news over the weekend. Part of the never play bunch that had walked from the field house. "Gentlemen, I have been in the education business for over thirty years. What has happened to this team, to this school, to our town, is unprecedented in all my years of experience. It is with deep sadness that I share with you that Coach Parks died early Saturday morning from his injuries in the accident with Coach Davis on Friday night." He paused and took a deep breath of the fall Georgia air. "There will be a memorial service at the stadium this Saturday at 1 p.m. for both men. I want all of you there and I want you in coat and tie. If you don't have one, let the coaches know so we can get you one. I have asked the State to make grief counselors available for all athletes and students." He paused again and chose his words carefully. "These men touched a lot of lives and were difference makers in their community. Boys, there is no shame in asking for help. We are all hurting right now."

Lee turned toward the coaches. Watters was getting anxious. He had rehearsed his first talk to the team since learning of his awkward promotion. Lee was stealing his thunder. Lee did not want to undermine the coaches, but he also wanted to make sure these boys knew they were not alone in their grief. Lee remained focused and continued. "Coach Davis and Coach Parks welcomed me to GA and Dance County fifteen years ago. I will always be grateful for their leadership and friendship. Please keep their families in your prayers."

Lee continued. "Coach Watters will be the interim head coach." Watters nodded his head toward the assembled group. "He is assisted by two great coaches, Griffin and Williams. We have a game at home this Friday night." Lee looked directly at Kyle Morgan, his voice pleading for the senior quarterback's leadership. "Let's honor these two men with our performance against Liberty in front of our people." He turned toward Watters ready to pass the baton, then decided to give the team some extra time. "Any questions?" Lee said to the team.

Ben Young was frustrated. He had seen the boosters start to congregate at the fence with the hope of overhearing the conversation. The same people would always circle the post-game field talk delivered by Coach Davis hoping to relive a celebratory message from their past high school experience. Young didn't care. He stared at Lee first, and then at Watters. Neither man was on his Christmas wish list. The tone was defensive, a little harsh. "Are we getting a new Head Coach?" he asked.

CHAPTER 9

The drapes had been pulled slightly back just enough for the sun to light the small hotel room. The coach stared at the street below. Last night had ended earlier than the previous. He had found another bar, but this time one with high definition flat screen televisions. They hung from the ceilings detailing to the patrons sporting events from all corners of the country. And this time he kept to himself and kept the small talk with the young waitress serving his dinner to a minimum.

He had gone light on the booze and heavy on the protein ingesting a grilled chicken salad and a cup of chili with his two draft beers. The combination had left him hungry this morning while he stared down once again at the tourists lining the sidewalks making their way toward the wharf of San Francisco.

Today was getting your butt moving day. A phrase he had used to motivate his players. The opportunity he would scream to get past your mistakes and get better. He was a little angry and a little disappointed in his self, concerning his lack of discipline on this whirlwind escape trip. Today he would make changes. Today he would start the process to getting his life back on track.

He had started the process before calling it a night. His legal pad was out of the backpack and on the small wooden table on the corner. The iPad was charged and next to his cell phone. A Delta text had hit his cellphone alerting him to the opportunity to check in for his flight later today.

He sat down at the table. He picked up the pen and started with his financials. He had nine thousand in a savings account and two thousand in his checking account. He had done a pretty good job managing his credit cards and owed less than two grand, between three accounts. His last employer provided a three month pay settlement after a very public and ugly departure from his head coaching position. He had managed to move most of it to a long-term savings account that combined with his retirement accounts amounted to just under ninety thousand dollars. His rent for the two -bedroom apartment just north of Savannah was nine hundred dollars. A car payment and other living expenses had his monthly nut at a hair below three thousand. His lease would expire in two months on the apartment. He knew a move out of state would not be difficult.

He next listed his contacts. The go to people that he would be comfortable reaching out to for work. Football season was in full bore. Jobs would not start popping up until late November and early December and by then for many if not all, those would have already been filled from backdoor agreements and long-term relationships. He scratched out three names on the pad and reminded himself to stay focused. Now was the time when the mind could easily drift to the rear- view mirror and not on the windshield that he knew he must be looking through.

He looked at the plastic single cup coffee maker beside the TV. He thought about enjoying a cup of a fresh made black brew. He didn't move fast enough. He gave in to the mental urges for a second and allowed the memories to flow.

His Dad was a decorated firefighter and moved up the ranks of quickly in thirty years of service retiring as a battalion chief in their north Florida community. His Mother had stayed at home and raised two kids. Dad stayed busy and had interest in several secondary business to supplement the family income. The upper middle-class lifestyle provided a very nice upbringing for the Coach and his family.

But they were not close. He secretly idolized his Father. He wanted to be like him from his earliest memory. He could match the vocal pitch of the sirens from the ladder truck and engines screaming down the oak tree lined roads as a toddler. He wore a plastic red hat in his early developmental years around the house to the point he would forget it was on and his Mother would have to remind him to remove it before dinner. In High School, a battalion chief allowed him to take the entrance exam for the Fire Academy, both the physical and written. His Dad never knew. His scores were top 5%.

The schedule kept his Father away from the early and formative events in his life. By late middle school, he was frustrated with the other kids having their parents in attendance at all of the after-school events. He appreciated his Mom being there at more than most but his sister needed her time as well. He stopped looking in the stands by his sophomore year. He was an accomplished baseball player that was soliciting college letters. But his passion was football, and he strived with his efforts and preparation day and night to play at the next level.

He played both sides of the ball in high school and was afforded the opportunity through his ability to pivot and turn on the afterburners. Coaches loved the speed he possessed in the open field but also remarked of his uncanny ability to deliver a hit and keep moving. Despite the talent, interest was later in football from the colleges. He played receiver and defensive back and with his class, and there were a high number of talented athletes. Some of the schools that sent representatives to his high school and always found a teammate were memorable; Arizona State, Northwestern, Kentucky, and Ole Miss. He yearned for that visit from the coaches at Florida State or from Georgia, but they never came.

One morning an assistant coach walked into his math class. All of the kids had previously witnessed the drill. One of the athletes was about to be pulled away for a recruit visit. The eyes from his teacher shot across the desk. He grabbed his books and headed toward the door. The assistant would not share with him anything as they walked toward the school cafeteria. He turned the corner and his heart skipped a beat. His breathing became hurried. Standing just a few feet from him was the legendary Coach of Georgia Southern University.

The Coach was the legendary former Defensive Coordinator and Assistant Head Coach for a major powerhouse. He had left the big school shortly after winning the National Championship to rebuild the football program at GSU. His players would run through walls for the Coach and there was not a helmet on a sideline his bald head was afraid to hit. He was dressed in khakis and school polo. He was recruiting for which would be his last year as a college football coach.

He extended his hand to the high school senior.

"Son, we have something very special going on up the road." His eyes locked on the young player. "I have watched quite a bit of film on you. I am very impressed with your speed and football acumen. You had a great game against Colquitt with that one-handed grab and return for a touchdown early in the first half." Coach Russell looked quickly at a closed GSU notebook before him. He then returned his focus back on the player. "You have a lot of decisions coming up in a very short time. I can tell you we might not have all the bells and whistles that the larger schools have but I can promise you this. We have a beautiful campus just north of here and we have proven we can go out and win National Championships." Coach paused and added, "We are not going to stop." He smiled. He asked him if he had any questions for him. The meeting had overwhelmed the seventeen-year old. He shook his head gingerly. The coach rose from his chair then extended his hand. "I would like for you to come play football with us." The continued the grin and turned away with the assistant. Ten months later he would see the legendary coach again, this time as a player for GSU.

He remembered the comment about the beautiful campus. He knew where the next memory would take him and in football language it was now time for his brain to call an audible.

CHAPTER 10

Liberty High School was a small private school in the Atlanta suburbs. The bus would bring around forty players with a wide variance in athletic talent. Coach Davis had agreed to play the small school a few years earlier. The decision came as a result of fulfilling a promise to a young coach who began pestering him at a conference in Destin, Florida some time ago. Strategically, Davis felt it would be a good chance to rest his key skill players in the early part of the season while keeping his word. He also knew his kids needed an easier match up at that point in the season. And in spite of all his accolades and talent he couldn't get them up and motivated to maximum levels for every game on the schedule.

Principal Lee walked the interior corridor underneath the home seats of the large stadium. He clutched a two-way radio that kept him linked with his staff scattered throughout the school property. A freakish tropical front had pushed thick hot air into the North Georgia area. Temperatures would be in the seventies at kick off on the last day of September. Humidity had followed the spike and it was miserably sticky for a fall evening. He looked toward the home team Patriots locker room. A couple of players were still in tee shirts and athletic shorts. There was some rap music coming from the inside. His experience told him to head toward the door and start dispensing some hardline instructions to the young men. He took one step toward the door. Any interaction with the team would undermine the interim coach. After a moment, he realized the best move was for him call the teacher assigned to the front gate and inquire on parking issues and attendance updates. He moved toward the stairs and let it go. Kickoff was less than thirty minutes away.

James Morgan and his wife Kathy made it to their seats. He carried a red cushion with the Patriots logo and placed it on the metal bleacher for him and his wife. They were just on the right side of the fifty-yard line and past games would have them completely surrounded by a loud boisterous crowd minutes before kick. They gave to the school in all aspects with their time and finances. They were an upper middle-class family and while not spoken, very appreciative and blessed of the pending full ride scholarship to a division one school for their only son.

Dan Green had taken his customary perch standing along the fence near the visitor goal post. His stature was imposing. Six foot- two and close to two hundred and sixty pounds. He liked his country vegetables and fried steak, but he also could outwork and out hustle the best of them. He kept a small gym in his basement and lifted weights many more times than most men half his age.

He had driven to the game in a recently purchased Cadillac Escalade which was by far the nicest ride in the parking lot. The booster stickers were already on full display and he arrogantly took up two parking spaces. Green's kids had long graduated but his ties to the community included several businesses and what seemed too many, unlimited revenue and resources.

His wife had joined the other parents in the stands when Green and his wife had first arrived, but it would be halftime or later before he would head up to sit with her. While Green missed the connection from his kids' earlier time here, his success in business and financial contributions to the school had launched him into a mysterious power position with the school board. Not on paper with a title but a behind the scenes influence. He never missed a Patriot Football game and if Coach Watters had any shot at replacing Coach Davis in a permanent role, his interview was tonight in a one-shot deal with Dan Green.

Sergeant Alexander wore khaki pants and a white polo with the same logo on the sleeve. He took the same cushion and placed it down on the top row of the bleachers next to the press box. He was a little intrigued with the fact the Liberty coaches had already made their way to the small cubicle to communicate with the sideline coaches. He saw no representation for the Patriots. The game announcer fumbled with his notes. The Methodist minister who had delivered the eulogy for both Davis and Parks was in the press box set to deliver the benediction. The clock on the scoreboard read 26:45 and counting downward.

Coach Watters sat in the back of the locker room. He looked at the game sheet one more time. His fiftieth time in the last two hours. His adrenaline had tapered down somewhat, and he had managed three hours of sleep the previous night. He stood up and walked toward the center of the room. "All right, gentlemen, let's get out there and get some pregame snaps in for the offense and some light hitting for the defense. Coaches, move to your stations. We will be back here in fifteen minutes."

The schedule was off, and the players felt it. The previous staff would have never allowed pre-game activities to get this off kilter. The players fell into single file and trotted toward the field.

A small applause lifted from the corner stands as some students and parents greeted the players running onto the field. Kyle Morgan shot a wave to his parents. Dante Alexander was all business and kept his eyes glued toward the field. The leadership from the players took over and the offense and defensive squads began their customary drills on the Patriots end zone line.

Principal Lee said hello to Watters as he made his way toward the Patriots bench. "Good luck tonight, Coach."

Watters shot him a quick glance. "Thank you, Sir," he managed to say.

Kyle Morgan was confident. He looked at the Liberty Team running plays on the visitor thirty- yard line. The defensive line had a couple of very large boys but a half ass film study earlier in the week by the senior QB had him assessing more trips to the dairy queen than weight room for the visiting players. He looked at the defensive backs. They were wiry and athletic. The weakness he looked to exploit was the size. The biggest back was less than six feet. He felt by halftime he would be on the bench joking with his skilled teammates and allowing the back up to get some work in.

Ben Young felt the sweat drip off his face. He spit some grass he had pulled from under the goal post to calm his nerves and substitute for the lack of nicotine dip that was usually stuck between his gum and lower lip. He wanted to get fired up. Scream enthusiastic messages to his team. Run over the nose guard assigned to him once the whistle blew and the game was underway. His mind raced. Was it the heat? The lackluster practice his teammates had walked through every day this week? A stadium he was now staring at that was less than sixty percent capacity 10 minutes from kick?

"Bring it in!" Watters yelled along with a quick shrill from his whistle. The players circled at the home 40-yard line. "All right, men, let's get back in the house and prepare to come back and get that third win of the season." He looked at the players from right to left. He chose to ignore the blank stare being returned by most. "Ok, Patriots on three." He extended his hand to the center.

46   L. Lee Stout

One followed slowly and covered his hand, then another. "1,2,3 Patriots!" eked out of about half the players' mouths.

William Alexander watched the circle break and slowly shook his head. The sound from the cheer had barely made it past the halfway point in the bleachers.

This team was a long way from recovering from the devastating loss in leadership and for the first time the thought of losing to an inferior opponent entered his mind.

CHAPTER 11

He had downloaded the ride sharing app as a revolt against the taxi company that had picked him up days earlier. The taxi had smelled of urine and the driver attempted a longer than needed trip hustle. This was a first for him with the phone technology and he was almost giddy with surprise when the SUV that matched the picture on the phone pulled in front of his hotel.

The time was just after lunch and the one last eastbound flight before the red eye schedule departed in less than two hours.

He handed the driver his backpack and duffle.

"What airline?"

"Delta," he responded.

"Headed home?"

He waited to answer. He was already thinking about the thirty-minute ride and this turning into a conversation to nowhere. Relax, he told himself. "Yes, Georgia."

The driver mentioned a drive through his state many years ago on a vacation to Florida. He tried to show interest with a head nod visible in the rear-view mirror to his sixty something year old moving him through the side streets of San Francisco.

"Good food down there in Georgia," the driver said. "I am diabetic, so I have to stay clear of the breads and potatoes or I can get in trouble quick."

The coach listened.

"I remember the corn bread in Savannah, fried chicken and salty collards fresh from the fields. Man, that was some good eating." Coach smiled. He suddenly missed a weekly treat of a meat and three. He had several options on a daily basis but stayed disciplined to limit his intake.

The Bay Bridge caught his attention. Cars inches apart lined the structure as far as the eye could see. A couple of more turns and the vehicle plowed north on the 101 en route to San Francisco International Airport.

The driver was busy with changing lanes and real taxis passing the vehicle at very high speeds. A conservative radio show was barely audible. Mid-term elections were the hot topic today and there was pending doom being blasted through the airwaves to the country if the other party gained control. He closed his eyes knowing this brief period of calm would last only a few more minutes. He always prepped for the worst outcome. The airport was ridiculously crowded. There would be lines of hapless travelers slowly pushing their way through the belted gates. He salvaged the thought with a reward that for this once in a blue moon flyer, a reason for several intoxicating beverages prior to the four-hour flight.

He had exercised some and felt better. An action plan was in place. He had approximately thirty contacts from his past that he would reach out for the list of opportunities. Confident he felt that bridges were still in place in spite of his rocket shot career climb followed by the crash. He had experienced a wicked turn that provided some humility and provided to some a laugh and satisfaction. No one told him it was an easy business.

He thanked the driver as he clumsily handed him the two bags. He felt almost guilty with the internal pay system and not having the customary fare transaction with the ride coming to an end. He handed the driver a crisp 20-dollar bill fresh from the ATM the previous evening. The driver lit up like a multi thousand-dollar bonus had hit his checking account. He extended his hand and said thank you at least twice.

He entered the terminal and recognized his growing prowess with technology. A carry-on bag and early check in with the app had his boarding pass ready to go. He took a cursory look at the ticket and baggage drop and kept walking toward security. Another positive moment followed. There were only twenty of so passengers in line. He walked toward the TSA pre-check which he was still not sure how he became eligible on such limited travel. He pulled out his license and scanned the phone for the officer.

The heavy-set officer easily could have benched press the next three passengers in line. His biceps stretched the fabric to their max on the tight uniform shirt. He held his license and his eyebrows tightened. "I believe I saw you on ESPN?"

Coach remained quiet. The agent looked him right in the eyes. "Yeah, High School out of Georgia, you were profiled for being the head coach at such a young age for a powerhouse." The guard then lit up exposing a toothy smile. He handed his license back to him. "Man, you had those kids running through walls. I wanted to grab my helmet and get back on the field."

The coach forced a slight smile. He was taken back by the recognition. Thankful the crowd behind him was growing, he extended his hand. "Nice to meet you, sir."

The TSA agent was appreciative. And like many men his age that coach had interacted with, would have loved the chance to take the field one more time.

The reminder of the rise and fall was getting to be a bit much. He looked at his watch. There was still way too much time to kill. He thought about a late lunch. He would have been lying to himself if he remotely believed he was hungry. He saw the bar and restaurant next to his gate. There were a few televisions and open seats. Decision made.

"What can I get you, sweetie?" she asked.

He didn't hesitate. "Beam and Diet."

She nodded like she had filled fifty in the last hour. "Would you like to make it a double for only six dollars more?" The math was agreeable and for the first time today he suddenly started to relax.

"Yes, that sounds good."

She handed him a menu and he gave it a quick glance then laid it flat against the table. The time difference had the games from the East Coast starting. The flat screen delivered high school football, national television, being played in a stadium large enough to house many of the current college football teams. Advertising was not being spared. The uniforms and equipment budget for these teams were simply off the charts and very hard for the older coaches to wrap their minds around. He tried to show interest in the two Texas powerhouse teams on the flat screen in front of him. He chuckled at the profile the network was featuring on the starting Quarterbacks. Bradshaw and Staubach got less time on Superbowl Sunday, and that was a different era and too damn long ago. He shook his head and stared at his drink.

"Would you like something to eat?" she asked. He was still staring at his drink. This time it was a little lighter, about half full.

He glanced at the phone, approximately one hour before boarding. He knew he needed to eat something. "Grilled chicken sandwich, please."

She picked up the menu. "Would you like to add fries or a salad with that?"

He considered it for a second. "Do you have sweet potato fries?"

She smiled. "Of course, for you, sweetie." He looked at his drink. She was still one step ahead of him. "Another, double for six more?" He nodded in agreement suddenly realizing he was going to miss the customer service in San Francisco.

She arrived with the second drink and within minutes laid the plate of food before him. He wanted to relax and put off the inevitable. He knew the work to be done waiting for him in Georgia. The isolation that would overtake him from the few call backs he would receive from his past colleagues. He was already psyching himself out. He knew it would take an onslaught of communication that would need to be repeated each day for a chance at one opportunity. It was going to be a lot of detail oriented, roll up your sleeve efforts, with no guarantees he would grace a sideline again.

He contemplated the loneliness that would hit him in the gut each night with being alone.

The second double was followed by a third. He asked for a fourth as the gate agent sent out the first announcement for pre-boards of families with young children and strollers. The glass was empty as the premium passengers lined up with their tickets prominently displayed on their smart phones. He paid his check, again tipping a lot more than necessary. He surveyed the half- eaten sandwich and one last fry staring at him from the plate.

He steadied himself as he rose from the stool. He grabbed the luggage with untimely awkwardness. He made his way out of the restaurant past the host stand and into the terminal. He found a wall and leaned against it until his boarding zone was the called. There was a lot of emotion swirling in his mind at the moment. A young man caught his eye. He was a few years younger and sat patiently in one of the terminal seats. There were young kids running in front of him playing a game of tag. One of them brushed his bag and by the grace of youth athleticism avoided a nasty spill. The man's glance to the commotion was very brief and without the coach's stare, never would have been noticed.

The coach caught himself gazing at the man's choice for literature. It was not a magazine, novel, nor newspaper. The man held a Bible. If there was an answer for the question that nagged him in his current state of mind, the man upstairs just gift wrapped it and handed it to him.

He heard the voice of the gate agent. He then took one last look at the red letters on the sign before him. What is displayed was simple and straight forward. Delta Flight 621 departing at 3:30 p.m. for Atlanta. Nathaniel Edward Jackson, Coach Nate, was coming home.

CHAPTER 12

Liberty had won the coin toss and elected to defer. Watters looked at his prized QB. "We are getting the ball first. Let's execute our plan and catch them off guard with our first two plays by running the ball. We establish the run and then we'll start taking shots downfield." Morgan gave him a lackadaisical look and stared back at the at the kickoff team getting into position. Watters let it go and turned his attention to the kickoff.

The fans had responded. A lackluster pregame crowd now was close to capacity with all on their feet. Dan Green had still not left his perch at the gate. A shrill from the whistle pierced the sticky Georgia air. The Liberty kicker delivered a pro level kick that easily made the end zone. First and ten for the home team at the twenty.

Ben Young lined the offense up at the 10. Morgan contemplated the tailback dive play for only a second. The players looked at him waiting for his response. "Y option 341." Ponder stared at his QB. He respected him but also knew the game plan being practiced all week was now off the table and something was amiss. The players took the direction and made their way to the line. Ponder looked at the goal post and the small DB waiting for his movement. He knew he would get the first look and if he was open the ball was his. He checked his alignment with the burly official and awaited the snap.

Watters stared at the game plan in front of him. Coach Williams' voice came through the headset. "Did you call for a pass coach?" Watters' eyes darted from the paper to the field. He saw the air raid look of a four-receiver set. Before he took it all in, Ponder shot down the sideline like a rocket making its way through the clouds. Two under-sized backs tried to match the speed but it was futile attempt. He had a five-yard separation as he crossed the opponents forty.

Kyle Morgan had taken the shotgun snap from Ben Young and was already looking to his left. He had a little pressure coming in from the middle of the line. There was no worry. He took one step and planted. The ball left his hand in a beautiful spiral thirty yards from pay dirt.

Ponder saw the pigskin hanging from the sky. He placed his hands in the air to connect for the long completion. Time seemed to all of a sudden stand still. The ball seemed to stop moving. He waited for the slap of the leather on the black textured gloves but it never came. The arm reached in front of him out of nowhere. The Liberty player, all five damn eight inches of him, had positioned himself to make a jump at the ball. He was successful. His slap pushed the football into the sideline.

A collective gasp echoed from the stands. Watters kept his eyes toward the field. Ponder jumped up and made his way back toward the huddle. Watters knew he had a problem. This was an open rejection to him and his game plan. He tried to take a deep breath. Send a message to all there were no issues. He wanted to shake his head and take a peek into the stands. He needed that reassuring look from his girlfriend that had supported him all week while he displayed childlike mood swings and finally apprehension toward tonight's game. He took a lesson from his mentor's playbook and kept his focus.

Watters grabbed a young receiver. "Get Ponder out and tell Morgan, Dive 46 is the play, run it!"

The receiver ran toward the huddle. He pointed at Chris then made a thumbs up gesture. Ponder didn't flinch and ran toward the sideline. Ben Young had not moved the huddle from the previous play. He was a tad winded. The Liberty defense had moved a backer close to the nose guard. They were putting a tremendous amount of pressure on the Patriot center. This would not be a cake walk and the burly lineman started searching for internal inspiration.

"Coach wants us to run, Dive 46."

The Senior QB nodded in agreement. "Ok, Dive 46, but Dante be ready, if they move the DBs in close, I am going to hit you on a post."

Alexander was not accustomed to going rogue and sure as hell didn't have any appetite in undermining the coach's authority. This type of behavior might be overlooked by Morgan's Dad but he knew where his Dad stood. The rules were clear in his house and the Alexander men were expected to follow them. "Break," the players screamed in unison and made their way to the line. Morgan lined up under center. He had two backs in I formation. Watters calmed down a little as the play matched his laminated sheet clutched tightly in his sweaty hands.

Morgan went just a little too long with the count. The Liberty players were not showing their cards and did not break from formation. Morgan did not want to run the ball. He wanted at least thirty passes on this hell hot sticky evening. Perspiration ran down his face as the internal conflict emerged. He wanted to send a message tonight that he could play at the highest level under any circumstance. He scanned the defense with piercing eyes. "Seattle, Seattle," screamed from the backfield. Watters could not believe what he was hearing. If he was wearing a visor he would have pulled a Steve Spurrier and let it fly down the sideline in contempt. He did not have a visor, did not have a cap, and the weightlessness of the laminated play card would not have had much impact.

Morgan took the snap and this time rolled to his right. He expected to see the athletic moves of Alexander pushing him open against the sideline. Not the case, as the defensive end had tied him up at the line of scrimmage. By the time Alexander was free, a defensive back from Morgan's backside had gambled on the run and was coming in fast from the right. Morgan clutched the ball tightly and kept moving toward the sideline. Alexander threw one hand toward the sky telling his QB to let it go. Morgan brought the ball back in a looping motion and set to fire. The thud of the helmet to his pads cascaded through the now silent stadium. Another gasp from the stands signaled bad things for the Patriot team. This time there was no second chances with a broken-up pass, no third down to regroup and keep the drive alive. The ball was jarred from Morgan's hands with the vicious backside hit. It bounced once on the seventeen and within seconds crossed the Patriot goal line in the hands of a Liberty Linebacker.

CHAPTER 13

Dan Green made his way to the parking lot. The stadium lights were now at full power. The sun had set early in the second quarter. The temperature had not dropped with it, maybe a degree or two but that was it. Green felt the moisture running from his forehead. He was not angry, but he was not jovial to the people lining the walkway along the stadium. There were some "Hey Dan" calls that screamed from the seats. He pretended not to hear them and kept moving toward the exit. He knew he would have to deal with the ladies at the ticket gate. Two women boosters that excelled at knowing all the gossip throughout the town would be his last barrier between the stadium and his car. Like Dan and his family, their kids had graduated several years earlier. But Friday night football was a key social event in Dance County and many would not miss it even without a vested interest on the field.

"Everything ok, Dan?" asked nosey number one. He failed to answer and acted like he did not hear her.

"You coming back, Dan?" asked nosey number two. He elected to answer not allowing the tension to continue.

"Yes, Joyce, I will be back in a few minutes."

Joyce wasn't stopping her interrogation so easily. "Boys looking a little flat, what do you think?" He had not stopped walking, his back now to the ladies.

"Just a slow start, they'll be fine," he said.

Dan found his truck a minute letter. He opened up the tailgate with a click of his key fob. He sat down inside the back of the extravagant SUV. He looked at his new loafers now covered in a thin layer of dust. He reached to his right and pulled a small nylon cooler toward him. He reached inside and pulled out a long neck Budweiser. He then pulled a red Solo cup and began the bottle to cup transfer. There was a mixture of ice and water in the cooler with three bottles anchored in the slush. He would finish the first in three long gulps.

He saw Officer Yates standing at the parking lot entrance. He placed his first empty behind the third row of seats out of view. Yates nodded in his direction and began walking toward the stadium just two rows over from the SUV. "How you doing, Dan?" said the man standing to his right. He had not heard him walk up and for someone not easily rattled, a little startled with the surprise. Dan Green took a long look at Principal Lee. He was curious if he was going to get the no alcohol policy on school grounds recited to him for the second time this year. He had promised to the veteran educator to comply but the last couple of weeks had everything off kilter.

Lee chose to ignore the cooler and the fact he had seen Green raise the bottle as he entered the lot. There were bigger fish to fry and he wanted to see where the biggest booster in the history of the school stood on the abysmal performance. He sat down next to him.

Dan Green did not mince words. He was a businessman and former athlete. He had no problems with brash behavior from himself and ninety nine percent of the time, he got what he wanted. "I am not sold on Watters in a leadership role," he said.

Lee was ready for this quick assessment. "One half of play, Dan," he said. "We have to give the kids and the coaches time, it has only been a week." Green thought about reaching for the second beer. Contemplated for a second and knew better than to push it.

"I get that and appreciate the situation, but I saw some very concerning behaviors from our top players, and I'm sorry that stems from leadership or lack thereof."

Lee got it. He didn't want to argue but he knew he was referring to Morgan's renegade performance. "This team needs a coach that is not going to baby them or kiss their ass. That is why the loss of Matt Davis is catastrophic. He had those kids on a tight leash. There was no bullshit and no half ass performance."

Lee listened patiently. He knew before he left the stadium and walked across that parking lot that this conversation was likely.

Principal Lee did not want an adversarial discussion this soon. He attempted to show empathy with limited verbal response and heavy eye contact. Green was slowly disarmed and took a deep breath and stared at his loafers. His eyes watered as he thought about the last time he had spent time with the two coaches. There had been a pancake breakfast and Green had been invited to sit at the coaches table. Matt Davis had valued Dan Green's friendship, in spite of his super booster reputation. People suspected favors for Green's generosity but outside of preferred parking and the VIP seating, there was not much gained from his heavy financial support. Lee patted him on the shoulder. "We will get through this, Dan," he said.

Principal Lee stood and thanked him for his support. He asked him if there was anything he needed, and Green responded with an all good through an affirmative nod. He slowly turned and began walking back toward the two nosey gate agents. Green looked at his watch and contemplated how long he was going to let his wife sit alone in the stands. He reached around the seat and decided to have one more.

The scar on his left hand caught his stare. He looked at it attempting to shake the memory of twenty plus years prior. The unwanted abrasion had come from a rope burn. He and his wife had been victims of a not well executed home invasion. The two losers had anticipated a deposit from one of Green's stores to travel home with the owner. They had awaited his return in some bushes by the garage. They had placed guns to his head and had him bring his wife to them from the kitchen where she was preparing dinner. The frightful ordeal took less than a few minutes after Green had given them three grand from a safe and convinced them the gold mine they were after was safely in the Citizens and Southern Bank night deposit.

The minute the armed thugs exited the house, Dan Green had already freed himself from the nylon rope dripping blood from his hand to the exported rug below his feet. His young wife knew what was next and she pleaded with her eyes for him to not leave. But Dan Green was determined. His teeth were clenched and his faced screamed boiling anger exiting his soul. He may not have been military or law enforcement, but he carried an all steel interior and the men that had just violated the sacred walls protecting his family were going to pay.

He grabbed a .270 long rifle and twisted the bolt chambering a round. He was on his front porch as the old Datsun barreled up the dirt road. He placed the rifle's butt against his shoulder and steadied the cross hairs on the driver. The thunderous clap of the discharge brought a blood curdling scream from inside his home. The driver's shoulder exploded as the bullet passed through the vehicle. The two thugs managed to keep the beater moving and would be captured later that night at a rural ER two counties away. The scar reminded him of the dark days that followed with a trial, battles with attorneys and prosecutors not happy with his brand of street justice, and a traumatized wife who would need long term pharmaceutical care and patience from a loving husband that he lacked.

He focused his stare back on his dirty loafers as Larry Brown approached after the third bottle had been emptied. Green was now upright and watching the lift gate being closed at the click of the fob. "Nice set of wheels, young man," Brown said. Green thanked him with a slight smile. "Not one of our best starts. Hopefully the offense can get moving," Brown said referencing the 14 to 7 score. The only time the Patriots had crossed the Liberty end zone was a fumble recovery and score by Dante Alexander. Green had yet to speak. He thought about pushing his friend on the young quarterback's mental state. Green knew that Brown's daughter Stephanie was Morgan's girlfriend and they spent a lot of time together. He didn't want to cross lines with his friend, but he was irritated with the young athlete's performance.

"Do you think an interim coach is the correct path for this team?" asked Green.

Brown had not put a lot of thought into it. "It's High School, Dan, this not a coaching decision to the levels seen at the University of Georgia or Georgia Tech." He regretted the response as soon as it left his mouth. He watched the wrinkles on Green's face cringe. The teeth were now clenched. Green stared at him for a second not willing to extend the same nicety's extended to the Principal minutes earlier.

"Larry, I appreciate your thoughts, but I disagree with that statement today, tomorrow, and next week. This is a playoff team with enough talent to make it to state. I lost a great friend last week and I am sure as not going to sit around and watch his and Park's efforts thrown away by some undeserving assistant."

Larry Brown took a step back. He was suddenly uncomfortable with his decision to approach his friend in the parking lot. He knew that Dan Green had spoken and when the whistles blew to start the second half, Coach Watters' tenure as the Dance County Head Coach would end with the fourth quarter.

CHAPTER 14

Coach Watters had watched the seconds tick off the scoreboard for the ending of the first half. "Back to the house!" he screamed in an authoritative tone as the clock hit 0. He placed his eyes on the small opening in the corner of the stadium. He thought about looking into the stands. Taking that one second to see his girlfriend, knowing the worried look she was now wearing.

He thought about the boosters. Again, he considered that one quick look at their faces with the hope of a little reassurance. He could not do it. He would not do it. Put it aside he thought. He had to focus on the team and getting them back on track.

He entered the locker room a few minutes later. Not seconds later because he had stopped at a trash can underneath a bleacher and violently threw up the pregame meal he had picked at hours earlier. A couple of small kids were staring at him through the gaps in the fiberglass. One started giggling at the sight while another screamed, gross. He wiped his mouth with the sleeve of his coach's shirt, spit toward the cement wall and headed for the door.

Now or never he thought as he slammed the door shut. The offensive linemen were huddled around center Ben Young. Their helmets were off and there was an almost relaxed look to them. Watters was having none of it. He walked up, grabbed the water bottle out of Young's hand and threw it toward a portable chalkboard in the corner. The ricochet narrowly missed Chris Ponder's head. "What the?" he screamed as he turned toward the front of the room.

Watters stood before the team. He clenched his teeth and forced a madman stare toward each player. Now or never he told himself. He walked a few steps toward a barrel shaped metal trash can. He grabbed it from the floor and threw it toward the lockers. Some of the players were about to lose it with laughter. They could not believe what they would later describe at an after game party among themselves as the shit show before them. A month earlier and before the tragic accident, Watters had conspired with a couple of players to play a joke on one of the defensive starters. They had moved his car from the student lot to a convenience store and told him the car had been stolen. The joke had not gone over well, and it took a long talk from Coach Parks to keep Coach Davis from firing him. A player's coach was not welcome on Matt Davis staff.

He could have trashed the whole stadium. In many players' minds, Watters was nowhere close to earning a tough guy hard charging disciplinarian reputation tonight.

"Liberty brought 40 players tonight," he screamed with a hoarse crackled voice. "40 players; undersized, with half the athletic talent of this team, in your house, whipping your ass." He stared at Morgan then threw the laminated play sheet toward him. The weightlessness of the card spun downward like a paper airplane with zero lift.

"How about QB 1?" Watters screamed. "You want to give the rest of the coaches a night off. You got this right. Running your own plays. Well where in the hell are we right now, Morgan? I'll tell you where we are, we are losing."

Morgan stared at Watters. He was a competitor and he knew his parents would be up his ass with questions if they did not turn it around tonight. He remained quiet.

"Ben Young!" Watters screamed. Young was placing a dip in his bottom lip when he heard his name screamed from Watters. He looked up at the coach. "Chicken shit blocking, young man, where is your head?" You are all region and your letting the interior lineman push you around at will. What is going on?"

Young stared in silence. He objected to Morgan's cavalier play style. He knew the offense was way out of sync. He knew he had to take a leadership role. He wanted to play for his coaches' memories and play for himself. Something was gone tonight. The internal drive that could push him through anything was just not there.

Watters knew the time to get back on the field was nearing. He had one last chance to send his message.

"Alright, gentlemen, the bad news is we lost the first half. The good news is we play two. It is time to cut the crap and focus on our game plan. We have to focus on fundamental football. Stay with our blocks, wrap up with our tackles. Get your ass out there and hit somebody. It is our house, our game, our time."

The team circled. Chris Ponder echoed the coach's wishes. They followed Kyle Morgan through the locker room door and trotted toward the end zone single file for warm ups.

Watters picked up his game plan and waited till the room was empty. He checked his phone for that reassuring text. The screen read the date and current time and that was all. He placed the phone back in his pocket and jogged toward the door. A local reporter was waiting for him as he crossed from under the stadium through the chain fence leading into the stadium. "Coach, any comment to start the second half?"

He looked at the reporter contemplating a response. "We got to put some points on the board. Liberty has a good team and they came to play." He regretted it the moment he said it knowing if they didn't win handily that comment alone would bite him in the ass with the boosters.

Kyle Morgan threw a couple of strikes to Chris Ponder and declared himself ready for the second half. Ben Young's leg was now cramping, and he had a lineman helping him stretch his leg underneath the goal post. The whistle from the officials and the exit of the Liberty Band from the field indicated the second half was ready to begin.

The Patriots wasted no time in tying the game. Dante Alexander returned a kick to the visitors' forty. Kyle Morgan adhered to the play call from the sideline and connected with a twenty yard out pass that turned into a touchdown with a missed tackle from an undersized back. The score was now even on the extra point. The stadium let out a collective sigh of relief.

The teams traded punts over the next two possessions. The coaches atop the press box saw opportunities in the now porous Liberty defense. The recommendation was to exploit an undersized defense with successive toss sweeps from the backfield. On third and five, a hole opened up and another touchdown had Dance County ahead by 7. There were eleven minutes left in the game.

Liberty subbed their starting QB with a young freshman to start their first possession of the fourth quarter. Watters screamed through the headset demanding to know who just entered the game. The kid may have been a freshman on the roster but the link ended there. He was at least six two and two twenty on the scale. The first play was from the shotgun and he delivered a rifle shot thirty yards downfield to a receiver who added another ten yards on the run. Suddenly Liberty was eleven yards from tying the football game.

There was confusion on the Dance County sideline. A defensive back had come off the field without his replacement. Liberty snapped on a quick count go and the officials let the play go with Dance County playing with only ten on the field. The receiver could have caught three passes from the young QB before a defender showed up. The scoreboard was again screaming upset.

Morgan assembled the offense on the sideline. His competitive juices were flowing. He knew this would be a devastating loss if it was not fixed. "Alright, offense, we need to move the ball. No mistakes. Extra speed on the routes receivers and I will hit you." The skill players nodded. The offensive line looked at Young. He stared at the QB with an emotionless glare.

Liberty made a huge stop on the kickoff return capturing Dante Alexander behind the twenty. Morgan yelled to the offense, "Let's go!"

The defensive linemen were talking shit now. Two lined up in the interior opposite Young's shoulder. He knew the blitz was coming. The play had been a short out pass to the tail coming out of the backfield. Young choose the play side of the ball and went for a chop block to give Morgan the time to complete the pass. It was just enough. The Patriot back caught the ball at the far sideline and escaped the defensive back. He saw pay dirt in front of him and was on his way. At the fifty, the most athletic Liberty defender had made up significant ground and was now behind the Patriot ball carrier. He raised his left hand to the sky and brought it toward the ground with all his strength. For Liberty, it was the play of the game. The ball was no match for the crushing blow and it popped from the runner's cradled arm and lay helpless on the opponent 45-yard line. A second Liberty back scooped up the ball and pushed across the fifty before Ben Young could take out three weeks of anger with a blood curdling helmet to helmet tackle.

Liberty expected the score and clock. The stadium fans were on their feet. Even the kids who looked at Friday night for the social and pre- party gathering were catching themselves staring at the field and the scoreboard. Watters expected pass all the way from the young Phenom. The coaches across the sideline were not giving in. They ran two straight run plays with success. They now had a first down at the Patriot 28.

Watters paced the sideline with surging adrenaline. He barked at the players for standing too close to the field. He screamed through his headsets at his assistants demanding that they be ready for the deep ball.

The coaches across the field still would still not give in, just yet. The play began as a simple end around. The receiver took the hand off and raced toward the opposite end of the field. The Patriot players sensed there was more and tried to correct by focusing their attention back on the QB. It was not fast enough. The receiver threw a rocket shot spiral behind the scrimmage line hitting the QB in the same spot when the play started. The QB looked immediately toward the corner. His tight end was five yards from a touchdown. He hit the receiver while he applied the brakes then carried it through the back of the end zone.

Approximately a hundred Liberty fans cheered their loudest. The rest of the packed stadium remained silent. Everything was now favoring the small school from Atlanta. Less than two minutes to go.

Watters screamed for his offense to get ready. He walked over to Morgan, lowered his voice and did his best attempt at remaining calm. "Ok, Kyle, we don't have to get it all in one play. Let's work the sidelines with some short out routes. Tell the receivers to focus on the catch first. We have timeouts and have plenty of time to win this thing." Morgan nodded his head in agreement. It took 46 minutes of game clock but he was now on the same page as his coach.

Watters was finally starting to relax. He knew a win would be enough. There were too many factors for tonight. The tragic loss, having to get back on the field so soon, it was blind luck the opponent was not a region peer that could have delivered a three-touchdown loss and added misery. Yes, he thought a win would have everything on track.

Liberty was still not ready to concede to the script being played out in Watters' mind. They had moved several of their skill players on to the line as the team prepared to kick to the Patriots. An assistant from the press box caught the change and screamed into the headset. Watters was confused at first then understood what was occurring. The Liberty kicker's toe met leather before Watters' voice was heard from the sideline. "Onside kick," he mumbled incoherently as the ball kicked end over end into the turf and bounced ten feet into the air. A Liberty player was under it and caught the ball just over the required ten yards.

The shrill whistle came from the officials. Watters was stunned. He stared at the field. The referee signaled with an outstretched arm toward the end zone that play would resume with Liberty on offense. Three offensive snaps and a fourth down run for a first was all Liberty needed to outrun the Patriot timeouts and Dance County scoreboard clock. The game was over.

CHAPTER 15

The flight from Atlanta landed in Savannah after midnight. It was an uneventful plane ride for both legs of the journey. A couple enjoying a Napa getaway for an anniversary had exchanged pleasantries just after takeoff from San Francisco but that was all for interaction and conversation for the Coach.

He had ordered a chicken salad wrap for seven dollars from the senior flight attendant somewhere over Oklahoma. He decided enough liquor was consumed at the airport and switched to water and ice. He contemplated a nap but was too wired. He continued to psych himself out for the days ahead.

He arrived at his apartment and took in the surroundings. Coach was very neat and particular about his living arrangements. Everything had a place. The kitchen sink never carried dishes. The trash was emptied on a too frequent basis. Little things he always told himself. Do the little things right and no one will ever question you on the big things.

He took 6 milligrams of melatonin to help with the jet lag and produce enough drowsiness to put him into sleep. Success was about four and half hours with deep enough REM to produce a dream of a beach trip with a lost love. He awoke to blurred vision and stared at his clock. As the cobwebs cleared he realized it was 4:52 in the morning. He would give it 10 minutes and if he was still awake would start his day.

He contemplated a run on the treadmill, deciding against it at 5:15 after his first sip of hot black coffee. He laced up his Nike's and headed toward the bike trails that circled his complex. Five miles at a leisurely pace could be done in 40 minutes. The air was sticky. Savannah in September. Humidity had to be close to 90 percent. He spat as a gnat touched his lip. He was sweating before the jog began. He reminded himself of the importance of exercise. The one agent to combat stress that did not require a doctor's visit or the booze. He knew he had been reckless in San Francisco. Knew the demons were knocking on his door. He acknowledged the problem in mile one.

At mile two he remembered the story of Erk Russell walking into the locker room with a burlap sack. Coach Russell had released a diamondback rattlesnake on the floor of the room. Players scattered, the message was simple. You mess with drugs, you might as well be messing with a rattlesnake. A helluva way to send a message. He cherished the memories of his college days and those first years of coaching. He felt the sweat pouring down his face. He was finding strength for the battle ahead. Mile 3.

He thought of her. Was she married? When was the last time he had seen her? How did she enjoy swimming with the sharks as a big-time attorney in DC? Was that what she really wanted? She was so smart. So talented. So beautiful. He had searched for her on social media after one to many in Frisco. She was in a relationship. He wasn't sure if she was married or if there were kids. He felt guilty for looking and slammed the iPad, almost breaking it.

She expected more out of life. Her parents damn sure expected more. And her father, damn him, would not have respected his occupation even if he had made to a Power 5 Head Coach role. Mile 4.

For the day ahead, his goal was 10 to 12 live conversations a day. He anticipated it would take at least thirty or so calls to get that many on the colleagues from his past on the phone. People were busy. Smart phones had caller ID. He was sure there were some that would return his call. The insecurities were back. He gritted his teeth and the eight mile a minute pace became seven. Mile 5.

He finished his run as the apartment complex began to wake up. Young professionals tied to weekend hours drove past him with expressionless faces. A young couple managed a stroller and two large dogs down the same path he had just taken. He made his way back in the house for that second cup of brewed coffee.

He rummaged through the refrigerator, looking at the date on the orange carton to ensure the eggs inside were still in the non-expiration range. He grabbed a pack of turkey and a slice of cheese. A large omelet and more coffee would be consumed before the network morning shows delivered the first batch of negative news to the nation.

A quick shower and he was ready to get going. He wore a freshly ironed polo and khaki pants. He organized his laptop and legal pad making sure he had a couple of fresh pens to take notes. Looked at the first name on the list, remembered a couple of ice breaker memories to ease the awkwardness of the conversation and dialed away.

By eleven that morning, he was right in the middle with his feelings against his expectations. Not too high, not too low. It was about where he expected, and he was ok with that. A horrendous start would have been crushing to the ego, conversely, a great start may have eased the sense of urgency.

He had spoken with five coaches from his past out of sixteen calls. Genuine enthusiasm filled the line from the voices on the other end. He thanked each and every one for the concerns and kindness. There were recommendations for different web sites and employment listings on line from sites he was not familiar with. Very helpful advice and he was appreciative.

The calls produced three solid leads. All unfortunately were out of state. Two were in Alabama and one in Mississippi. He knew he would have to move. It would come down to just how far. He had followed up calls that would be needed to move the process. He felt more confident than on the jogging trail earlier. He finished up around noon after searching the online employment listings recommended earlier.

The weather was getting hot. It was still too early for lunch. Coach usually skipped the midday meal and opted for a whey protein shake or protein chocolate bar and motored on with his day. He craved a fresh iced tea and thought about the combination gas station and deli that connected the city street with the bustling interstate. The beverage station would have what would seem a hundred choices for patrons suffering from the Southeast heat. He was not interested in the sugary soda but the four selections of iced tea. The store had a mango peach unsweet he would surround with chopped flakey ice. Very refreshing and Coach wasn't scared to grab a 44-ounce plastic cup to add it to.

He changed into shorts and gray tee-shirt. The running shoes were back on. He eyeballed a spinning reel and his tackle box sitting in the corner of his apartment just behind his desk. He shrugged his shoulder talking himself into his next move. "Why not?" he said aloud. He walked over and picked up both items. They were placed in the bed of the Ford pickup. He put on his sunglasses and headed toward the store and interstate.

Twenty minutes later and it was as if he had exited civilization. The interstate had led to an empty two -lane highway, a minute passed and the pickup was now barreling down a narrow dirt road. Large oak trees lined the path providing cover from the now intense Southern heat. He made a right turn through a field down following a road evolving from beaten down grass and truck traffic. A quarter of mile later he brought the vehicle to a stop.

He looked at the tiny waterway snaking its way through the farmland. A heavy cover of trees provided more shade from the heat. He grabbed his gut buster plastic container of iced tea juggling it with the fishing pole and tackle box and walked toward the water.

He had learned about the spot from one of his players. He knew of several players, mostly linemen, that loved to fish and hunt during their spare time. He would have loved to join them and enjoyed the interaction, but and there was always a roadblock, from a leadership and liability standpoint the negatives always outweighed the potential benefits.

He watched his step as he got closer to the river. While there was a striking stretch of sugar white sand that lined the river there would also be some thick brush to navigate. South Georgia was home to the cottonmouth moccasin and Coach had run across his unfair share. They were short and fat snakes that were meaner than a yard dog on a three day fast. He kept his eyes peeled as he moved forward. His attention not on the river almost made him not notice the elderly gentleman already in his targeted fishing spot.

He had to be pushing eighty. He had a brown cane pole with thick fishing line knotted to the end. He whipped the pole just under an outstretched oak tree within inches of tangle with a thicket of Spanish moss. The orange cork floated with the current just a few inches before violently being pulled under the black tinted tea colored water. The old man flicked his wrist and the fight was on. The bluegill was no match for the pole and sixteen pound test fishing line. The man jerked the fish from the water and into a free hand. Before Coach could speak, the fish was flopping around in the white bucket.

"Nice one," Coach said. The man responded with a nod. The Coach knew of the man but had not interacted with him. He had been at all the Friday night football games.

The old man was using live bait, crickets. He had caught two more while Coach was still eyeballing his many lures in the tackle box. Coach decided to go with a beetle spin. It was a yellow and black bodied insect replica with a shiny attachment. He didn't profess to understand what the panfish and largemouth bass saw in the lure. He thought it may just be the aggravation of the vibration under the water that pushed them to strike. The old man was on his fourth fish in ten minutes by the time Coach delivered his first cast. The old man still was not talking. Coach decided to let him be and focus on the fishing.

The competitive juices started flowing within the first few minutes. When the old man delivered another large bluegill, Coach nixed the spinner and changed the lure to a long black plastic worm. Coach was moving from the run game to the bomb pass play going after much larger species than the three- quarter pound bluegill. He tied the knot and made a perfect cast next to an exposed stump in the dark water.

He was immediately rewarded.

The line vibrated twice as if an electrical charge was shooting from the water. The line then tightened, and the fight was on. Coach gave it an extra second and set the hook into the large fish. The old man lowered his pole and looked toward the commotion in the water. Coach was using an ultralight combination. The four-pound largemouth was producing the same pole bend as a shark would on heavy sea tackle. This is what the Coach had wanted from this trip. An escape, where all that mattered was the experience before him. Just a battle between man and nature. No reporters, no inquires, no assault on privacy. Just a break.

He pulled the fish to the bank and placed his thumb on the fish's lip paralyzing the movements. It was a very nice catch. He admired it for a second and placed it back in the water. The fish moved away and headed back toward the stump. Success.

The old man mumbled. "Nice bass."

Coach looked over. "Thanks."

His next words were a surprise. Not they would have come from a neighbor or booster, or even a nosy reporter, but from the old man, a surprise.

"When are you going to be back on the sideline?" The man's voice had a raspy sound. Coach wondered if it was from years of smoking or just old age, or both. He looked at his fishing reel. He had placed the hook back into the plastic worm and was ready to cast. He delivered another perfect strike. This time he threw under the cover of a large oak.

He waited a few more seconds before responding.

"Not sure, soon I hope." The old man fished a can of snuff from his back pocket. He laid the cane pole at his feet to take care of the business at hand. Once he was satisfied with the amount of tobacco between his bottom lip and gum, he turned toward the Coach. "It was bullshit the way you were treated. That was not your fault. Everyone on that school board knows that you had nothing to do with that kid being allowed to transfer and play."

The Coach was stunned at the disclosure. He didn't want to say too much. He was still hurting, angry. Nothing good could come from where this conversation was headed. He tried to muster up a spit. The gallon of tea he was nursing was not hydrating at the pace of the suffocating heat.

The old man continued. "I hear these kids talk, I hear their parents. This mess was done by one rich white man. A lot older than you and sure as hell not a Coach. He is being protected. The Georgia way. Money fixes everything."

Coach didn't argue. He had enough of the Georgia way. He was tired. A last- minute bender from one coast to the other for not one good reason was not helping. He turned toward the old man.

"Like I tell the kids, you get knocked down, you get back up. Fair is something that comes to town in October. Hell, if it was easy everybody would be doing it."

The old man smiled. He was fishing again, and the bluegills were playing their part. He would leave with twenty pounds of the fat slabs and later serve them to a large extended family with fried hushpuppies and cheese grits.

"I respect what you did with those kids, Coach. You made sure they had a meal when no one was around. You gave them a father figure when many didn't have one. You prepared them for life and you can't pay someone enough for that."

Coach smiled, thankful that he was several feet from the man with the poor eyesight. Thankful that the old man did not see the tears well up in his eyes.

CHAPTER 16

Dan Green poked the eggs with the dull point of his fork. He was sitting in a booth normally reserved for two or more at the Waffle Stop. Rose Wilkes eyeballed him from the soda fountain. She had agreed to work the early morning shift for a young waitress that had a bridal shower she wanted to attend. Rose thought about heading over and filling the coffee cup for Green but saw from his body language he wanted to be left alone.

Green stared at the eggs laid perfectly stacked. He had ordered the same meal for twenty plus years. Two eggs sunny side up and runny laid atop a third egg cooked well. He wasn't sure why he became hooked on the combination. It was different, and the cooks had to work a little harder compared to the other orders coming in from the patrons. But Dan Green tipped well, and he was there, always on Saturday morning, and well before many residents of the Dance County community stirred to begin their day.

There was no appetite. The weather had changed. A cold front had pushed the sticky hot air toward the eastern half of the state. It was very comfortable when Green had climbed into his SUV earlier that morning. He wanted to appreciate it, knowing he wasn't getting younger. Too much on his mind and this time it wasn't work or family driving the fresh batch of worry.

He shouldn't have a stake in this he thought as he finally forked the first bite of eggs. His kids were grown. He didn't have a vested interest with the team or players. No, that's bullshit he thought. He did have a stake in this. Many of his businesses were featured with bright metallic signs lining the stadium fences. But this was not about money. It was about a close friendship with Coach Matt Davis. He wanted to honor the man and the efforts. All those years of getting up every day and doing the right thing. Pushing those kids like they had never been pushed. Knowing that with very few exceptions that the life lessons learned on a football field could be carried over to adult life and be the difference maker in success or failure.

"Good morning, Mr. Green." Dan looked up and saw the striking figure in the perfectly creased and starched uniform before him. "Sargent Alexander, Good morning. Please join me." Alexander was not expecting an invitation. He finished the overnight shift and decided on a quick breakfast before heading home. "Thank you," he said.

"Did you have a quiet night, Sergeant?" Dan asked.

"Please call me William, and yes, outside of a couple of speeding tickets, very quiet."

"Your boy decided where he is going to play college ball."

Alexander thought about his response. Rose Wilkes hurried over and poured him a stout cup of black coffee. Green had not touched his coffee or iced water. One egg was gone. The toast and other two eggs were losing temperature and still covered his plate. Rose asked Alexander if he wanted the usual. "Sure, Rose, but would you add some hash browns to the order." Green thanked Rose and kept his focus on Alexander. He was in the small talk stage of the conversation. There was another reason for the breakfast invite and Alexander had a feeling where this was going.

"I am hoping he is offered by the state schools. I am a little selfish. I'm hoping I can drive to see him play and not miss any games."

Green nodded in agreement. "Understood."

Green looked at the seasoned ranking officer before him. He had a tremendous amount of respect for Alexander. A single dad raising an academic and athletic gifted son in a small town while performing in very dangerous occupation. The Dance County residents were fortunate and blessed.

Rose delivered his breakfast. Alexander placed the napkin on his knee, added tabasco to the eggs, and then went to work on buttering the wheat toast. Rose brought him a glass of iced water and threw in a compliment for Dante's performance the night before. That was her only mention of the game this morning and Dan was appreciative.

"What are your concerns with the coaching staff, William?"

He expected and appreciated the bluntness. It was usually reserved for intoxicated drivers trying to use barroom learned legal maneuvers to avoid a DUI investigation. "It was rocky start, expected I guess. They should have turned it around in the second half and put them away." Alexander forked a bite of scrambled eggs. He was a little taken aback by the amount of tabasco he had used. He swallowed then reached for his water.

Green leaned forward in his seat. "We are at a crossroads here. The season is still young but now we have a loss to an inferior opponent. The heart of the regional schedule is upon us. If we don't turn this around, there will not only be no playoffs, but we could be looking at a sub 500 seasons. I am not trying to alarm you William but that could dry up the recruiting visits from the major schools for your son."

Green let the words sink in. Alexander had considered all of this when QB 1 Morgan went rogue on the first series of plays against Liberty. He knew sending Watters out there as the head coach was akin to sending a rookie officer to gang riot, alone.

"What are your thoughts, Mr. Green?" Alexander was trying to buy time in the awkward breakfast meeting. Dan looked at him with a slight smile.

"Please, call me Dan and simply William we have to make a change. Even if the new coach is knocking on the door of retirement and only able to lead for one or two seasons, we have to have someone come in here with immediate credibility and get these boys back on track."

Green paused, looked at Alexander with an exasperated stare. The type of look that screamed no sleep, no rest. Alexander tried to lighten the mood. "Let me call Nick Saban and see if he could take a leave from Alabama and help us this year." Green chuckled. Alexander was a little hesitant to throw out the smart- ass comment. Green had appreciated it and Alexander relaxed.

"I agree with you, Dan. This is not a job that an assistant can be thrown into. The school, the community, but most important the kids deserve a top-notch head coach."

Green switched gears. He asked Alexander about his college years. "You played down at GSU, correct?"

"Yes. I had a pretty significant injury that ended my football there, but there are some good memories."

"Any of the former players down there go on to coach?"

Alexander thought about it only for a second. "Yes, I would have to think about who and where they are today."

Green decided to give his breakfast another shot. He stabbed his fork in one of the two remaining eggs. Alexander nodded toward Rose. He was confident that the accompanying smile would bring forth another cup of coffee.

His mind briefly shot away from the breakfast. He remembered a dinner in Savannah. It was an awkward night some twenty plus and then some years ago. There were two teammates with their respective dates in a high end and very formal restaurant. The girls were not happy with the last- minute arrangement and showed little interest in making the dinner a repeat event. There was fighting in the end with the player and his girlfriend. Very clear that South Georgia was a place she went to college and that would be it. He thought about his former teammate. He had kept up with him through the internet and the teammate would not have known it. There was a close friendship, then the injury. One party felt left out. There was disappointment, then anger, then everyone went their separate ways.

Alexander begged the question of himself. Should he have done more? Should he have tried to reach out and let the insecurities and jealously go? The teammate always had the eye of the coaches. He was given additional opportunities on and off the sideline. He felt he never got that consideration and when his contributions ended due to his injury, he felt his value to the team in the coach's eyes ended, too.

Green finished his meal. He grabbed the check Rose had laid by the napkin dispenser. held it in a clenched hand and looked Alexander in the eye. "William, if there is anyone that you can think of that we can talk to about this opening, please call me."

Alexander gave a "will do" then asked for his portion of the check. Green told him he had it and no worries. Alexander didn't want an awkward scene but knew the State Patrol did not accept gratuities for their officers even when off duty. He told him he would take care of the table as a way to split the tab. Green nodded to accept the deal.

Alexander watched him leave. He pulled out his iPhone and began the white pages search.

It was time to move forward, let things go, and reach out to an old friend.

CHAPTER 17

C oach Watters stared at the flat screen. He was going over the fourth quarter of the game film. He kept stopping and then reversing the chain of events, hoping for a different outcome. It was Sunday afternoon and he was already behind. His assistants would be arriving at the top of the hour for the weekly meeting and to discuss and prepare for the week ahead. The grading process of individual performances would need to be completed then the dissection of the ugliness of Friday night.

The local paper was critical but hesitant to ask for a complete overhaul. It wasn't major media-assault but the negative innuendo was there if you looked for it. There was reference to the tragic events and the loss of the coaches after a lengthy tribute had been placed prior to the game and earlier in the week. The reporters acknowledged the somber feeling that had taken over the stadium. It still seemed too early for a few observers to be worried about a football game or season with such loss.

Watters made a cursory head glance toward the door as the two coaches entered the room. They had not slept very well since Friday night. A win would have kept the pressure at bay for at least through the bye week. Unfortunately, the worst-case scenario had occurred with a loss to a weaker opponent. Coaches lived with the carousel and potential for abrupt upheaval. Plans for both men were in the works in case the bottom fell out with their employment. Both had coaching experience in other sports and both were able to move to other schools if needed.

For Watters it was not as cut and dry. He had gambled with an out of state move. His girlfriend was from the area and with her community ties not likely to move more than a few miles away. He wanted to stay at the school but knew the performance Friday night was a problem. Niceties were shared by parents and boosters after the game, but he knew that would not be enough. He was not coaching elementary school age kids at the local Y. This was big time High School Football in the Deep South with college scholarships and state rings on the line.

Matt Davis had set a high bar as a hall of fame resumed coach. Another ugly loss and Watters would need to look for another profession if he wanted to stay in Dance County, Georgia.

"You men get any sleep this weekend?"

The tension had just been let out of the room. Coach Williams laughed while Coach Griffin smiled. Both men had left Friday night pretty upset but great spouses and some needed family time had helped with getting things back on track over the day and a half break.

"Let's break down Liberty first, then discuss the bye week and preparation, ok?" Watters looked at both men. He had learned from Coach Davis that rolling up the sleeves and getting back to work was the best way to get through the mental challenges of a negative outcome. He wanted to set an example with his staff right away.

Coach Williams elected to start with the offense first. He had been asked more times than usual about Morgan's performance and where you go from here. A friend from one of the division one schools recruiting Morgan had called on Saturday questioning the cavalier performance. Question marks were now being raised and social media recruiting sights had lit up literally hours after the dismal performance by QB 1.

Williams felt the community and the region were looking hard at the decisions that would come from the three men at the table. There would be additional scrutiny at the practice on Monday. It would not surprise Williams if a couple of hundred spectators showed up when the boys hit the field at four o'clock.

Watters decided it would be best to keep the emotional discussions at a minimum and focus on the film and the analytics.

"Did either of you from the press box or game film see any mechanical changes or deficiencies we haven't seen before with Morgan?" Griffin paused for a second.

"He did seem hurried with several of his passes, even when the pressure seemed at a minimum," Watters shot back. "Hell that would be expected when you are changing the play that is coming in from the sideline." Williams had spent a lot of time with Morgan. He had been a go to confident for the young QB when things went sideways with Davis or Parks. They had not talked over the weekend.

Williams addressed both coaches. "My opinion is business as usual. The kids read the social media and recruiting boards. We don't need to add any more pressure than what is coming externally. I say get these kids back on track with some intense practices like it is the beginning of the season and everyone is undefeated."

He decided to share a thought that had been on him from the early hours of Saturday morning after failing to fall asleep. "Guys we have a bye week coming up. Thoughts on ditching the customary pregame prep for the next opponent and having a week of summer camp type fundamental drills?" Watters looked at both men. It would take the pressure off the preparation and anxiety with a big regional game in two weeks. It would also show the kids and the community that he was willing to go outside the box in his coaching plans and styles.

Watters knew the drills and format would have risk.

"The big concern I have with that is injuries," said Watters. "We could do some modified work, maybe two days of intense hitting and two days of intense conditioning, I need to think about it. I like it, just can't afford to lose any depth."

"Let's break down the film and then we can move toward finalizing next week's practice schedule."

The men worked without a break. Around six that evening Watters girlfriend delivered a 12-piece family meal of fried chicken, biscuits, mashed potatoes, and cole slaw. The smell of the chicken was too much, and Watters gave the ok to load their plates while continuing to analyze the plays from the previous week. After the last of the eight biscuits was consumed, Williams asked for a break to stretch his legs and relieve himself of the bucket of iced tea he had been drinking since he arrived.

Coach Griffin spotted an opportunity when Williams left the room to ask Watters his opinion of their jobs and future prospects of keeping them. "I am thankful for this opportunity," he said to his new friend and boss. "But with that I am also concerned. Is the administration looking at us as permanent coaches or are we just a temporary fix?"

Watters knew to choose his words carefully. This was not a conversation that ended on Sunday night and could easily impact interactions and focus for not only the coaches but the entire team.

"I can't predict the future. Hell, if any of us could we would probably be doing something else right now. I am not trying to take anything away from your concerns. I have them and I am sure Coach Williams does as well. We are human and have families. The best thing that I can share with you is what I was told when I entered this profession. One game at a time and winning that is what we need to focus on."

Williams came into the room. He looked at both men realizing he had walked in on a backdoor conversation. He awkwardly paused then moved to take his seat at the table. Watters made an on the fly decision to address the proverbial elephant in the room with both coaches.

"Guys, I know this is not how we expected our career trajectory to play out. I heard a talk show host the other day tell a recent college grad that in spite of, her best planning her life would take at least 8 to 10 unexpected detours from the life script she had laid out in her early twenties. I thought long and hard about that feedback and agreed that I have seen the same thing happen with me."

Watters paused. The room was quiet. He had the undivided attention of both men. "I look at this office and realize what has happened to this team and each of us. The void that is now present here at this school. There was something very comforting about walking in to this locker room knowing Matt Davis was your head football coach. You just knew that whoever lined up across that field, you could play with them, hell you could beat them."

Williams and Griffin nodded in agreement, both reliving their favorite Davis and Parks memories. Watters knew this was therapeutic for all as they had not had a chance to truly express their emotions from the tragedy.

Watters looked at the two men. "Gentlemen, we have a job to do. Parks and Davis are enjoying a beer right now just north of the pearly gates with all eyes on us. They showed us how to work, how to lead, and how to be better men. Let's honor them with a great week of practice and preparation for the season ahead."

For a moment all three felt secure. They took that feeling as emotional fuel to work well past midnight toward a practice plan that would challenge even the most athletic and talented Dance County Patriot.

CHAPTER 18

Monday morning and the alarm had been set to wake the house at six a.m. William Alexander was up at five and moved from the kitchen table back to the bedroom to turn the device off. He was on his second cup of coffee and had started his day reviewing the local and Atlanta papers online. He had moved to the kitchen and was preparing breakfast. A television was muted with a morning show filled with countless weather and traffic updates from the city to the south. He paused for a moment thankful he lived in a small town. He moved toward his son's bedroom and gave the shout out for his son to get up and start getting ready for school.

Dante Alexander lowered himself from the bed. He glanced at the clock and wondered why the earlier than usual shout out from his dad. His question was answered as he smelled the first whiff of bacon from the kitchen. He walked toward the room. "What's up, Dad?" His dad looked at him with that proud father smile. The small tabletop griddle had strips of bacon to one side and four blueberry pancakes cooking on the left.

"Good morning, Son." Dante looked confused then pointed at the food. "Is it a holiday? Am I getting the day off?"

The smile from the lawman continued. "No, just wanted to get your week off to a good start. We haven't had a lot of time together. I thought we could enjoy a good meal before school," he said.

Dante smiled and told his dad he was going to grab a quick shower and dress. He was at the table ten minutes later. William Alexander poured a large glass of orange juice for both men. He laid out two plates complete with scrambled eggs, two pancakes, and four slices of bacon. A lone banana peeled sat on a small plate next to Dante's breakfast. Both men did not hesitate to start immediately with the bacon.

William looked at his son. "I know we haven't talked about it much, but how are you doing? What has happened over the last few weeks would be traumatic for anyone. Are you ok? Do you need to talk to anyone?" William had worried about pressuring his son. He wished he didn't have to go at this alone. He had talked to his mother after the accident. She had mentioned a visit in a few weeks and had called Dante right after the wreck.

"Yeah, Dad, I'm ok. It feels weird with practice and stuff. The kids are trying to do their best but you can see where it affects some more than others. I miss the coaches. I know Coach Watters is doing his best, but you can feel it's just not the same," Dante said.

Alexander looked at his son man to man eyeball to eyeball. "I understand, you keep doing what you are doing. Don't let up and be the absolute best you can be. That is all anyone can ask."

Dante nodded his head.

"Dad, how do you handle seeing what you have seen as an officer so many times, the accidents and people dying in front of you?"

Alexander had remembered a similar question from Dante when he was four, maybe five years old. They were on a family trip and had passed a fatal wreck scene. His parents told him not to look at the mangled vehicles and the tarp covering the body on the roadway. To this day he had believed his son had complied with his wishes. His answer twelve years later would remain the same. "I pray, Son. I ask God for His help in understanding tragedy and giving me the tools to help people impacted get through their challenges. Just remember a problem shared is a problem halved. Don't hesitate to talk with others."

Dante smiled. He remembered his dad was off work. "What's on your schedule today?"

William looked at his son. "Well I am going to drop you off at the school and head down to South GA to see an old friend. It will be late tonight before I am back. Any problems with getting a ride home from practice?"

Dante said that would not be an issue and the two men finished their breakfast.

Alexander dropped his son off ten minutes before the first school bell. He had given instructions the fridge had plenty of fresh turkey meat and cheese for a large sub sandwich after practice. The men were used to fending for themselves when it came to meals and Dad worked hard to ensure the ice box was fully stocked.

He made his way toward the interstate. His personal car was a Ford Mustang. He was not hesitant to let Dante drive it to school as the Patrol vehicle would always be parked outside when he was off duty. This time he was at the wheel and within the time it took for Dante

to complete home room and his first class of math study, William was already in stop and go traffic just south of Atlanta.

He decided his first bathroom break would occur just north of Dublin off 1-16. He knew the area well and had a few friends that he hadn't seen in a while. They were not the focus for this visit, but he hoped he would have time to at least call.

He spotted a fellow trooper creeping off the same exit he had chosen for his pit stop. He was two car lengths behind as the trooper brought the charger to a stop. The car was definitely older and in not as good as shape as the patrol unit he had back home. He looked at the long scratches along the bumper. Dirt roads and rocks were not kind to a car's body. He continued to follow the car.

Fortunately for Alexander and his kidneys the officer was not far from his stop. He turned into a parking lot of a gas station. Alexander turned the Mustang and parked three spaces from the trooper.

The officer was oblivious to the Mustang. He got out of the car and put on his wide brimmed hat. He was a large boned man with a body frame that screamed wasn't afraid of a good meal. He looked like he could push his car for several miles without breaking a sweat. It would take knee knocking drunk before someone to have the courage to challenge this man physically. Alexander made a whistling sound as the officer grabbed the door to make his way into the combination convenience store and deli. He stopped and looked back toward the sound.

"Trooper First Class Doug Brown," he said. Trooper Brown looked with a squint in his eyes mindful the sun glasses had been left in the car.

"William?" he said then paused with the surprise. "What brings you to middle Georgia? You haven't been transferred to God's country have you?"

Alexander responded with a toothy smile and extended his hand. "No, Doug, just wanted to come down and make sure you were still writing tickets to the poor dads driving their families to the beach."

Brown rolled his eyes. "Yeah right."

"Can I buy you a cup of coffee?"

Alexander nodded and asked for a minute while he excused himself for the men's room. When he returned, they both pulled sixteen-ounce Styrofoam cups from the dispenser. Alexander reached for his wallet and Brown waived him off and quickly gave three dollars to the cashier. Alexander tipped his cup in appreciation and spotted a small table between the window and the frozen yogurt bar conveniently in the middle of the large store.

"Seriously, how have you been?" Brown said as he positioned his frame on the tiny plastic chair.

"It's so good to see you, William." Brown smiled.

Alexander was now deep in thought as he turned the memory bank on and he tried to remember the last time they had seen each other. "Ten years, advanced training class in Forsyth?"

Brown shook his head in agreement. "I believe that's it. Are you able to grab dinner with us tonight? Amy would love to see you."

Alexander thought hard about the invitation. He would love to spend time with his old friend and his family. Then he remembered how tight the schedule was and there was a work shift closing in. "Brother, I would love to, but I have to get back, I'm sorry, but I promise a better job of scheduling next time."

Brown smiled, happy for just those few minutes to spend time with a fellow trooper and more importantly an old friend.

"How's, Dante? I remember just yesterday it seems when he was born. Man, I bet he got his momma's good looks and your athleticism. That young man is going to be some kind of athlete and ladies man."

Alexander shot a follow up smile at the praise. He caught Brown up on Dante's season and the quest for the next level and college ball. Brown's face became suddenly serious and the smile evaporated. "We heard about the wreck, I know that has to be a hardship on your son and that town. I heard you worked it. That had to be tough."

Alexander chose not to let the memory of the night take over. "Yeah, we are all healing right now. One day at a time."

The curiosity question from Brown finally came as Alexander took a long sip of the dark coffee. "So, what brings you all the way down here?"

"I thought I would head down Savannah and reconnect with one of our former teammates." Alexander had nothing to hide.

Brown remembered quickly how transparent the senior officer conducted himself on and off duty. "Nate Jackson?" It was a win by Brown on the memory challenge.

Alexander shook his head in the affirmative not ready to say his name. "Now I know I haven't seen you in a while, how long has that separation been?" Alexander still hadn't come to terms with his actions for the day. He shook his head and didn't respond.

Brown had played football with both men. He knew how close

they had been and suddenly remembered how the relationship ended in an abrupt fashion.

"Doug, I got a question for you? How much do you know about the situation down in Savannah?" Brown was quickly putting the pieces together. This was more than seeing an old friend. It didn't take a PhD to know the situation the town was in losing their coach and what was involved in the search for a replacement. Brown chose his words carefully. He knew more than most. He followed sports at the college and high school level with a passion.

"I have talked to a few people and without a doubt Nate was not treated fairly. On a scale of 1 to 10 on role in the scandal that caused everything, I would say a negative 1 on any involvement by him. He ran a clean program. He pushed those kids, yes, there were a few issues for him personally, but he didn't deserve to lose his job."

Alexander nursed his coffee. He wasn't excited about another pit stop before his arrival. He chose his words carefully. "Well is he ok with the State and his ability to take another job elsewhere?" Brown appreciated his friend's direct nature. "I am not aware of any issues that would stop him from coaching again especially in Georgia. To my knowledge after the proactive manner and speed in disposition by the principal and school board that pretty much closed any other action. It was obvious there were some political favors to protect whoever was involved that kept the board from pushing the matter publicly."

Alexander thought about the reference to the personal matters and decided against bringing it up. We all have our cross to bear he reminded himself.

The plastic chairs screeched as the men shifted their bodies to exit. Alexander extended his hand. "Let's not let this many years slip by us again. Let me know when you head north, and I will treat you to a Braves or Falcons game, whatever season we are in."

Brown smiled and thanked his friend. They made their way to their cars. "Be careful out there, William," Brown said and pulled away in his vehicle headed back toward the interstate.

CHAPTER 19

The players huddled at the forty-yard line. As expected, there were several dads standing at the fence line of the practice field. For a Monday, the mood was upbeat. Kyle Morgan was asking about a rumored party for the weekend. He received mixed answers from two different players. Dante Alexander kidded Chris Ponder about mix matched socks he was wearing. "Where did you get those socks dude?" Ponder ignored him and adjusted the brightly colored fabric pulled close to his knee downward to his ankle.

Coach Watters ran through the goal post followed by his two assistants. The screech of the whistle reverberated across the field bringing silence from the huddled team. "Line em up," he screamed. "Stretch drills, gentlemen, get loose. We have a big day today." The enthusiasm dropped two levels as the players stood to take their place along the field. Helmets were now on and chinstraps were being buckled. Two senior players began barking the stretch drill instructions for the team members to follow. Ten different stretch exercises with the players pairing up to help each other for the last four. The first order of business lasted close to ten minutes.

"Everyone on the thirty!" Watters screamed. The players started looking at each other with a quizzical look. This was definitely off schedule. "Three lines, full speed to the goal line and back," he yelled to the team. Now the enthusiasm was on par with a trip to the dentist. Heads hung downward. Feet shuffled slowly. Players looked at each other as they were still on the field after the Liberty loss.

"Today, gentlemen." The skill players took the line first. The whistle blew, and fifteen players raced toward the end zone. Coach Williams put the effort at seventy percent. The backers and defensive backs were in line two and delivered a slightly better effort. Line three included all the big men. The linemen were showing wear and tear as they motored the thirty yards toward the goal line. Ben Young was throwing off mixed messages. Was he nursing an injury from Friday night? Was his attitude toward the coaching staff reaching a negative high? Coach

Griffin ran alongside with him. "What's up Young? You need to see the trainer? Young ignored the coach and took his pace up just a notch. A competitive shot to the coach that if he wanted to run alongside him the speed would have to increase. Griffin got the message and turned away and jogged back to the sideline.

The drill continued for three more sets. There was now labored breathing. The temperature was unseasonably cool for September but for the players it felt like July conditioning all over again.

"Take a knee," Watters yelled at the players. The helmets were off, and the heaviness of the breathing drowned out the vehicle traffic and noise from the younger kids playing near the practice field. "I am not going to rehash Friday night. Liberty came in a beat us, period. We regained our focus late in the game, but it was too little and too late. Today and moving forward we are going to get back to the fundamentals. When teams play us, they are going to remember how hard we hit, how well we tackled, and how we moved the ball up and down the field." He paused for a second as the players began to catch their breath. He had their attention.

"Some call the drill we will be doing today Oklahoma, my high school coach called it hamburger. Regardless we are going to run, tackle, and block today like it's the most important thing in the world. Backs and receivers, you will be with me, lineman with Coach Griffin, and defense backers and secondary with Coach Williams. Let's move, gentlemen."

James Morgan had left work early to take in Monday's practice. He stood with three other dads' near the fence line. In ordinary times the players would be in their position drills and Kyle would be slinging pass routes to his receiving corp. Today, James was watching is only son await coaching instructions next to a blocking dummy that had been positioned horizontal with seven other dummies forming a narrow chute and creating a very tight path in the middle of the practice field.

Watters voiced echoed. "Once again, gentlemen, the drill is simple. On my whistle, QB hands off to the running back while linemen square off. Simple goals, here, gentlemen, offense score and defense stop them. Line up and on my whistle."

James Morgan started thinking about college recruiters and scholarships. He could not believe he was watching his son participate in a middle school blocking and tackling drill.

Ben Young jumped in and was rewarded with the chance to hit one of the largest defensive players on the roster. The whistle blew, and Kyle Morgan handed off to his starting running back. Young was able to get lower than his defensive foe and started to drive the player down the field. The big lineman was not happy with the starting center getting the best of him. He drove his arm upward catching Young under his face mask. The movement was now at a standstill. The back was barreling down the chute. The defensive back twisted and was able to break free from Young's drive. He dove toward the running backs feet and the offensive surge was stopped.

Watters' whistle blew. "Nice start, Young, but not enough. Good play, defense. We have to hold those blocks." Young shot him a disapproving stare and walked over to the end of the line. Mentally he was in a bad place and not sure where his heart was. Morgan gave way to the second-string quarterback and made a disapproving hand gesture to his starting center. The timing could not have been worse. Young looked back at QB 1 and told him to stick it.

Watters ignored the banter. The third set of players were executing the drill. The offensive line was holding momentarily but the defense was making tackles. The running backs' moves became less explosive as everyone completed the first series of hits. James Morgan looked at his son then looked at his watch. He wondered how long the exercise was going to continue. He watched Young deliver a great hit on an underclass defensive linebacker then drive him ten yards down the field. The running back moving down the chute could have stopped and had a drink and still scored.

Forty-five minutes later and the scheduled water break had been ignored. James Morgan was pacing up the fence line. His starched shirt was rolled at the sleeves. The colorful tie that he had walked out of his house at daybreak was wrapped around a hanger holding his sports coat in the back seat of his car. He avoided the conversations from the other fathers and older siblings that watched practice with wonder. There were a couple of fathers who openly questioned the exercise. Morgan didn't take the bait and fall into the conversation. He kept pacing.

A crushing tackle had one lineman favor his knee and limp toward the sideline. Watters looked briefly at the player and signaled with his whistle to keep the drill going. The third player to move slowly from the pile and show a potential injury caused Morgan to stop his pacing and throw and angry stare toward the coaching staff.

Principal Lee had made his way from a staff meeting to the practice fields. After a few minutes watching the band rehearse, he made his way to the football field. He saw Morgan and approached QB 1's father. "Mr. Morgan, how are you today?" Morgan looked at the principal. He was not used to this type of deviation in a practice schedule at this point of the season.

"Ok, Mr. Lee, how are you?" The tone was not warm and fuzzy, not that is what Lee expected from Morgan, but he knew there was more. The principal turned his attention toward the field. Saw the players showing injuries by lying on the sideline with their helmets off favoring various knees and legs. Injuries were now starting to pile on with the count at six players.

"I understand the thought behind this practice, but I'm not sold it should go this long," said Morgan without provocation. Lee looked at Morgan and smiled. "Let's give it some time, James. He is a new coach following some big footsteps. He is trying to put his stamp on this program and team." Morgan halfheartedly accepted Lee's explanation. He was concerned about his son and the season. He turned toward the stands hoping to catch a glimpse of a recruiter. "I know, I know."

Lee moved away and made his way down the fence line. A couple of students said hello. The parents waited for the principal to acknowledge them with a greeting. Lee was the quintessential school leader. He carried an infectious smile and worked to greet everyone at practice. "Thank you all for coming out today. This means a lot to these players, we greatly appreciate your support."

Dan Green had been busy with a land deal meeting. He had looked at his watch and debated swinging by the practice field. Curiosity had won over and he had turned the SUV into the dusty parking lot. He was dressed in similar attire as the other working Dads' minus the tie. He was a simple dresser. He loved a nice khaki colored pant and either a golf polo or simple button-down shirt. The shoes would again take a beating with the dust and dirt of the parking lot, but it was football season and shoes could be polished or replaced.

Green spotted Morgan and headed in his direction. He ignored the other parents and slapped him across the shoulder blade. "James, how are you?" Morgan looked quickly to his left. He didn't have to hear the voice or see the large man now standing next to him to identify. There was only one man that greeted with a shoulder slap and that was Dan Green. If you felt the sting from your flesh across your backside you were in good company. He liked you and that was a good friend to have.

"Well Dan, Watters has had the team in some archaic hitting drill for at least the last hour. By the time this damn thing ends we will probably have half the team on the injured list." Green absorbed the update. "Trying to toughen them up."

Green responded, "Looks like Coach is trying to regain some control from the lack of respect Friday night." Morgan bristled at the statement. He knew it started with his kid. Kyle's behavior toward the new coach was indefensible. He ordinarily would respond if Green said something he disagreed with. He decided to let it go.

"We have a big regional game coming up in less than two weeks. There will be college recruiters there, representatives that could impact several kids on this team's future. I just hope we are not seeing the beginning of a blown season."

Green responded with another back slap, this time not as forceful. He wanted to show understanding to his friend. "These things have a way of working out," he said. Morgan's head shot from the field toward the larger than life booster. He knew something, probably had already orchestrated some big change. Morgan thought to himself and smiled. The man is always one step ahead of everybody. And that is why he was simply one of the most powerful in the region.

CHAPTER 20

Coach Nate Jackson had risen before dawn and completed another run. This time he added a mile and was under fifty minutes. He had taken longer than usual on the cool down and enjoyed the rest of his eggs from the fridge, this time scrambled. His coffee intake had increased, downing three twenty-ounce Styrofoam cups by eight am. He had been promising to add bible study to his routine. A promise he had made to himself after the scene at the gate in San Francisco on his journey back to Georgia. Today he delivered.

By lunchtime his calls were delivering more promise. There were now a total of six leads in three states. The last call was to an assistant he had worked with several years prior in Savannah. He was now in North Florida. He was being recruited by a small Catholic school that wanted to start a football program. The assistant on the phone did not want the head coaching position. He had been a lifetime assistant head coach and greatly enjoyed the x's and o's without the overall responsibilities and additional scrutiny. It did not hurt that his wife was a Physician and the dual income provided a very nice living for his family.

Coach was very appreciative. This opportunity was the most intriguing one of all that he had been presented and considered. It was a fresh start and that more than anything was what he needed.

He skipped lunch and motored through the day. He found a resume service online and reached out with all the dates and achievements from his background. He knew the next steps would involve many interviews and endless miles of paperwork. It was the process and dealing with the bureaucracy that would be an enormous test of his will and patience. He reminded himself of the reward. There was simply that chance to be back on that sideline, in his office, leading his kids and his team into battle. It was one of the hardest jobs and one of the most rewarding.

The clock got away from him. He had found some old playbooks and that had him now strategizing for the opponents. He was way ahead of himself and he knew it. It was early afternoon and he needed a break. He massaged his temples at his desk. He then looked around at the sparse apartment. He was ready for a change. His legal pad caught his eye. There were three more coaches that he wanted to connect with. He looked at the first name then grabbed his phone. Before the second digit could be hit, a loud rap came from the door. He ended the call and cleared the screen. He sat the phone down and turned toward the door.

Alexander had played the scenario over in his mind a dozen times since he left Trooper Brown and the coffee in Dublin. He knew what he wanted to say. He kept telling himself he was there for the kids. This was not about him and their relationship years ago. This was about having the best coach for the team and that man was Nate Jackson.

He had pulled Coach's address from the White Pages. He thought about just picking up the phone, but he knew that what he would be asking from Nate Jackson deserved a face to face. He wanted to see the facial reaction from the coach. He wanted to summarize the situation in North Georgia with the thoroughness and respect that the football program in Dance County deserved. This would be a twenty-hour work day for William Alexander and he had given many to the Great State of Georgia. He internalized the importance as he parked the car in front of the apartment.

When Coach answered the door, he was surprised to see the large figure standing before him. The man was imposing. He had a chiseled face, large pulsating biceps, and almost zero body fat. He removed the Ray Ban aviator sunglasses before Coach could speak.

"May I help you?" Coach asked. He hadn't got to the word you when he connected almost twenty years of separation.

"William, William Alexander."

Alexander looked at the coach and formed a slight smile. "How are you doing, Nate?"

Coach stood for just a second then opened the apartment door. "Please come in."

After an awkward handshake, Alexander walked in to the two-bedroom apartment. He thought briefly how the man had not changed since their college days. Everything was in place. The desk in the corner caught his attention. Not a stray book or paper. All neatly organized and tied to a purpose. He turned around to look at the Coach. Still working out, great shape like always he thought. The man could run, and he had always been impressed and jealous of that.

"Can I get you something to drink? Water, tea?"

Alexander responded with a no thanks and stood by the sofa in the living room.

"Please have a seat."

Alexander adjusted his body frame on the sofa, thinking how firm the fabric stood. Definitely not much wear. Nor would he expect that with the hours that Coach recently kept away from the small apartment.

Coach didn't carry his textbook infectious grin. He was still stunned by the sudden and out of nowhere visit. He broke the awkward silence that was now developing. "What's it been, William, nineteen, twenty years?"

Alexander nodded his head. Neither of the men were fans of small talk. Coach kept the dialogue moving. "I last heard you were in Atlanta working in Law enforcement."

"Yes, I have been a trooper for several years. Actually, I am now in North Georgia, Dance County."

Coach smiled, non-verbally thanking him for his service. "And your family?"

Coach asked. "I have one son, Dante. He is a senior. Just the two of us bachelors."

"You got any pictures? I bet he is one talented and athletic young man."

Alexander pulled his phone and shared a couple of photos of Dante in action on the grid iron.

Coach smiled. "I know you are proud."

Alexander slid his phone back into his pocket. He acknowledged the comments with a thank you, then decided to cut to the chase.

"Nate, I am not here to get into your business. I am here to see if there may be interest in a potential opportunity in North Georgia. We lost two fine coaches to a tragic automobile accident. We have interim assistants in place now, but I can assure you the folks that make the decisions will be moving soon on an experienced and highly successful head coach."

Alexander let the words sink in. He was seeing from his old friend something that had come with age and not always demonstrated during their college years, listening skills and patience. Coach seemed to hang on each word. He showed empathy in his non-verbal cues to the delicacy of the conversation. Alexander continued.

"I am not going to hold anything back from you. I know we all went our separate ways and I regretted that we haven't spoken in a long time. I carried some bitterness and anger from my injury and I didn't feel that anyone had my back once I could no longer contribute on the field. I know that is a burden to carry and yes that was a very long time ago and water under the bridge. I am here now for a team that needs help and I am here for my son. I have kept up with your coaching, I know you are the one for this team. I can't offer you this job. All I can say, I believe it will be there for you, if you want it."

Coach got up from the lone chair across from his former team-mate. He stretched his legs as if he had been sitting the last twelve hours. He walked over to a window and adjusted the blind to regulate the scorching sun trying to get into the room. He spoke after a second awkward pause.

"I knew Coach Davis and Coach Parks, would see them at the various coaches' clinics. They were Hall of Famers, no doubt." He paused for a moment then continued.

"I was aware of the tragedy. I hurt for the families, the players, and the community. No doubt this is a tough situation." He paused. "William, I am sorry that things moved in different directions for us. I was a young and selfish player looking back all those years ago. I know that now and I guess that is why I am drawn to coaching, to overcome those faults I have carried."

He looked at William then walked back over to the chair and sat down. "I need a job, I am not going to try to hide that from anyone. I can tell you that this one concerns me on several fronts. I am not sure that even a get everything back on track performance means I am coaching there two years from now. I know the boosters in Dance County. I know them because those same ones down here accelerated and destroyed my career so fast it would make your head spin like a bullet ride at a carnival."

William anticipated push back as drove somewhere between the Ogeechee River Bridge and the Chatham County line on the interstate. "Coach, I have followed your efforts and I have seen your work. You may have been one of the biggest assholes but you know how to win. You can keep these kids on track. More importantly, there are several players that have a chance to play at the next level. If the season craps out, then some of the scholarships may disappear. That would be devastating for these kids and they sure as hell don't deserve that because they lost their coaches in a car wreck."

He let the words set in, then raised his large frame from the sofa.

"Nate, I need you to coach my son."

Coach looked at the large man before him. He had stood up to make his most important point. It was now personal. There was a slight watering to his eyes. If he hadn't carried 100 percent of the Coach's attention he had it now. "It has been just he and I the last few years. He has not had it easy. But he has a shot at D1 program. There is one man I would trust with his future outside of Matt Davis, God rest his soul, and I am looking at him. I am asking, please consider being the next Head Coach of Dance County."

CHAPTER 21

Tuesday night in Dance County and the quarterly meeting of the school board was in session. There was a very sparse audience. The local media was represented by a first-year newspaper reporter. There was no agenda that included coaching changes at the county high school.

William Alexander was plowing through the evening on three hours of sleep. He had pushed the limits with his personal vehicle and had made it home the previous night as Dante was watching TV and knocking out some math homework. He inhaled a half a sandwich then changed to his uniform to work an overnight shift ending at 8 a.m. the next day. He had thought long and hard about his visit with Coach Nate Jackson. He knew it was a gamble, not quite a Hail-Mary, but still a significant one to reach out to Dan Green. As soon as he had changed he decided to go with his gut and meet the booster prior to the quarterly meeting. They had met back at the Waffle Stop over coffee. Alexander shared the meeting with his old friend and gave a highly favorable summary of what Coach could bring to the team. There were few questions from Dan Green. He excitedly moved his head up and down and flashed a toothy grin when he connected the Coach with the ESPN piece. He knew this man and knew this would be a rising star for the Patriots. He also knew there would be push back.

An hour later, Dan Green had sat patiently in the back of the room. The board plowed through the usual items up for discussion. At eight thirty it seemed the meeting would end quite a bit earlier than usual. Dan Green made his way to a podium facing the school board seats reserved for public comment. Three of the six board members looked at him with quizzical expressions. The other three scrambled their written papers before them looking for the edit in the agenda. No one had any idea why he was there or what was next.

"Good evening ladies and gentlemen of the school board," he said. "My name is Dan Green and I would respectfully request a few minutes of your time this evening."

All eyes found their way to the Chairman of the School Board. Hugh Davis was a stickler for rules and this was way outside of the box. He removed his glasses and laid them in front of him. He shot a cursory look first to his left then to his right, though he did not seek the approval of anyone sitting with him on the board.

"Ok, Mr. Green, we have a few minutes for you, go ahead."

Dan Green had not had many opportunities for public speaking in his past. He was used to speaking in small groups or one on one. He carried a great deal of swagger and confidence and that was apparent in his chosen words.

"Thank you, Mr. Chairman. I will get right to the point of my request. Less than two weeks ago, this community and our County High School suffered a tremendous loss with the sudden and tragic deaths of Coach Davis and Coach Parks. These men were pillars of the community and outstanding role models and leaders for our town and football team. I am here today asking for you to honor these men by expediting the hiring of a top notch coach to continue their legacy and work with our championship caliber football team."

Hugh Davis was interested in a lot of things but not football. He grudgingly had attended games but not with any consistency or routine. He was the father of two daughters that had graduated from the city school ten years earlier. There was interest but not the passion that other board members and parents carried for the sport.

Davis knew this was a potential time bomb. He could nip it right here with a wrong place and wrong time or kick the can down the road with a handoff to his colleagues for discussion. He gambled with indecisiveness and did not immediately respond.

"I have not had any discussions or request from the high school regarding this," he said. Dan Green was ready for the response.

"I understand, but with all due respect, sir, this is a program that has and should compete at the highest level. Please do not take this the wrong way, but we have an interim staff in place and there needs to be a national search in place to find the best coach for our county high school."

Two miles from the meeting, Coach Watters sat behind the former desk of Matt Davis. He looked at his roster with several black lines drawn through player's names. His gamble with the two intense practices had backfired. He was looking at least eight to ten injuries with some highly questionable for the next game. He had fielded three calls from concerned parents and his student trainer. He watched two non-starters clean out their lockers and quit.

He had sent the other two coaches home shortly after practice. He had not discussed the mid-week session. He knew he had to get the team back on track and start to build the kids back up again. The large number of players on the sideline would be a distraction and hurt the ability to shadow the opposing team during practice. He tried to put his mind in Matt Davis mode and come up with game plan for the next afternoon.

Back at the school board meeting, Dan Green was not satisfied with the board's response. They committed to taking it under advisement and a follow up discussion. There were no concrete timelines or plans for it to supersede any of the other actions for future agendas. Dan Green left the meeting and headed for his vehicle. He spied Principal Lee in the corner of the room and decided it was important that they have a discussion. He waited for him to finish his conversation with a wife of a school board member.

Lee nodded his head at Green and motioned for him to walk with him toward the parking lot. Green did not waste anyone's time. "I am a little concerned with the lack of urgency of this board," he said.

Lee kept his eyes forward. "Dan, everyone is feeling the pressure. I had several calls from parents just today regarding the practices the last two days. There are some that are concerned with promoting an assistant that is just not ready to take on this role."

Green liked what he heard. His message was finally being shared by others. He wanted a change by halftime of the first game following the tragedy. He also knew want and get were two words that had different meetings.

He wanted Lee to shake the Southern gentleman persona and give him the North End of Boston bottom line. "What's next, Mr. Lee?" They had made their way to the parking lot. Only a handful of cars had remained

The weather was cool and there was a slight breeze. Lee ran his fingers through his thick white hair. He slightly leaned against the large SUV sitting spotless in the sparse lot.

"I don't think you are going to see a change this season," he said.

CHAPTER 22

The interview had been arranged after one phone call. Coach Nate was on his way to meet with the Catholic school in North Florida. They had several assistants ready to go. They needed a head coach and his colleague and friend had delivered a referral and recommendation that had the principal and ultimate decision maker on the phone extending a face to face the following afternoon.

Coach was careful with his coffee. He was mindful of the starched white shirt sticking to his body and how disastrous a spill of the coffee would be. This was not attire that he enjoyed but came with the professionalism of the position. Three hundred plus day a year in assorted sweats, t shirts, and polos with khakis was the norm, but there would also be a handful of days you would have to don the suit and all its accessories. He wore a multi colored tie. It was very trendy and eye catching. Maybe a little too stylish for an interview but the colors had caught his stare at his last trip clothes shopping. He knew he needed three or four in his closet and had made the selection with the approval of the young and very cute sales clerk.

He took a long sip of the strong and hot brew. His speed was sixty-five and his timing was good. He told himself he needed to relax and take in the surroundings. He was on interstate 95 heading south to Florida and the Duval County line. He was driving through one of the most beautiful and peaceful areas of the southeastern US. Waterways were lined with towering poles of grass. Confederate soldier and poet Sydney Lanier described his experience with the stunning views so eloquently, the Marshes of Glynn.

The dark orange sun peeked above the treetops. The waters beneath the bridge rippled. A dark object came through in the middle of the waterway. An alligator, about six feet, surfaced for a moment and disappeared. The abundance of grass sticks emerged from the water and protected the land. A picture-perfect morning in southeast Georgia and Coach reminded himself again on his second pull from the Styrofoam as he crossed another bridge to enjoy it, embrace it, and leave the worry and the pain behind.

He was in Jacksonville morning traffic an hour later. Nature was calling and he did not see any good opportunities to leave the interstate and relieve his coffee-filled bladder. He lived with the growing pain and dialed in a sports radio station. The jocks were local and juggling three topics with little affiliation for the professional and college teams on hand. He was hoping for some good banter on the gators and jaguars. He got golf, love life, and diet advice. None of which interested him. He switched to a country station with a behemoth signal. Alan Jackson sang about a famous muddy Georgia waterway and Coach's attention to his bladder was diverted.

Another thirty minutes and Coach had found a suburban exit off the multilane interstate. He pulled into a Panera Bread restaurant lot and secured his attaché case, a coaching gift several years and survivor of several moves. He felt a surge of adrenaline leaving the men's room after exiting with the multiple ounces of coffee he had consumed during the drive. His second stop was to the order line and register to secure a second cup for a more expensive and flavorful brew, this time it would be small paper cup and not the thirty-two-ounce Styrofoam he had filled usually reserved for iced tea and sweltering heat.

The legal pad was out. He had made some prep notes the night before over bites of a grilled cheese and lays potato chips. He worked through his accomplishments. There were the customary wins and losses. The offensive and defensive mindset and how complicated schemes could be articulated to young players. His POA was simple. Coach, counsel, and develop. He made notes of specific incidents where he demonstrated all three. He thought about one of his kids that he had kicked off the team in his early years of coaching. It brought back strong memories and caused him to pause and put down his pen.

Laney Jefferson had not had it easy. Eight out of ten of his players fell under similar backgrounds. These were very tough environment to live in. These were also very tough environment to overcome for success in later life. An old story, told too many times, missing father, single mom doing everything to keep a roof and food on the table. Normalcy was that most got into trouble. You overlooked some of it, some you couldn't. Coach had a hardline against theft and violence. There were no exceptions. Laney had started some fights at school borderline bullying mixed with downright violence and aggression. He had been warned. The thefts came later. Coach witnessed one. He was dismissed from the team immediately.

Coach Nate didn't let him fall off the cliff. He would pull the kid out of the hallway and talk to him. He told him he cared about him and that he and only he could change his life. The kid bristled at first, resistant to the efforts. He was not a feel-good story to a white coach. Nate did not give two shits about what the kid thought about him or his motives. Coach was a difference maker and internally he lived where results were expected on and off the field.

On a February afternoon, Coach picked Laney up in the parking lot of the school. He drove him to a local sporting goods store. He paid for a pair of Nike shoes and a flashy running shirt that the kid approved with a skeptical look. He handed the kid the bag as they climbed back into the pick-up. They drove back to the school and parked next to the stadium. Laney looked at him, then, mumbled, "Thanks."

Coach shook his head. "Not that easy, Son, now you earn it." Every day the two ran after school. Sometimes a couple of miles, sometimes more. When spring football training started in March, Laney Jackson was second on the depth chart for an outside linebacker position. He graduated one year later to a full ride at a Division II school. Coach pulled a sip from the Panera hazelnut. That is what he needed to focus on, Laney Jefferson and the opportunity to positively influence fifty or so more.

His smart phone vibrated on the table surface a few minutes later. That was his appointment reminder for his interview. He gathered his belongings and headed toward his truck. He pulled into the parking lot five minutes before the hour. He had reminded himself while tossing and turning the night before not to be comparing the facilities to the large public school he had left. The only similarities would be the measurements of the grid iron and the goal post, stark differences for the rest.

He looked at the cars in the lot. There were mostly late model Hondas and Toyotas, a few European imports as usual serving as economic distinction among the students. He grabbed his attaché case. He made sure his phone was silent, even though his incoming calls were limited and walked to the front of the school. He couldn't help looking toward the field house. A practice field was surrounded by a few pines and trails most likely used by the cross-country team. A field house separated the practice field from the stadium. He guessed the maximum attendance for Friday night would be capped at 2,500 fans.

This would be a big difference from his previous lives.

The door was locked. A small rectangular box was mounted on the wall. Before he could react, a voice full of static greeted him and asked his business. He relayed his appointment with the principal. A buzzing sound followed, and he pulled the heavy door toward him. The office was to the right. He looked at the middle-aged woman behind the desk. She had dark hair and a disapproving look. He suddenly felt awkward, worrying some of the many ounces of coffee had hit his shirt or tie. He flashed a warm smile and realized the look was not for him.

Two students were in the hallway. He turned toward them. Their uniforms were impressive. Gray slacks and starched white shirts. A maroon tie and black shoes completed the attire. A young girl wore a dark sweater even though the temperature in north Florida was expected to be eighty-eight degrees that day. The admin was now standing. "Where is your hall pass?"

The male student responded, "Ms. Green sent us up here to let you know the AC is not working in her classroom."

The admin shook her head. "I'll call maintenance, now please return to class."

The kids nodded and turned toward the hallway. Coach stood still and waited for the admin.

"May I help you?" Now the smile was there. "How is your day going?"

She chuckled, appreciative of the acknowledgement. "Well, it feels like a Monday."

Coach kept his grin. "We will get to Friday, I promise." He paused for a second. "I have a ten am meeting with Principal McNamee."

She looked at her computer, checking the online calendar for the meeting. "Yes, Coach Jackson, please have a seat he will be right with you.

He was ushered into the office after a two-minute break. A short and slender man arose from behind a large wooden desk. The craftsmanship was remarkable and unlike any desk he had seen in a public school. Principal McNamee caught his stare at the woodwork. "This has traveled with me from Boston to Virginia, and now here. It might look a little out of place, but it is almost like an old friend, that favorite coffee cup. I just could not imagine having an office without it."

Coach smiled with an instinctive understanding nod toward the Principal. Coach had watched his share of home shows on cable when the news and sports channels would not hold his interest. He had a new appreciation for design and furnishings. "Please have a seat," said Principal McNamee. His hair was white and neatly trimmed. He had a toothy smile and a voice that was smooth and similar to the radio newscaster Coach would sometime listen to in Savannah.

They exchanged pleasantries and discussed upbringing, values, and how their paths had finally crossed. It was a mutual discussion with both men doing as much listening as talking. The subtle but skillful questions was on par for any high-profile Division 1 College Coach that he had agreed to meet with that had entered his office with the goal of signing one of his kids. This meeting did not feel like an interview nor did the Principal have any desire for it to. He had a monumental interest in the Coach before him and wanted to know as much as he could to confirm if this was the right fit for his school.

One concern for the McNamee was the move from a state powerhouse to a small private school. They discussed the obvious first. "What are your concerns with budgeting for the program? We are solely funded through our tuition and annual fundraisers. I don't know what you had to spend in Georgia, but I can assure you that you want have a fraction of that here."

Coach remained firm and direct in his response. "I will do what it takes to put the best effort forward with the team. If I am short on equipment, or practice or game needs, I will work with my staff and do what we need to do to raise the necessary monies." Coach paused and contemplated if now was the time to let the Principal know that his path back to the sideline was not about the money or what a school could offer. The loss of his job and career trajectory had been humbling. But in the absence, he had been reminded of why he chose coaching.

McNamee had done his homework. Not quite the analysis of for a background investigation for a future FBI agent, but pretty close. He asked some traditional questions to gauge work ethic, attention to detail, and key performance accomplishments. Coach showed humility in his responses while allowing specific examples to shine through for each question. Both men were enjoying the interaction and Coach had positive thoughts.

A knock on the door was followed by the admin reminding McNamee he was needed in another meeting. He responded with a request for one more minute. She smiled and shut the door. He crossed his arms across the desk. He looked Coach directly in the eyes. "Mr. Jackson, what questions do you have for me?"

Nate smiled. "Principal McNamee. Is there any unanswered question that would keep me from being the next Head Football Coach?"

The stunning grasslands separate the coastal islands of the Glynn County coast.

CHAPTER 23

The players milled around the practice field. Some were engaged in conversation from the previous school day. Others sat quietly on one knee awaiting the first whistle. The fatigue was building in. The end of the week was nearing. It was cool in North Georgia and had rained earlier. A passing front had brought chilly air. Some of the players had moved to long sleeve undershirts to combat the changing elements.

Dante Alexander pushed Kyle Morgan to throw him some passes. His head was not into this session. He had thought of Stephanie and her absence for the upcoming weekend. She would be making a college visit with her parents and leave on Friday. The Friday was their first and only day off during the season. He had had not been his charming self with her or her friends at school somewhat pissed that her parents had not allowed him to travel with them. He felt he had a very good relationship with the family and tagging along would be a no brainer. He would have enjoyed a trip to Atlanta and seeing Georgia Tech and Emory, two schools she was considering. His name never came up and it appeared a weekend with the boys in Dance County was now being forced on the schedule.

The whistle interrupted his thoughts. Coach Watters stood at the fifty flanked by Williams and Griffin. "Let's go, men, we have only a couple of more practices left before our bye week officially ends. Let's get moving. Alexander, lead us in stretching."

Dante ran toward the thirty. The players moved to arrange four lines ten yards apart. Dante screamed right leg over left and the choreography was on. Stretching lasted about ten minutes then a second shrill of the whistle sent the players to their respective position groups. The offensive skill players waited in the middle of the field for Williams to take them through their warm up exercises.

Williams charged toward them with his whistle blowing in three pops in rapid session. The men instinctively lined up three across and trotted across the field doing high knee raises in unison. A pop of the whistle signaled the next line. The players would line up at the boundary line facing the stands and repeat the exercise. Four more exercises would follow and then practice was officially underway.

Williams took some ribbing from a couple of his players as they discussed the preparation for their next opponent. The challenge would be so much greater than what Liberty had brought to Dance County. It would be a very serious week of practice and learning. The kids were not ready to focus. "What you got planned this weekend, Coach?" a backup receiver asked.

"Film study, son, we got to get ready for some football a week from Friday." One of the kids chuckled almost as if to say he didn't believe the Coach would spend a perfectly good weekend camped out in front of a screen watching game film. Williams turned toward the young player.

"What type of defense does Clayton run?" he stared at the kid his mannerisms and persona becoming very cold in a second. "What type of coverage can our wideouts expect on third down?" The kid had panic in his eyes. There had been talk of a film study among the players, but it ended there. Since Griffin and Davis had died, the attention to detail had been the first to go from the younger players.

Watters had witnessed a similar exchange on the defensive side of the practice field. He was on a short fuse and carried with him some emotional baggage from a particularly tough day at school. His whistle interrupted the sounds of the wind whipping through the sparsely leaved trees lining the practice field.

"Bring it together, now!" The players trotted toward the middle of the field. Some stood, and others took a knee with apprehension in front of the three coaches. "Alright, gentlemen we have been out here for less than thirty minutes and I am not seeing the level of focus that is needed from this team. We are headed for another piss poor start if we continue down this road." Number 1 offense to my left, Number 1 defense to my right. Gentlemen, we are going to scrimmage the rest of the practice and more importantly we are going to practice our plays until they are damn perfect. Do we understand each other?"

The players could not believe what they were hearing. Full contact practices were always earlier in the week. By Thursday, the routine was never blocking and tackling and high-speed contact. Once again, the perceived normal had blown up in front of them.

Kyle Morgan moved toward the sideline. He was looking for the red vest that signaled to the defense he was not to be touched during live drills. Watters anticipated the move. He met the kid at the sideline. "Live scrimmage QB 1, No vest." Morgan shot him an angry stare and then trotted toward the huddle. He was one of the strongest kids in the weight room but getting hurt before he had a chance to play college ball was a frequent concern to both he and his parents.

"Looks like you're in the same boat with us common folks, Kyle," Ben Young said from the huddle.

He shrugged off the comment. "All right, let's light these boys up." The offense broke the circle and trotted toward the line. The defensive line looked at the formation and adjusted their stance. Morgan barked the cadence while a receiver went in motion left to right. Ben Young snapped the ball and the first play was underway.

Several fathers had lined up along the practice field fence. There was chatter on the practice schedule. A scrimmage this late in the week not only was not the norm but would have never been ordered by Davis or Parks.

A blitz had been called to test the offense right off the bat. Ben Young dug his heels in after the snap and had no trouble with the first man that crossed the line. He was positioned with his hand clenching the defensive lineman's jersey at the letters. Young was pushing him forward. All was good until a linebacker had exploded from his outside position and barreling ahead through the interior of the line. The right guard attempted a last-minute move toward him to slow the onslaught.

Morgan was surprised at the sudden collapse of the pocket. He was in trouble, desperately looking for an escape route first hoping to launch a pass to a secondary receiver. The big backer had speed and momentum. He placed his helmet into Morgan's numbers. The thud of Morgan landing on his backside was heard throughout the sideline. Morgan's dad witnessed it from the fence. He waited patiently for his son to pop up, to show everyone that hit was clean and now an afterthought. Morgan's head violently hit the hard turf. He was slow to get up. He pushed himself off the grass. He knocked the dirt off his knees and spit the dust from his mouth. He shot an angry glare at his offensive line now circled ten yards back from the huddle one play earlier.

"What the was that?" Morgan stared at his line.

Young shot back, "It was a blitz, idiot, you need to get rid of the ball."

Morgan shook his head. "Hold their butts this time and keep them out of this backfield." They broke the huddle a second time attempting a simple run play. Number 1 defense was feeling good. Chatter started at the line before the line was even in formation. A secondary back had moved up toward the interior linemen. The offense felt the pressure of a back to back blitz. This was no ordinary end of the week practice. Things were very serious and very full speed.

Morgan took the snap from under center and handed the ball to his big tailback rocketing toward the mass of players in front of him. The handoff was only a second old when a defensive back ordered to disrupt the play placed his helmet on Morgan's shoulder. He drove QB 1 to the ground while the defensive line shut down the ball carrier behind the line of scrimmage.

Morgan's dad had seen enough. He waited for his son to get up, taking a deep breath as he worried about multiple body parts on his only son, now seeing the two plays delivering so much force. Kyle Morgan did get up, this time much slower. And this time there was no bounce or eagerness to take the huddle. He grabbed his shoulder and stared at Watters and Williams.

Morgan's dad walked toward his car. His cell phone was about to be out of his wallet as he internally debated on who to call first. The task was not necessary because his phone vibrated in his pocket. He clicked the key fob auto starting his vehicle. Looking down at the phone, Dan Green's name appeared on the screen. There were no pleasantries on Morgan's mind when he swiped the screen to answer. The response was not "hello, how are you?" Or what can I do for you?" The response was direct and to the point. "Dan, we got a big problem."

CHAPTER 24

Coach Nate had driven back to Savannah from Jacksonville and arrived just as the traffic was starting to pick up. His starched shirt was rolled at the sleeves. The tie was now in a loose ball and was on the passenger seat. He contemplated his next move. He had not worked out but did not care for exercise this late in the day. He was a morning person through and through. If the run or weight lifting did not happen before daybreak it was postponed to the following day.

He thought about fishing, but sundown was close, and he did no desire to fight the bugs and critters after dark. His stomach growled, and he remembered he had not had anything to eat outside of a protein bar when he left the interview.

The traffic on the four-lane was nearing bumper to bumper. He made a decision at the next intersection to u turn it and head in the opposite direction of his apartment and away from the work and school commuters heading for the suburbs. The neon sign was the only marker on the dirt road intersecting with the busy highway. He turned the truck right. The suspension held as the cab bucked up and down with the uneven surface. A dozen or so cars and pickups lined the single level wood framed building. A covered porch wrapped around the structure providing cover from the scorching son and too frequent rain showers. A lone white sign in desperate need of maintenance and a fresh coat of paint alerted visitors they had arrived a Gentleman Jack's Oyster Bar and Seafood. He parked the truck and hurried inside.

He recognized a few regulars perched at the bar. There was eye contact as a couple of electricians still in uniform raised a longneck Bud in his direction. He acknowledged the gesture with a head nod. He eyeballed a chair at the opposite end with several empty stools and grabbed one.

The bartender was in her mid-thirties and mesmerized the patrons with striking beauty and quick wit. Something one may have found unexpected for a shack bar and grill buried on a dirt road in South Georgia, at least for any first-time visitors, which he was not. She had dark fire streaked red hair that ran long down her back. Dark eyes complemented ageless facial features. She had long tanned legs and not one imperfection with her body. She could have easily adorned a television screen, but life has many roadways and hers led her here. He had always liked her, and she knew it. As the booze flowed and the men became bolder, she became stronger and acted without hesitation. No one hit on this young lady and there was plenty of back up if needed.

She spotted Coach and walked over with a cold longneck. He gave the approval and she flung the metal cap toward a trash can making a pinging sound. "How are you tonight?"

He smiled, thankful for the interest. "Not bad, any recommendations for dinner pretty lady?"

She was receptive to the compliment but only from him and responded with a white toothy smile. There was a brief pause and then the sultry southern voice. "I had the gumbo for lunch, and it was pretty good."

Nate smiled at the thought of dark spicy rue and fresh seafood. "That sounds good, no rush, I'll probably have a couple of these first," as he raised the cold bottle toward her.

He finished the first one in four deep gulps. The crowd at the end of the bar was changing shifts. The electricians had been joined by some other skilled laborers tasked with new housing development along the interstate. Dinner was at home with their families. The limit was two maybe no more than three drinks and they were gone. Young professionals, some from the apartment complex Coach lived in, were now making their way on to the stools. Coach contemplated his third beer before giving the go ahead on the food order. He shifted his attention toward the flat screens. Football. It was everywhere.

He felt a hand on his shoulder. Ordinarily he would have turned quickly to see who had been able to make their way up behind him. He had consumed two beers in very quick fashion. The empty stomach and the adrenaline of the day had allowed the booze to circulate quickly. He was buzzed and did not want to admit it to himself.

"How are you, Nate?" He turned and looked at his former boss. Paul Edmonson was dressed in similar attire. He wore dark pants and white shirt. There may have been a tie and sport coat on earlier, but it was now gone. Nate looked around before responding. He was curious if Paul was alone or with others. Confident there was no other surprise visitors he made a hand gesture toward the open stool beside him. Paul appreciated the first sign of welcome and sat down.

Nate pushed the empty bottle away. She recognized the man sitting to his left. She walked over this time with two bottles and placed them before them. She acknowledged his presence but the temperature in her attitude toward the visitor had dropped twenty degrees. The pinging sound was louder as two bottle caps ricocheted off the can. Nate turned toward Paul. "How are you, Sir? I haven't seen you in a while."

The response was expected but still formal and cold. Paul realized the wounds were deep and fresh. "I'm sorry, I should have called."

Nate was tired of uncomfortable. He liked Paul. He knew he was in a tough spot and just following orders from his superiors. It wasn't personal, it was just business. There was a family, kids, responsibility. He was not going to punish him. Both men had been through enough. "How's Becky? And the kids?" Coach said.

Paul's facial expression loosened. He relaxed. "They are good. They ask about you, want to know how you are doing."

Nate kept his eyes forward. He was staring at the bartender keep up with thirty or so patrons and mix drinks for the rest of the diners away from the bar. Skilled athleticism on display. "I appreciate that, Paul, please let them know I said hello."

Beer two for Paul and number four for Coach arrived. Paul was on borrowed time and looked nervously at his watch. He had a message he wanted to deliver. For Coach, he was appreciative, but it wasn't necessary. The fact the man had the courage to approach him when so many would not be good enough in his book.

"I am your friend," he said. "If you need anything, a referral, letter of recommendation, anything, please let me know."

Coach turned to him as Paul stood up. He laid a twenty by the bottle. Coach waved it toward him and said, "No worries, I got this." Paul nodded, put the bill in his front pocket and turned toward the door. Coach let him get about ten feet toward the exit. "Paul."

He turned around and looked at the Coach. "Thanks."

The gumbo arrived, and Coach asked the beauty behind the bar for hot-sauce and pepper. He opened a pack of saltines and crushed them in his hand adding a top layer to the meaty gumbo. She asked him if he needed anything else. He took one look at his beer and she turned toward the cooler. He polished off his fourth Miller Lite before the bottle cap hit the trash can.

Decision time came thirty minutes later. The younger crowd that had replaced the men with early wake up calls had started to thin. The third shift at the bar would take it to closing time. The professional drinkers took up a third of the bar, some with lives to get to later on, others in question. Coach was at his decision time. He was right at the line on whether or not he should drive home. He had been there for some time, had alternated his last drinks with water, and conned the sexy barkeep for seconds on the gumbo.

She walked toward him, having finished cashing out a group of three twenty somethings at the end of the bar. He was surprised their attention was on their phones and not the beauty before them. Her curvaceous figure not lost on his stare. The shorts were very tight, and he tried to block the thoughts coming from multiple influencers. She broke his silence with a simple smile and question about his plans for the evening. She was now being flirtatious, and he no longer questioned the booze or his insecurities.

She grabbed a bottle and poured a couple of shots. He waved his hand at first, but she kept pushing. The liquid burned as it hit the back of his throat. He grimaced at first then forced a fake smile. She was effortless in her movements. There was a slight clinking sound as the glass hit the aged bar top. The drop dead gorgeous look was on full display behind the bar and this time it carried a wink.

He looked at his phone, saw the ridesharing app, and asked for another round.

CHAPTER 25

Dance County High School had a two- bell system to start the day. The first was a warning bell. It signaled the students had five minutes to make their way from the hallways or for some the parking lots to their homeroom classes. The second bell was final, and teachers had full support to write as many tardies as necessary to keep order for the twenty-seven hundred kids enrolled.

Kyle Morgan didn't need the first or second bell to have him at his seat this morning. He had got to school early. He didn't want to get caught in the pending drama. His body was sore, and he still carried some after effects of being slammed to the turf during the impromptu scrimmage ordered by Watters. He sat quietly in his homeroom chair ignoring the chatter around him.

Down the hallway, his father had assembled with six other parents awaiting entry into the Principal's office. The door leading to Principal Lee had been shut. He had been warned of the upcoming meeting demands through a text from his loyal administrator. The parent group represented players injured during the practices of the previous week. The majority were strains and sprains with the most serious including a possible ACL tear and concussion.

Watters had no idea of the pending firestorm as he pulled into campus at his usual time one hour before the first warning bell. He had thrown a couple of good mornings at two of his players that were forced by busing to arrive on property way before school started. There was a "sup coach" response from one and a distrusting stare from the other one. Watters shrugged it off and blamed it on the typical lack of sleep and early wake-up call as he made his way into the offices adjoining the gym and stadium.

Watters shuffled through some lesson planning. He had classes he was responsible for before he could turn his attention toward the afternoon and the upcoming practice schedule. He confirmed that he could play a movie to fulfill the class lesson plans for the day and shuffled his pile on his desk. He looked at the practice schedule agreed upon after the scrimmage from the following evening. The attire was shorts, t shirts, and helmets for the Patriots. They would run through their game plan for the upcoming regional game that would take place one week from Friday. This was the make or break game, and everyone had doubts. The gamble on the scrimmage was backfiring before him and he knew it. Too many players were hurt and his read on Kyle Morgan was that he had pushed him too far. He knew he had to pull back hard on the intensity and find a way to build the kids back up.

His alarm rang signaling him to make his way to the main building. He entered a side door and was walking to his classroom. He looked at the main office to his left as he made his way down the hall. James Morgan and several players' parents were being led into the office by Principal Lee's secretary. His heart jumped. He felt a sudden wave of fear and panic shoot through his body. He kept walking, head high, "keep your cool" he told himself. He was breathing almost normal when another figure appeared almost hitting him as he walked through the last mass of kids scrambling for their classes with the ringing of the warning bell. Dan Green made eye contact with the first year Coach. That was it. He found the teacher's lounge and walked right into the men's room. He found an empty stall, sat on the toilet, then proceeded to bury his face into his hands.

Dan Green had entered Principal Lee's office last. There were extra chairs in the room, but he decided to stand. His plan for this meeting was to let the parents make the case. He would participate if needed but he felt the strongest points would come from those directly impacted.

James Morgan did not let him down. He detailed the practices that happened not once but over and over since the Liberty game. He eloquently described how the tried and true coaching plans were not being remotely followed and how what seemed to be barbaric rituals had made their way onto the Dance County practice field. He laid out specific examples of the drills that were continued after several injuries followed by extensive detail of a full contact scrimmage normally occurring during the preseason had happened just yesterday.

The other men in attendance were hesitant at first. They knew what was occurring was unchartered waters for all involved. Going after a Georgia Football coach at this stage, where so much has happened already. And it is football, a response from one of the dads when the meeting was being planned, where full contact drills and bloodied scrimmages were expected.

Lee listened patiently. He was eyeballing Dan Green hoping not to be noticed by the parents in the room. He wondered when the most influential booster was going to share his opinions. He knew that this many parents, with this much passion had a leader driving this meeting. He guessed he could give credit to Morgan but with Green in attendance he knew that was not the case.

Morgan stopped his plea to allow two of the moms detail their concern with the pain their sons were in when they arrived home. They spoke of difficulty walking and one not being able to concentrate during dinner. Morgan looked around the room then waited to deliver the home run punch.

"Kyle was not allowed to wear the colored vest during the scrimmage," he said. "He tried to put it on, but Watters stopped him at the sideline. That vest ordered by Coach Davis tells every player on that field that the quarterback was not to be touched."

Lee looked down at his notebook in front of him. He scratched at it with a Mont Blanc pen that had been a Christmas present from his wife. He knew the vest worn to protect quarterbacks was not unique to Coach Davis. It had been used when he played high school ball in the Northeast. Details he didn't have to go in to. He continued to listen patiently.

"Watters' assistants dialed up several blitzes, Kyle and that offensive line never had a chance." Morgan paused then continued. "He took some very bad hits, Mr. Lee. I am very concerned about his physical and emotional health right now. Right now, with all the nationwide media attention on head injuries, football is not winning any popularity contest with the public right now."

Morgan's wife sat very still with an ashen look on her face. She couldn't believe the twist and turn beginning with the horrific car accident that had taken the lives of Davis and Parks. A crashing blow to a small town that had impacted everyone.

Dan Green moved forward from the back of the room. It was now his stage to bring it all together and provide the school and Principal Lee a solution.

"Mr. Lee, we can't have our all region QB hurt at practice. Mr. Lee we all know the great recognition this young man brings this great school with his potential to play at a Power Five university," Green said. He was still standing at the back of the room with his arms folded in almost a defiant stance.

Lee spoke for the first time on the subject. "I speak not only for myself but my faculty, we care about every student athlete that steps on that field." Lee paused. "These are concerning actions and I appreciate all of you taking time out of your busy schedules to bring them to my attention. I can assure you I will have a discussion with the Coaches," Lee said.

Dan Green unfolded his arms. He approached the desk. The parents noticed his non-verbal cues. This was not going to be a comfortable conversation they were now privy to. One mom looked at the door considering an escape route. Several sets of eyes looked down suddenly interested in the condition of the shoes they were wearing. James Morgan stared at a picture of Principal Lee handing a regional trophy to Coach Davis at a football banquet two years earlier.

"No disrespect, Principal Lee but that is not good enough. This is a crisis now and these kids and this town do not deserve this," Green said. He paused for a moment at a crossroads. He had opened the door now and there was no turning back. He could give Lee the push to do the right thing in his mind or close the door and take over everything. When Dan Green walked into the school that morning he was fully prepared to do the latter.

"Principal Lee, we are asking you to request an emergency board meeting tonight, based on the facts that you have been presented today. We have a coach in waiting that would surpass any national expectations. He has significant experience coaching young men and documented outstanding performance. We need you to set the stage with the board and get the approval to move forward."

Green paused and threw his last punch to the gut, planting that imaginary seed there were a hundred lawyers waiting by the phone for that green light to start filing lawsuits. "We can't have any more young men hurt."

Lee was seething inside. He was outweighed by Green by easily sixty or so pounds and at least three inches. Any other setting, he may not have cared and flung himself across the desk, letting the Boston street-baller come out with a in your face challenge and maybe a swing to the face. He knew it was best to look away from Green. He tried to read the expressions in the faces of the mothers before him. The hurt and pain was enough. He gave Green his victory.

Lee stood up. He committed to moving the process forward to the group. "I will take all of this under advisement. This is a fluid situation and will involve many people at different levels. I understand the urgency but also ask for your patience."

Lee went on to thank everyone again for their time and attendance. His admin opened the door leading the contingent of parents out of his office.

He shook everyone's hand as they proceeded to the door except Green. He motioned for him to stay.

CHAPTER 26

Nate had rolled out of bed just after seven a.m. This was the latest he had slept in quite some time. Even with the years he was employed he never got close to being in bed this time of the morning. He did a survey of the room. The sheets were crumpled at the end of the mattress. A pillow had made its way to the floor.

She had left around four am. He thought he felt a kiss on his cheek. He definitely remembered the shutting of the door as she exited the apartment. He wanted to find wrong in the decision making. He wanted to beat himself up for his lapse in control. It was not going to happen this morning. He too busy now thinking of her.

They had left the bar on the wrong side of midnight. She had driven to his apartment with Coach riding shotgun. He remembered a late model Honda or maybe a Toyota. There was loud music screaming from the speakers, a catchy tune from the eighties. They both were singing like kids taking the family car out without permission. He remembered a pretty voice that could hit the high notes, he couldn't.

When they arrived at the apartment, she kidded him about his bachelor furnishings and attention to detail. Not a hair out of place is how she may have described it. She asked him if there was a girlfriend. He dodged the answer and she let it go. He was down to a six pack of longneck bottles in his fridge. He offered her one. When he handed her an open one she sat it down on the coffee table and leaned toward him.

It was his first kiss in quite some time.

He smiled as he made coffee. The television was on in the background, but he wasn't paying attention. He was hungry, but he had not been to a grocery store. Outside of the remaining six pack and a gallon of spring water, the fridge was empty. He pulled at a drawer out next to the silverware. He found a protein bar advertising 20 grams of whey protein. He tore the package and took his first bite as the sounds of the coffee hitting the glass pot began.

Coach was on his second cup when the phone rang. "Hello, Nate Jackson?" he said using the speaker phone key.

Principal McNamee's voice boomed from the tiny speaker. "Good morning, Nate, how are you?

Coach smiled. He was thankful he had caffeine and a little food now in his system. "I am doing well, Sir, how are you?"

McNamee responded quickly and was very direct. "I am doing well, thank you. Nate, I was very impressed with our meeting. I know you have a lot of options in front of you and you are a going to bring a great deal of skill sets to your next employer." He paused momentarily. "Nate, I would like for you to bring that talent to our High School, I would like to offer you the opportunity to be our Head Football Coach."

Coach smiled. A whirlwind of emotions over the last few weeks had seemed to last for an eternity. He realized how much he had prayed and when all had been lost had turned it over to God, realized he still had a ways to go.

His pause in the conversation was longer than normal. He knew he needed to say something.

"Thank you, Mr. McNamee, your words and this opportunity mean a great deal to me. I can't thank you enough for this call," he said.

"You are welcome, Nate. My admin will be putting together a letter and official offer package for you that will be overnighted to your address tonight. Please take a look and let us know if you have any questions."

Coach paused. "Thank you, sir, I look forward to receiving and will follow up as soon as possible."

They exchanged pleasantries again. It was clear that the Principal wanted an answer in line with Coach's response as soon as possible following receipt of the documents. He told McNamee he would call him after he received the package and they ended their call. Coach sat his coffee down on the table and walked over to the sofa. He didn't sit down. He kneeled by the cushions, interlocked his fingers, stared at the sky, then closed his eyes and prayed.

He got up and walked over to his desk. This was the point when his mind went into overdrive. He looked at the legal pad. There was fresh page awaiting his game plan for him to scribe. There were personal decisions and the checklist associated with a move to another state. Then there were the professional decisions. A staff would need to be hired. He had the referral that brought him to the lead. Would there be other coaches that would be part of the deal. His previous staff had stayed on at the school he was let go. There was agreement he would not come back for them. Friendships had been tested and steady paychecks had won. Going back and fighting that battle was not even a second thought.

He loved the surge of adrenaline he was now feeling. He reminded himself how important it was to enjoy the moment. He had coached his kids on this, now it was his time.

His stomach growled. The booze was still circulating. He knew he needed more than the protein bar he had just consumed. Grease, eggs and bacon with some toast and juice was what his body needed. Clear his mind with a big breakfast. He grabbed his keys and walked out of the apartment. The giddiness disappeared when he realized he would first have to hire a ride to his parked truck at the bar from last night.

Forty minutes later and one-half baked explanation to a twenty something Uber driver, he pulled his truck in front of the small diner. The crowd from earlier had dissipated as the clock was well into the workday. An older waitress was cleaning up from the previous rush. She saw him and made her way toward him. He politely asked for a coffee and water, and then hurriedly went through a large breakfast request. The waitress smiled and disappeared with his order.

He eyeballed a newspaper stand. He fished fifty cents from his pocket and walked over and engaged the stand. He pulled the state paper from Atlanta from the rack and walked back to the booth. The headline told of a very tight and nasty Mayoral race in the Capital City. What was new there he thought to himself. He separated the sections. Sports would be read first, then local, followed by business then lifestyle. The waitress returned with his food and he cleared an area just big enough for the large plate in front of him.

He admired the food on the table. Three eggs scrambled, cooked just right, were at the centerpiece, three slices of thick smoked bacon lining one side of the plate with a cup of perfectly cooked grits holding a rectangular shaped block of butter lined up opposite. The waitress returned with a fresh cup of juice, and extra water, and a small round plate with two buttermilk biscuits.

He was on page four of the sports page. The area normally reserved for high school sports and non-headline stories. He was about to lay the paper down and dig into his king size meal. The small ink had the story buried in the corner of the page. He had scanned by it at first then looked at it again. The headline read, "Dance County Patriots looking South for new Football Coach."

He read the story twice and folded the paper and moved it aside. The food smelled so good, but he was suddenly not hungry. His great news, minus the hangover, had been robbed by a story quoting anonymous sources.

His name was in the second sentence just after the line reminding everyone of the school's tragic loss of Coach Davis and Parks. The reporter had rehashed his winning percentage and his team's feature on ESPN. The story finished with guarded words on the separation citing an undisclosed recruiting violation.

He scanned his internal memory bank. He then reached for his phone and checked the call log. He was featured in a story in the Southeast US's largest paper and no one had reached out to him. He shook his head and remembered why his mentor had warned him about the media.

He pulled a twenty from his wallet. He took one long sip of the water as he ignored the rest of the food before him. Ordinarily there would not be this showing of waste. Ordinarily he would use the mealtime to strategize, and formulate a plan. But this morning he was pissed and, unfortunately. he knew this was just the beginning. He pushed the twenty underneath the plate and made his way to the door.

CHAPTER 27

The Dance County Government was now moving at supersonic speed. The mud of bureaucracy normally associated with any types of changes, especially in education, was not present at this given moment. Nevertheless, political capital had been burned. Principal Lee had stuck his neck out. And now an emergency board meeting was scheduled for two that afternoon just hours after the parents had left the school office.

Lee had not going let the biggest booster off easy. His conversation with Green that morning was stern. He was not happy how Green was forcing the situation at mid-season and undermining his leadership. Lee saw it as a critical juncture in his tenure and he was not going to take a back seat.

"What makes you so confident he is going to accept our offer to coach here?" Lee asked. Green shared with him that he had ties to the community. He was close friends with the Alexander family and that he had watched that young man grow up. He wanted to help him achieve his dreams and play at the next level. Lee bought the response with hesitancy. He was still not sure at the time he would be able to corral an emergency gathering of the school board. It would take a mountain to be moved and he knew that before the parents entered his office that morning.

Green looked hard at the Principal. A reverse to where the conversation was heading. "What are your concerns, Principal Lee? I mean you have a top-rated Coach with a national reputation that you have a shot at landing on your sideline."

Lee stared at his top booster remaining silent. "When you were in Boston and there was any mention of high school football in the South. Do you remember any of the schools that were mentioned? I bet you heard the name Valdosta and I bet it was because they were winning so much and had been recognized countless times as having the best teams in the nation." Green paused then continued. "You have that chance here, today, with this Coach. He can continue the

work of Matt Davis, potentially taking it to the next level, and ensuring
the reputation to this school and all the positive academic and influ-
ences a winning program has on the students."

Principal Lee took it all in. He had made his decision to reach out
to the board after the second parent's plea earlier that morning. This
time with Dan Green was simply to reestablish boundaries.

Principal Lee leaned forward in his chair. He placed his elbows
on his desk. His posture was perfect and eye contact was dead center
with Dance County's biggest booster. He was not going to lay down a
speech, but nor what the few words he was about to say, would never
be misunderstood.

"Dan, I appreciate all that you do for this school and I appreciate all of the work in assisting with this search. But please understand
one thing, any offers to any teachers or coaches or anyone that is employed at Dance County High School will come from me. Understood?" Green nodded at the veteran educator. The look on his face
was enough. Lee responded, "Thank you."

The impromptu meeting of the board was held at the elementary
school auditorium. The local newspaper had sent a first-year reporter
over to the school to cover the event. Dan Green sat in the back row
along with a handful of parents that had met with Lee earlier. The meeting was called to order by Chair Hugh Davis at 2:05 p.m. as sounds
from the hallways of kids headed for carpool were heard through the
aging facility.

"I call this meeting to order," Davis said. "It is my understanding that we have had some developments concerning one of our high
school programs and Principal Lee would like to address the committee with an urgent request." Davis paused. He looked at each of his
board members then continued. "Principal Lee, the floor is yours."

Lee stood and walked up to the table that had been arranged for
the board on the auditorium stage. He double checked to make sure
he was not missing a podium or a microphone. "Chairman Davis, our
honorable board of education, thank you for allowing me the opportunity to stand before you today." He quickly scanned the faces of the
board. "Can everyone hear me ok?" he asked. There were a couple of
quick nods from the members. A female board member Lee had met at
on the holiday events smiled at him. He continued.

"I am here today requesting that the board expedite today the approval for the hiring of a Head Football Coach. Dance County experi-

enced a tragic and devastating loss with the sudden passing of our head coach and assistant head coach just weeks ago. We will never be able to replace what Matt Davis and Sam Parks brought to our community. These gentlemen were makers of men and their efforts have had profound effects on generations of Dance County Students."

Lee paused for only a second and continued.

"With all of the pain this community has been through, we must move forward. Life does move on. The football schedule has continued. There are fifty plus young men that deserve a chance to play a sport that they love, and to have the absolute best in leadership on the field with them when they are doing it."

Hugh Davis appreciated the tribute. He felt that the board should do more to recognize the heralded efforts of both of these men. He was not aware of what was going on behind the scenes with a new coach, nor did he quite understand the sense of urgency when three coaches were already leading the team.

Jim Harrison was a senior board member that lived in Greenwood. He followed football but had attended the City High School twenty years earlier. His two kids were enrolled at Greenwood High School. He did not feel he would be out of place to address the Principal.

"Principal Lee, I am sure I speak for everyone when extending our heartfelt sympathy to you and your school over the tragic loss of Coach Davis and Coach Parks," Harrison said. Lee looked directly at Harrison and acknowledged him with a head nod. "I realize that the first game back did not go well, but I don't understand why the men that are coaching now are not getting more time with the team. We have three coaches there now. Shouldn't we give this some time?"

There was buy in to Harrison's comments from the board members. Hugh Davis also appreciated the comments from Harrison. He made a mental note to share that with him after the meeting.

Principal Lee was at a crossroads. He could go all in and share everything from the Parent meetings. That could push the board for the hiring but also kill the career of his three recently promoted assistants. He could give Dan Green a greenlight to address the committee a second time. He cringed at that thought and moved on. He looked at the board members one at a time. He knew a pause here would not hurt. This was a very delicate conversation in addition to an urgent plea and he was not going to be pushed into acceptance by the fact he was now looking up at the board holding all of the power from their raised chairs on the stage which made all of them seem like giants to the audience.

"Mr. Harrison, I appreciate the thoughts extended from you and the board. It is my recommendation that we move forward with an offer to a highly successful and seasoned football coach that can provide immediate contributions to our program." Lee paused for a moment then continued.

"I have personally observed recent football practices and today I met with several parents. As we are all very much aware, there is a learning curve when anyone takes on something new. Coaches are no different than a teacher or any other professional promoted. A teacher can be promoted to a leadership position and they may be the best teacher in the world. But at that same a teacher may have several months or even years before they are performing at expectations with complex adult personnel issues. This is no different from what we have today. We have coaches that are now the architect of practices and fully responsible for game time decisions leading our young men. These coaches were not doing that just weeks ago. There have been mistakes. And these mistakes we can overcome today, by not forcing these changes and bringing in a highly regarded Coach to mentor our assistants and most importantly mentor our young players."

Lee paused again, hoping his message was resonating. "Football is a dangerous sport. Players get injured. Now more than ever we need the absolute best on that sideline leading these men."

Lee looked at the board. He pleaded with his eyes. He was dressed in his best dark suit and a baby blue tie. He could have passed for a CEO making a corporate pitch to the best and brightest in a board room in Boston's financial district among sidewalks and skyscrapers. Today he was in North Georgia, Dance County, where the pine trees and farm rows smother the city. This was his biggest pitch of his educational career. Get this one right and the gray skies that had encapsulated the school just might be giving way to some much-needed sunshine.

"I come before you today, honorable members of the school board, with the urgent and timely request that you please approve the hiring of a new head football coach for Dance County High School."

CHAPTER 28

The Beechcraft Twin Air took off from an executive airport just north of Atlanta at 6:30 on a sun-drenched morning. At the controls was a seasoned and high-priced attorney that had piloted as a hobby since he was in his teens. He was also the first call for any contracts or legal issues that the man sitting to his right in the copilot seat would contact.

Principal Lee was in the second row of seats. He nursed a coffee the men had picked up at a Dunkin Donuts near the airport just north of the field. He was mindful he was not flying commercial and that an aging prostate called for him to hit the bathroom more than most. He had made it a point to hit the head one more time before they boarded the plane. To his right and taking up an unfair amount of room was William Alexander. He was Dan Green's ace in the hole. Any difficulty or pushback from the Coach, and William would be summoned to save the day and get the commitment for the boosters and parents of Dance County. Green had turned around at least three times in the flight and smiled at Alexander to insure he was comfortable and enjoying his trip to South Georgia.

The flight took fifty-eight minutes wheels up to wheels down. There was not a great deal of conversation amongst the four men. The flight was unusually smooth for a propeller aircraft and the men were enjoying the view from 18,000 feet. There were very few clouds and Principal Lee took it upon himself to name all the small towns from the north to the south.

The captain would not be going with them to their meeting. He had some impromptu business in Savannah and agreed to meet them back at the plane at two that afternoon to fly them back to Atlanta. He had pointed out a Delta commercial jet climbing from Savannah Hilton Head International Airport en route to Atlanta. The men were impressed with the speed of the MD 88 as it traveled in the opposite direction as they were making their descent into the airport.

The plane landed, and the three men transferred to a rental car. The

Chevy Equinox was the only SUV available and Green took it. It was
a tight fit for Alexander and Lee, like the plane, but this was without
surprise Dan Green's trip and the two men would have to decide which
one would take the backseat. Alexander being the Southern gentleman
graciously waved toward the front passenger door for Lee. A standoff
ensued and he said no and pleaded for Alexander to take it. Green became fidgety and wanted to get moving. Alexander stalled another few
seconds then opened the front door.

Green playfully slapped Alexander on the shoulder. "Looking a
little sickly, Sergeant. You ok?" Alexander said.

"Absolutely, I have had my share of helicopter rides with the patrol,
a twin air is luxury flying for me." Lee stared through the back passenger windshield. He was curious how all of this was going to play out.
He did not get the warm and fuzzies from his conversation with Nate
Jackson just after the board meeting.

The call to Nate's apartment from the Dance County Principal had
come in around 5:30 in the afternoon the previous day. He was staring at the FedEx package that had arrived from Jacksonville. It was the
paperwork outlining the offer from the Catholic high school. It was
sitting on his kitchen table unopened. All of the thoughts; the newspaper article, the call from North Georgia, and the potential to remain
in state coaching a high school powerhouse, were now doing jumping
jacks in his extremely fatigued mind.

He had enjoyed speaking with Principal Lee even with the earlier
impression the boosters were calling all the shots. He was very upfront
and shared with him there was an offer from a private school on the
table. Principal Lee had responded with a chamber of commerce de-
scription of Dance County and the opportunity to live and work there.
He spoke of the high caliber students and athletes he would have the
chance to lead. When he added that he would like to meet with him
and was flying down the next day, it was the closing statement that a
man coming off weeks of unemployment could not say no.

They agreed to meet at a local IHOP. The restaurant was busy as
expected for a Saturday morning. Families enjoying the weekend with
an incredulous carbohydrate load to provide them endless energy for
the weekend. Obnoxious stacks of pancakes were being served by over-
worked waitresses. Kid's voices reached extreme decibel levels and immediately there were second thoughts on the meeting location when
Lee, Green, and Alexander made their way into the packed restaurant.

Green had asked Lee to give them an extra thirty minutes before scheduling the meeting. The coach was supposed to meet them at nine a.m. They had arrived at the restaurant at just after 8:30. Plenty of time for Green to propose a short-term rental for a private room in the back of the restaurant normally held for community meetings. Alexander excused himself to hit the restroom, leaving Lee and Green alone by their temporary meeting location.

Coach Nate arrived at the restaurant seconds later, fifteen minutes early than their agreed time. Nate was a stickler for Lombardi time and this was no exception. He was going to grab a seat at the counter on a bar stool and collect his thoughts over a cup of fresh brewed coffee. His attention was diverted when he saw two men standing by a temporary partition that had been pulled to isolate a private room. A thin man with a white shirt and stained tie made his way over to him and asked if he was Mr. Jackson. Nate said yes, and he was led over to the men.

He assumed the heavy-set man dressed in a starched button down and pressed khakis was the booster and the more lean of the two with the grayish hair wearing the gray suit combination missing the tie, was Principal Lee. He extended his hand. "I'm Nate Jackson," he said.

Principal Lee smiled. He shook Nate's hand as if they were fraternity brothers reuniting after several years. "I'm Brian Lee, I would like to introduce you to Dan Green, one of our biggest supporters of Dance County Schools and Athletics and a local businessman." Nate made eye contact and extended his hand. Principal Lee gestured for the men to make themselves into the room and take a seat at the lone table.

Lee and Green sat on the opposite side of Nate. The assistant manager was back now, to take their beverage orders. Nate and Lee ordered coffee, black. Dan Green asked for a sweet iced tea with extra lemon. As the assistant manager was leaving, he went to close the partition to provide privacy for the meeting. The door was caught inches before the close by the mammoth sized hand. Alexander pushed the door back and entered the room. Nate looked up at his old friend. Any doubt on the full press on the pending job offer was just removed.

Alexander was wearing khaki pants and a white polo. Covering the shirt was a pull over that had the Georgia State Patrol insignia on the left pocket. It was a striking windbreaker and Alexander's physical stature elicited many stares from the patrons and actually lowered the decibel level from a few of the tables. He asked the assistant manager for an ice water as he was leaving. The server acknowledged the request and scooted toward the kitchen. Alexander sat next to Nate.

Nate turned to Alexander. "How have you been, William?"

Alexander smiled. This was not his show and he was careful with his words.

"Good, Coach, I'm very happy to see you this morning."

Green looked at Lee then spoke. "How long have you guys known each other? Y'all did some great things just up interstate 16 in a few years back."

Nate forced a slight grin. "That was a long time ago, but yes, there are some very good memories."

The drinks arrived. Nate looked at the teaspoon in the middle of the dark brew. He swirled it around while Lee and Green stared at the heralded coach before them.

"Coach, I know there are a lot of opportunities before you. You are a young man with a tremendous amount of talent and proven performance." Lee paused. "I wish we were here in January or February and we were working off a retirement of two legendary coaches. Unfortunately, we are here in October following a horrific tragedy and a season up in the air for fifty young men.

"I can speak from years of experience; I have never seen a school board move with such acceleration. There is a great deal on the table right now and I am here today asking for your involvement. I am asking you to join us and lead our football team."

Nate Jackson took a long look at Principal Lee, then a quick look at Dan Green. He had played the scenario over and over in his head. He wanted to bring up the newspaper article. Ask probing questions on who he would be reporting to, was it Lee? Was it the booster sitting next to him? He backtracked and changed his direction.

He chose his words carefully.

"Gentlemen, I am flattered for the consideration. There will always be better circumstances when coaching changes happen and no doubt this is the hardest one I have ever been a part of." Green smiled at Nate. With that one statement, Green's mind screamed to himself he was accepting the position. All the anxiety of the last few weeks was taking its toll emotionally and physically on the Dance County Booster. He sneaked a wink at Alexander while Nate was looking at Lee.

"I have an offer on the table to lead a program in Jacksonville. I am going to need some time on this one."

Green felt a surge of energy leave his body. He was about to go into a full press. He immediately remembered the conversation from Lee's office. Keep smiling he told himself. These things always find a way to work out.

Lee leaned forward in his chair. He knew at any time the partition would open and the assistant manager would be barging in to take their food order. He did not want to lose any momentum in the conversation.

"I am sure that is a good opportunity down in Duval County. But, Coach, with all due respect that is a private school in Florida. I am presenting an opportunity for you to stay in Georgia at a high region classification where your kids will play against the best and have the chance to demonstrate they are the best.

"You will not be selling kids on coming out to play football. You will be taking kids that have been playing for a long time to the next level." Lee paused. "I need a championship level Coach to continue the efforts of two hall of fame coaches.

Green was impressed with Lee's sudden demonstration of selling skills. He decided to remain quiet.

He had an attaché on the floor that had been hidden from view. He pulled it up and removed a file folder. "Inside you will find an offer letter, benefit and retirement information, and application. There is a ten percent raise over your previous salary at your last position. The challenges are there, and I wanted you to be compensated for them. The start date is this Monday and as you are aware we have a regional game Friday night." Lee paused. "I would like for you to be on that sideline."

Green added to the conversation. "I can help with the move and temporary housing. I can have a truck and new apartment lined up tomorrow. All you would have to do is pack a few days of clothes and drive up tomorrow."

It was exciting, and Nate was not lost on the despair that had come with the unknown prior to the job offerings.

"Is there a number I can reach you tonight?" Nate asked Lee.

Lee's face tightened. He felt he had his man but had been around enough recruiting that a pause was a maybe and maybes are fifty-fifty. The flight home might not be as enjoyable.

The assistant manager arrived at the table. He asked if they were ready to order. Each of the men ordered the Saturday special which included pancakes, eggs, and sausage. Nate had run six miles while the men were flying south. He was best suited to metabolize the mammoth combination plus had had not eaten a solid meal in the last twenty-four hours. Green on the other hand had polished off a twenty-four-ounce ribeye Friday evening in spite of his wife's wishes to lose some weight.

Nate excused himself to go to the bathroom. Green saw it as an opportunity. He motioned for Alexander to follow him. There was still one more card to play.

CHAPTER 29

Nate was washing his hands when Alexander walked in. He went to the sink beside him and did the same.

"You guys have given me a lot to think about," Nate said.

Alexander looked at his old friend. He forced a slight smile. He dried his hands with the large silver dryer attached to the wall. The jet engine noise of the machine drowned out the sounds from the men's restroom. Nate pushed the door open and headed back toward the meeting room. Alexander placed his hand on his shoulder. "Let's grab some fresh air, let the senior leadership at the table catch up."

The men made their way out into the parking lot. Multiple lines of SUVs and mini vans patrolled the parking lanes. There were some leaving, some arriving. There were dads already scrambling for parking spaces with stressed expressions. Families knowing the restaurant would be overflowing, still arriving seeing the alternative of cooking at home as less desirable. The men stood next at the corner of the restaurant. A line had formed at the entrance and a few of the parents had recognized the Coach. They were now safely out of earshot. Nate looked at the sky guessing the temperature would still be close to eighty for the high of the day.

Alexander looked at Nate. "I spoke to Pam yesterday." Pam was Alexander's ex-wife and Nate remembered her fondly from their college days. He knew she would be successful and he also knew, like the once love of his life, the boundaries of Georgia would not contain her.

"How is she doing?" Nate asked.

"She is doing well. She knows Dante will be graduating soon and would like to increase her time with him." He paused. "In spite of everything, we are finding a way to make it work the best we can."

Nate smiled at Alexander. He could not believe there had been that much separation in their relationship. He wished he could have changed that.

"Pam ran into Stacy last night." The words flew from the sky and grabbed Nate. He felt his heart jump through his throat. He couldn't believe a relationship from that long ago could spark such a reaction. Nate remained silent.

"They both were in a restaurant in Georgetown, one of those powerbroker spots with herds of pretty people and Washington elite." Alexander continued. "You know the place where the drinks are double digits and you need a pair of readers to see the food portions."

Nate awkwardly smiled, impressed at the critique. Alexander continued.

"Stacy recognized Pam and approached her, well one thing led to another and a couple glasses of wine later, you and I were the topic of conversation."

Nate tried to not let on any signs feelings or emotion. He was guarded in his response. He looked up at Alexander and smiled. "That was a long time ago, William, I hope she is doing well."

Alexander didn't buy the generic response from his old friend. He had two more bombshells and debated when to drop them. He thought about the maybe on the Dance County Head Coach offer that Nate had delivered just a few minutes ago. He was not going to hold back. Not the muscular Trooper's style.

"Stacy asked about you, she wanted to know how you are doing. I guess she tried to find you on Social Media and told Pam you had not joined the rest of America yet. She had seen the piece on ESPN." Nate remained quiet. Anxiety, excitement, coupled with heart wrenching fear would how he would have to respond if asked to gauge his emotional level at present.

"Nate, Stacy is moving back to Georgia. She has accepted a position in Atlanta." He let the words hang. "And she is single."

William Alexander looked around the exterior of the restaurant. He wanted to make sure what he was about to say was between the two men standing on the concrete lip of the restaurant.

"I drove down here days ago to ask you for your help. Nothing has changed except you have other opportunities before you. You can go to Florida. Work with a bunch of entitled kids and parents that will make your life a nightmare if you don't give in to their every whim. Or you can stay home, come up to North Georgia and make a difference. With kids that don't always know where their next meal is coming from. With kids that are not always assured of a Christmas tree or Christmas present when December rolls around. Most importantly you can give these kids opportunities that they will have never seen, if you had not made the decision you are going to make today.

"You got a chance to keep the dream alive for the kids, the community, and now with you."

Nate's eyes looked hard at Alexander. He had never heard the man speak so eloquently. He put his arm around the massive shoulders. "Let's get back inside before our eggs get cold."

CHAPTER 30

Alexander and Jackson entered the restaurant. A new batch of customers found themselves waiting for tables to open up. Older kids kept themselves busy with hand held electronics. The noise level of the restaurant had dropped dramatically. Alexander slid the partition back and the men entered to find Lee and Green buttering their pancakes.

The four men would spend another forty-five minutes enjoying the food and engaging in small talk. Dan Green was comfortable in leading the conversation. He wanted to zone in on Coach and find out more about the man. What made him tick? What where his dreams? If he could walk away from football, what would his perfect job be? If all jobs paid the same would he be content with selling suntan lotion down in the Caribbean or coaching football for the youth league in downtown Atlanta.

"So, Coach, what do you like to do in those rare moments you have some time to yourself?" Jackson surprised Dance County's largest booster with the speed of his response. "I like to fish."

Green smiled. "You have a lot of options this part of the world; do you prefer salt water angling or fresh water?" Nate was cutting his pancakes mindful of the extra butter that was now oozing over the sides. "Fresh water, there is a little river just south of where I live I like to escape to." He paused for a moment to add just a tad of syrup to the sliced cake pieces on his plate. "Some bream, mostly bass, I use an ultralight rig and very partial to beetle spins and plastic worms with a Texas rig."

Principal Lee was surprised at the level of detail a conversation on fishing in South Georgia was now taking. He smiled electing to let the conversation stay between Green and Jackson.

"No salt water action, Coach?"

Nate shook his head. "I have been a couple of times, always when the seas have swelled and the motion gets a little ridiculous." He paused to take a bite of his cake, syrup, and butter creation. "I will definitely take a ride in a john boat or bank fishing over 6-8 foot swells any day."

Green notched a win. He thought there might be some draw to the Atlantic or coastal living that might be a barrier to Jackson moving north and away from Southeast Georgia.

"Well, I can understand that. I am partial to freshwater fishing as well. We have a lot of options up in our neck of the woods. I have access to several private farm ponds that offer some pretty good largemouth fishing and I have access to some property in the mountains that offer world class trout fishing. Coach, you ever done any fly fishing?"

Nate smiled. He was enjoying the company. It had been a while since he had sat at a table with like aged men talking topics outside of defensive schemes and zone blitzes.

"I can learn and would look forward to it," he said.

Green notched a second win in his mind.

Jackson knew their time together this morning was fleeting. There would be a decision that would have to be made; Today. He was leaning toward taking it when he first walked into the door of the restaurant. Now Alexander had delivered a bombshell. The opportunity in Florida was fading fast in his mind, and for the first time he thought about committing. But there was more, he had to know what he was walking into and there was no better time to ask the questions than now.

"What are the plans for the coaches that are in place now?"

Principal Lee took that one. "I know we don't have any time and I am asking for a lot from our next Coach. That would be your decision, if you could have staff join you in time to make a seven thirty kick next Friday night, I would support it. If not, the three men that in place now are well qualified and well thought of." Lee continued. "And you would have the opportunity to retain them."

The next question was a test for Green. Jackson knew the answer. He wasn't sure if Lee would know. "What is the roster right now, how many kids are injured or have quit since the accident?"

Green didn't blink "We are down to 42 players."

Jackson looked less than a second at Lee then Green. His second question was about to be delivered and he knew the answer was 77 with 1 injured. "How many players will Clayton bring to your stadium Friday night?"

Green did not wait for Lee to answer. He looked Jackson deep into his lightly colored eyes. "76" he calmly said.

The assistant manager brought the check and laid it in front of Lee.

Green asked Lee to pass it to him and Lee pretended to not hear him. He wanted one more minute to plead his case to Coach Nate Jackson.

"This is not the ideal situation as I said earlier. There is going to be a great deal of pain before it gets better. The kids are down, the community is down, I guess I may be expecting too much from the man that walks in the door to be the next Coach, but that is who we are. We will not sacrifice our standards of excellence."

Jackson nodded. Green was able to capture the bill during the dialogue. Jackson thanked the men again and they stood to make their way toward the exit.

Two of Jackson's former players were at the exit. One of them held the door for an elderly couple entering the restaurant. They kept the door open for the four men to exit. Coach Nate Jackson was not going to let there be any awkwardness this morning.

"Gentlemen, how are we doing this beautiful morning?" David Brunson was a captain on his former team and missed the coach greatly. He smiled, remembering that Coach used the word beautiful often, especially before a practice that would end up far from it.

"Doing great Coach, how are you?"

Jackson looked at his running mate. Xavier Payton would not start until his senior year. Jackson was always impressed with his work ethic and determination. He extended his hand to both men. "It is good to see both of you. Did you gentlemen have a good week of practice?"

Both players nodded at the coach in the affirmative. "Waycross is going to bring some big and strong players to your field on Friday. You are faster and pound for pound stronger. Have yourselves a good game and bring us a victory."

The boys smiled. Payton looked at his former Coach. "We sure miss you," he said. Jackson smiled, and the two players disappeared in the restaurant. Lee exchanged glances with Green. The player's expressions toward their former coach said everything. Any doubts on who they wanted as their next coach were far from the mind. It had to be Nate Jackson.

He walked toward the vehicle in the second line of spaces from the crowded restaurant. Lee turned to him and handed him his business card. He pointed out a cell number at the bottom of the card. This is the number he wanted Coach to call him as soon as possible. Jackson committed to the call only. He shook each of their hands and thanked them again for giving up their Saturday to travel to Savannah. They were in the SUV and headed toward downtown a few minutes later for some sightseeing at the request of Dan Green.

Jackson made his way to his truck. He couldn't get his mind off her. How long had it been? He thought of their weekend in San Francisco, how perfect it was and how his recent trip had told him two things. One, he missed and still loved her, and his life was very upside down at the moment.

He pressed the start button on his pick up and turned toward the interstate. The country music station was playing a song from Toby Keith. He was at an intersection waiting for the green light to turn left and make the four-mile trip to his apartment. He tried to remember the separation. She had so much opportunity. He didn't understand why it had to be Washington over so many other cities in the South. He could not remember her answers, but she was leaving and there was nothing he could do about it.

The horn screamed behind him. He looked at the light, then realized it had changed. He looked at the older man slapping his wheel then pointing with anger from a reddened face in his rear-view mirror. "I see it you jerk," Coach grumbled to himself before slowly pulling into the intersection.

CHAPTER 31

Coach Nate had skipped the turn toward his apartment and continued to head away from the city. It was Saturday and the sun was shining. Plus, Dan Green had promised all the help he needed to move his things. He shook his head at the commitment thought that had just been made. He wasn't ready to make the decision. Or was he?

He continued to drive, listening to the country station throwing out their play list. He listened for songs that he could relate to, hell, just something familiar. He thought at one time there was a twenty-five-year age gap with the singers providing the tunes through his dashboard with him being on the wrong side. He reached to turn off the radio when a Toby Keith song started. That bought him more time with the music and he kept driving.

Tybee Island was just ahead. He knew memories were now fueling this drive. He didn't fight it and continued the journey east. He found a side street and parked the truck. The clock was nearing midday. The sun was out, and it was warm enough to ditch the shoes and head for the water. He made his way out on the beach. There was a slight crashing sound as the waves met the shoreline. He loved to look across the water and dream of escape. A boat trip to nowhere free of responsibility and the pain and anguish that came with challenges and adversity. The dreams were always moments of time with no seriousness or second thought. When it came down to it, he was a fighter, embraced those challenges knowing a victory was always within reach.

He had walked almost a mile when he stopped to take in his surroundings. He couldn't believe he had almost found the spot. His senior year in college was the last time he had been here, with her. They had discovered Sunday afternoons and Tybee a year earlier. The families would be leaving as the sun began the descent and the beach would be returned to a handful of patrons and small groups of making their way along the shoreline.

They would lay a couple of beach towels down on the hard surface.

There was always a small radio playing her favorite pop station out of Savannah. They would be very close to each other. Sometimes she would only agree to the trip if he didn't pester her while she appeared to be studying a thick textbook she had brought along in her large carry on. At first, he complied, then the surroundings would kick in and he would head for the water, come back, and put the full court press for her to hit the dark water.

He always brought a small cooler. He would pour her wine coolers in a hard shell plastic cup with her sorority letters beaming across the label. His beverage was a lite beer, or a beam and diet poured into a solo cup. There were days when only one or two were consumed. Many days, there was much more. When that happened, a red-faced Nate would find himself renting one of the tired hotel rooms on the island as the sun made its last appearance along the beach.

He smiled at the memory then walked closer to the water. He looked at the dark waters of the Atlantic and thought again what exactly Alexander had told him. She was coming to Atlanta. She had taken a job with a law firm there. She was single, and she had asked about him. His heart jumped again. Like a kid. He couldn't believe it. Stuff like that did not happen to people his age. He was supposed to be in a suburb, in a four-bedroom house, with a wife and a couple of kids, and coaching on Saturday. But life loves a detour especially when human beings have a hand at the wheel. Now his road had led him to this ocean with a damn big decision. He had made it when he left the restaurant after seeing his former players, but he couldn't say it aloud. Not yet.

It was after lunch now and he should be hungry. There were more stops and he needed to get moving. He looked at one of the old hotels along the beach. He remembered how he never took for granted their time on the beach. He knew it was a moment in time, and even then, knew in his heart would not be continued. While they were so much alike, there were differences, and differences lead to separation. He needed to focus and being on this beach was not helping. He found his truck and the highway and headed home.

Thirty miles away the Beechcraft was being fueled for the ride north toward Atlanta. The attorney had finished his business early and had called Green and asked him if they were still a go for an early afternoon departure. Green told him they were leaving downtown and would be there in twenty minutes.

The men had left the breakfast with Coach Nate and had driven downtown and parked at one of the River Street hotels. They walked along the busy tourist destination hoping to burn off the high calorie breakfast. Lee had picked up a cookbook and a tee shirt for his wife. Alexander pretended to show interest while longing to board the plane and get back to North Georgia.

Dan Green had another surprise for them. Just before noon they ended up at a local favorite restaurant known for their caloric busting entrees and southern vegetables. The popular lunch spot was packed, and a line formed outside the restaurant. Lee did not say anything as they approached. Alexander spoke up.

"Dan, do we have time to wait in this line?" Green smiled but that was all the attention he was giving to the question. He ignored the line of tourists. Some gave disapproving looks as the three men walked into the restaurant openly ignoring protocol. Dan asked to speak to the manager and the three men moved toward the corner of the restaurant as away from the large crowd as possible.

A few minutes later they were seated. Dan had ties in Savannah and had prearranged the meal. He was in full recruiting mode and wanted to be ready if the meeting with Coach had extended into the afternoon.

The men were given a choice between menu items and the buffet. Alexander had decided he would try to go mostly protein with this meal and heavily restrict his calories for at least the next twelve hours. Principal Lee was enjoying the trip. He never realized the diversity of Georgia's geography. He was used to rolling hills, thick forest, and green meadows. He loved the city he was now in. He immensely enjoyed his walk along the river and flat topography, seeing the historic buildings and quaint cobblestone streets. The air was thick and yes it was hot. But he again he loved it all. During their stroll, he eyed several hotels that he promised himself he would bring his wife of thirty-five years for the weekend. It was full indulgence at this point and he with his voice exhibiting enthusiasm ordered the buffet.

The iced tea garnished with green julips arrived first and the men engaged in small talk. They gave it a few minutes and with Green providing the guidance they moved toward the buffet table. The line was significant but moving. Visitors filled their plates as if this was the last meal. Heaping servings of starches hung on the side of the glassware. Extremely large pieces of fried chicken dangled atop mounds of macaroni and cheese as the visitors looked for any openings to scoop more food.

Back at the table, the men waited for the question to be asked. Would he take it? Was the trip a success? If he did not take it, what was plan B?

Lee looked at Green and asked after devouring a piece of fried chicken. "What do you think, Dan?"

Green didn't hesitate. "I think he takes it, too much riding on this one," he said.

Lee looked at Alexander. "William, what are your thoughts?"

"There was a lot said this morning. I believe seeing those kids, his former players, when we walked out of breakfast helped." Alexander paused. He was not hungry when he walked into the restaurant. He was now staring at 2600 calories of protein and starches before him that he did not want to waste nor feel in his gut at eighteen thousand feet. "The private school job has a lot of unknowns, new state, new types of players, new budget constraints. I don't believe that supersedes what was offered to him this morning." Dan Green thought that Alexander might bring up Coach's former girlfriend. He didn't and Green didn't either.

Both men were happy with Alexander's assessment. They turned their focus to enjoying the best of Southern cooking.

An airplane ride home would follow soon enough. And the ride would carry the uncertainty of a coach's decision and impact on their beloved high school football team.

CHAPTER 32

Nate had dialed Principal Lee during his drive from the airport back to his home in Dance County. The conversation was brief and to the point with his acceptance of the offer to be the next Head Football Coach of Dance County. Lee was ecstatic. The last few weeks had been very stressful externally and internally. He now felt like the sun was coming up on a new chapter and the pain would move past the school and the community. He also felt a surge of new found power. The call had come to him. For the first time, an outsider had news before one of the most powerful men in the county. It was professional and personal satisfaction even as slight as it was.

Lee savored the moment. Still thirty miles from home, he stopped at a convenience store and grabbed a liter sized bottled water, trying to fight the full feeling from two mammoth meals in South Georgia. He got back into his car and cranked the engine. He looked at his phone screen on the dash. He raced through his contacts, found Dan Green, and hit the connect button.

Green answered on the third ring as Lee pulled his car back on the interstate. "Dan, Principal Lee. Can you help our new Head Coach down in Savannah with a move tomorrow to Dance County?"

Green smiled. He was at a favorite gun store in Atlanta looking at new rifles for the upcoming season. He excused himself from the clerk and made his way out of the busy store into the parking lot. "Absolutely I can, that is great news Principal Lee."

An hour later a text arrives from a number that Coach Nate doesn't recognize. It is a request for him to provide an email for him to receive the information for the timing of the movers and the address and logistics for his move north into his new apartment. He is impressed with the speed and organization and complies.

Nate transitioned into work mode back in his apartment in Savannah. He placed all the clothes that he would need for the next three weeks on his bed. He grabbed two large suitcases from the closet and began his packing. He made a quick survey of the furniture that would be moved north and realized a small U-Haul would do the trick. He made a mental note to share that with Dan Green's representatives. He looked at his watch, still midafternoon. He finished the clothes and necessities packing and walked over to the leasing office to share with the agents his abrupt plans to vacate the apartment. They were sad to see him go and give him a slight break on the financial implications for early termination on the lease.

Back in his apartment, Nate went through his desk and drawers for personal effects he knows he should box and carry in the truck. There were financial documents and employment papers that now found themselves in yellow files and placed in a backpack. He packed his laptop and iPad in that same carryon.

He came across a family picture on his desk. He looked at the picture taken with his dad, mom, and sister. It was just a couple of years ago outside a restaurant in Destin Florida. He and his sister had argued about bringing the family together for a vacation and the logistics. Petty things such as where was the best location? And how they would make the schedules work with different vacation times. She had kids and a husband, and this would be a very big deal for them from a travel perspective and financial commitment. He was single man and in the grand scheme of planning family outings in their eyes, he had the easiest schedule to manipulate.

There was a coaching camp the school and boosters wanted him to attend during the only week that he and his sister could make the trip work. He always told his players that family came first, yet he had not seen any of his family more than a year prior. He told the school and boosters that assistants would be taking the skill players to the camp and he went on the vacation.

He held the small silver framed 5 by 7 in his hands. He smiled at the thought of how much his sister's kids, now living in the Midwest, enjoyed seeing the white sand for the first time, one even remarking how it was the looked like the color of snow.

He fondly remembered the golf that he played with his dad at the municipal course near the beach. His dad told a few of the old firehouse stories and he felt that overwhelming sense of pride and admiration toward him. His dad had aged and he felt the guilt of not spending more time with him. A week with them in North Florida had meant a lot, to all of them. He made a mental note to pick up the phone and call all of them, tomorrow.

The time got away from him. He felt the rush that came with anxiety at the thought of this being his last night in Savannah. He tried to temper the nerves with planning. He made a decision on what time to leave. He did not want to pull into North Georgia at a late hour. He knew the trip would take at least 5 hours depending on the traffic in Atlanta. The coffee would be set to brew by six. He made a mental note to pack the machine in the truck. Keys would be delivered to local movers via the apartment complex on Monday. His new apartment was already furnished. All he had to do was pick up the keys. A thank you to Dan Green, but as Coach knew and despised came with a price.

The Savannah sun was disappearing. Coach looked at his boxes and suitcases neatly stacked by the door. There was nothing left to take care of. He thought about dinner and how he would spend that last night. He grabbed the keys and headed for the door.

A few minutes later he pulled into the Oyster Bar. The parking lot was full. He thought to himself that the lunch crowd on a Saturday afternoon had decided not to leave. It was football season, in the South, and college football would be dominating the flat screens inside. It took a little longer than usual to find space for the truck. He admitted to himself that he was looking for her car. He didn't see it.

He entered the bar and looked for his usual spot. It was crowded with the only exception being a couple of empty stools next to the waitress station. He recognized one with short blonde hair. He smiled, said hello.

She responded with a warm smile and, "Hey."

He sat down and looked across the bar, thinking he recognized the night manager taking orders at the other end. He looked around again wondering if she was there. It was Saturday night and no doubt the busiest day of the week for the restaurant. After a few minutes the manager would walk over and ask what he can get for him. "Miller lite," said Coach Nate. The manager nodded and headed over toward the ice chest. He grabbed the bottle and flipped the top with a flick of his thumb. The top sailed toward the trash can and pinged the other empty bottles. He handed the fresh brew to the Coach and asked him if he needed a menu.

Coach smiled. "Just a beer, thank you."

He keeps it at one. He was not hungry. More importantly he did not have any idea why he was there. William Alexander had rocked his world with the news Stacy was moving back to Georgia. No, he thought, and that was not the news that blew him away but the additional information that she had asked about him. There was so much time between them he thought. What would he even say to her? He shook his head. He tried to show interest in the college game that was on the screen. Florida State was playing a huge ACC game against Clemson. The Tigers were having their way with the Noles and the Seminole fans in the bar were not happy with anything at the moment. He finished his beer, left eight bucks on the counter and headed for his truck.

CHAPTER 33

Monday Morning

Coach Watters stared at the cardboard box that had been hidden in a classroom over the last two days. He had cleaned out the office formerly held by Coach Matt Davis when he was texted the news from his girlfriend that the deal was done, and Jackson would be the next Head Football Coach of Dance County. The cleaning had taken place late at night with an empty parking lot. He almost felt like he was breaking into the place. The only thought that had kept his sanity was the memory of the long hours studying film in this same office that had monopolized his time over the last few weeks.

At the top of the box was a playbook, documenting the game plan for Friday night. He had put a tremendous amount of effort into the work. He saw it as his chance for retribution. A chance to show the administration and the boosters he was the man for the job and the Liberty game was a one-time aberration. He picked up the box, and made his way to the Coach's office.

Nate Jackson was setting up a laptop on the desk. The door leading in to the office was open. Watters stood at the door. Nate looked up and made eye contact. He immediately stood and motioned for Watters to come in. Watters slowly walked in with the box in front of him. He sat it on the desk and looked up at Jackson.

His girlfriend had made him watch the ESPN special on Jackson and his South Georgia Team from their desktop computer on YouTube. Coach Watters was extremely impressed with the style exhibited in the reality piece, but he didn't let on to anyone. He had longed for that type of respect and admiration from his players in just his few weeks as the top guy. His ego said he was close. His timeline needed was not going to be given.

Coach Jackson extended his hand. "Nate Jackson, it is a pleasure to meet you, Coach Watters. Please have a seat." Watters was a little slow in responding to the kindness. He looked at the chair and awkwardly made his way into it. He nervously looked at the box then up at the Coach.

"Thank you, Coach, I wanted to come by and bring you the files and tapes for the team. I have all the game video included as well as the offense and defense plays, along with a game performance grade for each of the players. I thought you or your staff may be asking about this and I wanted to have it all organized when you were ready."

Jackson looked at Watters. Things were moving at a hundred miles an hour. His new apartment was still a mix of boxes and out of place rented furniture.

"I appreciate all of this, Coach Watters, this will keep me up most of the night and I will probably be wearing the same clothes considering everything I have is packed away in a box somewhere."

Watters laughed appreciating the sense of humor. Nate did a quick inventory of the box then resumed his focus on Watters. He stood up and walked around the desk. He pulled up a chair and moved a small table from the corner of the room toward Watters. They were now talking at the same level.

Nate looked at Watters in the eyes. He shared with him the story of when he was let go by the powerhouse team in Savannah. He talked of the conversation with his former boss and the kick in the gut along with the fear and anger that did everything to overwhelm him. Now was not the time to make rash decisions and respond to emotions he said to the young coach before him.

"I watched the Liberty game, Coach, from different perspectives. The first time I watched as a fan, the second time as a Coach. I saw a lot of positives from both perspectives. Sure, on paper you were bigger and a lot better and should have easily won by three scores. But last time I checked these games are played on a field and not on a computer screen or decided beforehand."

Jackson paused, and then he continued. "Coach Watters, you walked on that field with those players weighed down from tremendous adversity. Just stepping on that field took a helluva lot of courage from all involved."

Watters shifted uncomfortably in his chair, he was ready to stand up, move on, and put it all in the rear-view mirror. He had made up his mind to quit after watching the ESPN piece. There would be no room for him or his assistants. A top coach like Jackson would have his pick of the best of the best.

Jackson leaned forward in his chair, looking Watters in his eyes. "I would like for you to be a part of my staff, I would like for you to be my assistant head coach and offensive coordinator."

Watters was stunned. He fully expected Jackson to thank him for the box and his efforts and move him away from the team and school as fast as possible. Watters sat in stunned silence.

Jackson continued. "I am sure you didn't take on the role of head coach to hand it back a couple of weeks later. And, I am sure there are a lot of things going through your head right now." Jackson paused. "You take this position, and let me help you, I can promise you that you will be a head coach again and we will one day look back and talk about all you learned from that Liberty game."

Watters immediately thought of his other coaches, Griffin and Williams. "I am prepared to offer them as well," said Jackson.

Watters smiled. The opportunity before him was a good one. He knew deep down inside he needed a mentor like Nate Jackson to not only teach him but provide him the instant credibility that his recommendation would bring to future administrators. He did not leave him hanging.

"What time is practice, Coach?"

CHAPTER 34

The members of the Dance County Football team were summoned by Principal Lee via the school's public-address system to report to the gymnasium after second period. The players made their way slowly into the aging facility draped with tired regional and state banners screaming the achievements for the basketball and wrestling teams.

Kyle Morgan found a seat in the first row of bleachers. Chris Ponder sat beside him. The rest of the team filled the remaining first four rows of the seats. Ben Young sauntered in last. He was still nursing a dip and not ready to part ways with it. He looked at his available seating, placed his hand on Dante Alexander's shoulder, and lifted himself up to a spot at the end on the second row.

Principal Lee stood about ten feet from the front row, flanked by Watters, Williams, and Griffin. The man to the right of the group stood alone. The players did not recognize him. He wore a starched white shirt and khaki pants. The shirt was rolled at both wrist and there was no tie or jacket. Players exchanged glances. The developments from the weekend had remained a closely guarded secret that the administration wanted to announce today. The players would learn first.

"Can everyone hear me ok?" The players shook their heads in the affirmative. A few of the kids said yes from the back row. "Ok, Gentlemen, we are here today to announce the hiring of a new Head Football Coach." He paused just a second. "Coach Nate Jackson comes to us by way of Savannah, Georgia where his team constantly competed at the highest level and won several region titles. His team last year was a state finalist in the playoffs. We are honored that he has accepted the opportunity to be our new Football Coach for the Patriots. Without further ado, it's my pleasure to present to you Coach Nate Jackson."

Nate eyeballed the team. He wasn't expecting any warm and fuzzes from this group, not anytime soon.

He didn't waste any time and immediately went to work. "Thank you, Principal Lee, first and foremost I want to thank you and the school board for this opportunity. It is my honor to stand before each of you. I have followed this program for a long time and have tremendous respect for the history and the leadership that has graced this school and program. Men, I had the opportunity to spend time with both Coach Davis and Coach Parks over the years in camps and competition, and I will always be indebted to them for all that they brought to this great state and to you the players and families."

"I am pleased to share with all of you that I have met with the three coaches this morning standing with me today, Coaches; Watters, Griffin, and Williams, and they have all accepted positions to continue their coaching positions here at Dance County."

Nate separated himself further from Lee and the other coaches. He moved closer to the team. He lowered his voice by a decibel. "Gentlemen, I was raised in a family where my Dad was a firefighter. One of the brave men he served with when I was kid we referred to as 'Uncle Jimmy.' When I was growing up Uncle Jim was always around, and he was loved immensely by the town. When my dad couldn't make one of my games as a kid, I knew I could look in the stands and see Uncle Jimmy. Our families were inseparable, and he brought a tremendous amount of good through service and dedication to many families and the community. One day when I was twelve there was a bad fire at a grocery store. Uncle Jimmy went in and rescued six people. When he went back into the store to check for any others, a ceiling collapsed, and he was killed. The impact on all us was devastating. I share all this for one reason. There came a day when I was a few years older, I asked my dad how he got over Uncle Jim's death. His response was very simple at the time but I never forgot it. He said, 'Son, I went back to work.' The loss of your two coaches was devastating and it would break most teams. Today I am going to ask you to place trust in the men in front of you today. I know you don't know me and I know trust is a two-way street and must be earned. But I can tell you this, every waking moment, I am going to work to earn that trust and work to help each of you to be the absolute best that you can be. I ask simply, Let's go to work, Gentlemen."

With that said, Nate moved back toward the group. Watters stepped forward, reiterated the starting time, and reminded that team that the attire was helmets, shorts, and tee shirts for the afternoon practice.

The players stood. A few of the players approached the new coach and introduced themselves. It was awkward, but Nate knew it would be. It would take time, a commodity that he nor the team had.

Principal Lee had called for an assembly of the student body just before lunchtime on Monday. When the kids entered the auditorium, they found six chairs atop the school stage. Sitting to the far left was the Chairman of the School Board; to his right was Coach Watters. Sitting beside Watters was Coach Griffin and beside him was Coach Williams. Next to Williams and the empty seat by the adjoining podium was someone new to the kids and faculty. Behind the podium was Principal Lee.

Dan Green stood at the back of the auditorium. His large frame leaning against the wall. A couple of kids acknowledged his presence by saying good morning. The majority of them were oblivious to his presence and made their way to their seats.

The students stared at the mystery man in the chair next to the podium. His heavily starched white shirt was now sporting a light purple and white tie. He wore a navy-blue jacket and ten years earlier may have gotten away with giving the appearance of a fraternity president. He wore Johnson and Murphy loafers that probably had been worn about the same number of times as the sports coat. He had a slight smile as he looked across the auditorium.

This time the announcement was more formal. Lee announced the Coach and spent more time on his prior achievements. Lee told the student body that like Davis, Jackson would be coaching three PE classes focused on strength and conditioning. He also mentioned the reality show piece on ESPN and encouraged the kids to take a look on YouTube when they were at home and not in class. He addressed the positive developments for the three assistants and their continued roles on the team. Most of the kids applauded out of respect to the three coaches, letting the loss to Liberty expire in their memory.

When Coach took the podium, there was no mention of Uncle Jimmy or attempts to connect with the team. He spoke of his admiration for Davis and Parks and the rich history of Dance County. He was very upfront that Clayton would bring a lot of kids, speed, and talent to their house this Friday night and now more than ever the Patriots needed that 12th man. He asked the kids if they were ready to accept the challenge. The cheers and applause from the student body was well received by the leaders on stage.

Dan Green smiled. The new Coach was connecting.

CHAPTER 35

The forty-two players referenced during their breakfast meeting and interview on Saturday held true for the first practice under the leadership of new Coach Nate Jackson. All 42 were on time, in the middle of the field, awaiting instruction five minutes before the hour of 4:00.

He had met with the assistants over lunch at his desk and laid out their plans for the day. This would not be a typical Monday practice. There would be no rehash of previous games. Coach had meticulously scheduled work stations to be led by one of the three assistant coaches. The players would rotate among the stations following a whistle from a student trainer using a stop watch to keep the practice moving. Coach would rotate from the offense to the defensive stations giving him a look at all his players.

He had been on the phone during his drive the day before from Savannah to North Georgia. He had called William Alexander first and asked for his help with any scouting information he could get on the next opponent. He had played Clayton one time and he had access to the film, but he was looking for more. He knew he was walking in with a very thin roster up against a lot of depth. Even if Dance County was at maximum roster and had no injuries they still would be looking at a ten-point underdog to Clayton.

At practice, Jackson did not engage in a great deal of talk. He gave simple commands and tried to accent the positive. There was a lot of Coach Speak he could have thrown on them at this practice, but he felt for now less was more. Let's get to work Gentlemen was the catch phrase of the day.

The players were impressed and challenged with the work stations. It was mid-season and some of the drills seemed reserved for spring practice or early-summer but it was also a chance to show the new coach their abilities. A couple of the players had watched the ESPN clip at lunch and for those that had watched found instant street cred with the new Coach.

Coach Nate made his way to an offensive drill involving QB 1 Morgan and the receivers. He watched the mechanics of his starting quarterback. "Clayton is going to put at least seven maybe eight up front and force us to throw it. I need you to shorten your drop and get rid of it. We have to reverse our mindset and use the pass to set up the run first."

Morgan looked at the Coach. "Yes sir," he said.

Nate moved over to the offensive line. He watched his starting five push the sled. Watters was barking at Center Ben Young, not happy with his efforts. He blew his whistle causing the players and Watters to turn in his direction. "Gentlemen, you are the catalyst for our ability to move the ball Friday night. We are going to have to play a hurry up offense and get off the line. How we hit that sled today is how we will hit those big-ass Clayton linemen on Friday night." He paused and hit the whistle again. "Let's go, Gentlemen."

They practiced for two hours. The players were not allowed to walk between stations. It was constant movement and built in intense physical conditioning that came with the practice.

At just after six the whistle blew for the final time and Coach addressed the team.

"Gentlemen, good work today. We had a lot of moving parts and I was impressed with the focus. I have had a chance to take an in-depth look at Clayton. I am not going to sugarcoat it, they are big, and they are strong. They are going to bring almost twice the bodies to their sideline Friday night.

"Gentlemen, we will not be intimidated. Tomorrow we are going to come out here in full pads and put together our plan for Clayton. We are not going to hold back on anything. When they expect us to run we are going to throw it. When they expect us to throw it, we are going to run their damn ass over. When they have the ball, they aren't going to know which direction we will be coming, but rest assured we will be coming and bringing the hat with it.

"Nice job, everyone, Nice job coaches. Get your homework done tonight, get your protein in, and at least eight hours sleep. Seniors, take us out."

The coaches remained on the field while the players ran for the lockers. Coach Nate reiterated his appreciation for the Coaches' efforts. He asked each of them to take a look at the film on Clayton after dinner for their respective positions. He wanted to meet from breakfast in his office at six a.m. for a full report and to hash out the final practice schedule. The men thanked each other and headed toward the school.

Dan Green stood at the fence line patiently awaiting Coaches transition to the locker room. "Do you have a second, Coach?" Coach Nate nodded toward Dan and jogged toward him. He quickly extended his hand and asked how he was doing.

"Is there anything you need, Coach?" Green asked.

"No, I appreciate all of the help with the move. I am working on getting settled, but as you can imagine, a lot going on right now." Dan smiled.

"Yessir, no doubt you are one of the busiest in the whole county, please let me know if I can help?"

"Actually, I did have a question for you. Pregame meals for home games?"

Dan said, "Yes, our cafeteria staff from the school that handles the student lunches stays late on Friday and prepares the team meals for home games. It has usually been a hamburger, potato, salad, and tea."

Nate was a little surprised at first and thought the boosters may have catered the meal.

Green sensed that and added. "For away games, we pick a restaurant and have a room reserved with a fixed menu."

Nate said, "Thanks, I would like to change the pregame meal to a baked chicken and switch the potato to a sweet potato and add a green vegetable in addition to the salad. I prefer the lean proteins and complex carbs before a game." Green said he would take care of it and both men shook hands again and went their separate ways.

A half hour later, Ben Young wrapped his knuckles from his right hand on the office door. "Come in," he heard from the other side. He walked in slowly, second guessing his decision from earlier.

"May I help you, Son?" said the voice from behind the desk. Young was slow to look at the coach. He stared at a partially eaten protein bar aside a can of sugar free red bull. Coach straightened the papers on his desk. The nervousness of the big offensive lineman had his undivided attention.

"What's on your mind, Young?' The player was immediately captured by the tone and remembrance of his name. He was a starter. He had received college interest. Not to the level of QB 1 Morgan, but there was football after high school if he wanted it. He didn't expect the coach to be on top of the roster in his first week and moments after the first practice. Not with the player in street clothes and without a numbered jersey staring at him.

"Things aren't working out, Coach," Young managed to say.

Coach looked at the starting center. He rose from the metal chair and made his way toward the player. He found a corner of the desk and leaned against it with his arms folded. "I'm not sure I'm following you."

Young looked at his feet then back up at the Coach. "I am not sure if I want to finish out the season," he said. Coach unfolded his arms, stood straight and then walked over to the blank wall. Only a few days earlier, Coach Davis' daughter had removed all the personal effects and pictures from the office. Coach had thought briefly about hanging some of his own memories against the institutional and cold surface but decided it could wait. He turned back toward Young.

"You did not have a quality game against Liberty," he said. "Actually, I would have to grade you somewhere between poor and downright garbage."

Young was stunned with the colorful language. He knew he missed some assignments and for the most part had finally owned up to his self that he was going through the motions. There was no intensity or passion to his play. He gave the Coach that one but was surprised and not accustomed to being called on it.

"You did not have your weight balanced correctly prior to the snap. I saw delayed reaction time with several pass plays and your execution on two run plays just prior to the half was sloppy at best." Young was in awe of the young coach before him in spite of the criticism. There were rumors among the team of an unmatched work ethic and relentless film study by the Coach. He had never been given that much critical feedback from someone that only hours before he questioned how well the man even he knew him. He stood in silence.

"Son, I am not even going to try to wrap my head around what you or anyone else on this team has been through or feeling right now. I am not a counselor or psychologist. I am a football coach and as simple as it sounds life is not fair, period." Coach paused for a second then continued. "Adversity makes men and it breaks men." He let his words be absorbed by the offensive lineman.

"I watched the film from last season. You played a key role on this team and have demonstrated at times excellent field leadership. With that said, Son, you have a future in this game, but I am not going to sugar coat recent play and more importantly hold your hand or kiss your ass. I am simply a football coach, not a Tony Robbins, not your dad, not your buddy that you chase women with on Saturday night. I will promise you and you can take this to the bank. I will not tolerate half-baked preparation or practice. You want to go through the motions with me and your butt won't leave the bench. I expect 100 percent all the time. If I have to go into Friday night with thirty players, so be it. Clayton will not give a rat's ass if we dress forty or twenty. But I can assure you one thing, just as the sun will rise in the morning, I will only put on the field the best players." The coach walked toward Young. He was now only inches from the kids face. He lowered his voice and pitch then continued. "I say all this for one reason. You have a decision. You can walk out of here and move on with your life and one day you might regret it. Or you can come back to practice tomorrow with that chin strap buckled up and get your ass on the field and be the team leader I know you can be." Coach paused for a moment. He extended his hand. "I will support your decision either way, Young."

The speed of the dialogue stunned Young at first. He shook the coach's hand distracted momentarily with the vise grip strength of the man before him. He mumbled, "Thanks, Coach," and turned to exit the room.

Young shut the Coach's office door and made his way through the locker room. Alexander had been with the trainer after practice and still had a towel wrapped around his waist. He turned from his locker and looked at Young. "Everything ok, man?"

Young looked at his good friend. "Yeah, just had a question for the Coach. I'll see you tomorrow." Alexander nodded his head in return then pulled the headphones from his locker.

Kyle Morgan stood by the exit door. Young saw him and walked toward him. "Sup, man?"

Young looked at him then extended his hand toward the QB's shoulder. "I'm sorry I haven't been at my best. I was pretty pissed about everything and didn't handle it well. I promise you will get my best next game."

Morgan was taken back by the admission coupled with the brutal honesty. He knew his center was more mature than most, but the humility was impressive. Morgan was not going to let it fester. "Don't sweat it, man, we will be alright." Morgan extended the fist pump.

For the first time in several days, Ben Young smiled.

CHAPTER 36

Game week always produced countless checklists. He knew he should be using the technology on his phone to keep his life simpler and stay away from the sticky notes plastered across his desk and dashboard of his truck. Old habits were not going to change today. He stared at the yellow post it note next to the radio that reminded him to pay his cell phone bill. He was headed home after the practice had run late. It was still Monday he said to himself.

The players had given a good effort, but they were a long way from a win on Friday night.

He thought back to himself. He wasn't hungry but doubted there was any food in his fridge. He wanted a beer to go with the game film that waited to eat up the remaining evening hours.

He spotted a convenience store and turned in. The dinner time hour and the rural back road produced few customers. He held the door open for a kid wearing a pair of jeans hanging below his butt. The kid gave him a disapproving look and walked toward the front of the store. The coach eyeballed the sliding cooler doors and moved in the opposite direction. Three aisles over and unknown to the coach, his QB and star receiver were eyeballing a sack of potato chips to go with the twelve pack of Budweiser sitting at their feet. Kyle elbowed Chris who was choosing between the bag of Lays and the spicy Doritos. Chris looked at him and nodded toward the beer cooler. "Looks who's here," he said.

"You want to get out of here?" Kyle said. "No, just sit tight."

The coach was quick. He grabbed a six pack of Miller Lite and made his way to the front. The kid with the pants that would not fit had removed his headsets and was standing in front of the young female clerk working the register. Coach saw the kid fumble with some change and figured it might not be a bad idea to grab a newspaper. He politely waited by the stand of *USA Today* until the first profanity sailed through the air. The clerk was being as polite as her limited training and small-town upbringing would allow. The coach had overheard the question that was bringing the response. "I have to see an ID with a cigarette purchase," she said.

"I ain't got no ID!" The clerk moved back a step and was getting nervous with the tone. "Here is your money, give me the smokes!" Her voice dropped several decibels. The two players still in the back of the store inched forward. A bread rack stood between them and the coach. The kid became almost delirious. He moved his body back in forth as if he was on a dance stage. His arms swung wildly from side to side. His lanky frame was intimidating to the young clerk. She offered one last bit of reasoning.

"Please, I will get fired, I cannot sell you these." The law being stated drove the customer into further rage. He grabbed a pack of gum and threw it at the clerk catching her in the chest.

"Woman, sell me the cigarettes!"

Coach moved inches behind the kid. He looked at his pockets and waistband first. Then he looked down at his ankles. He thought only for a moment of the chance a weapon was somewhere in the over-sized jeans resting halfway down the kid's legs. The persistence did not stop. "I'm 21, now give me the dang cigarettes!" The clerk continued her movement backward. This was the nightmare that she had been warned about before taking the job. Money was tight and employment opportunities even tighter. She had reasoned with herself that she could tough it through any situation.

Coach had no problems with the element of surprise. The kid was eighteen at best and soaking wet weighed no more than 150 pounds. He grabbed the jeans with three fingers around a belt loop. He then executed the perfect wedgie. "What the?" the kid screamed. He thought just for a second of swinging his arms at the man behind him but knew it was futile. Older man strength was on display and the Coach was in complete control. The kid did not have any angle for which to break lose.

"All right, young man," Coach whispered in his ear as he pushed him toward the door. "I don't know what rock you crawled out from under, but you are going to learn right now you are not going to talk to a young lady like that." The kid didn't move. He was frozen. Coach had his belt loop midway up his back. He pushed hard and forced the kid through the heavy glass door. Only three vehicles graced the parking lot.

He pushed the kid forward and it took the wiry soul all his athleticism to keep from scraping the pavement with his front side. He tried desperately to keep his composure and not appear rattled. Coach did not move. He stood at the door and waited for any response. The kid shot him a quick look of disapproval, again, turned toward the road and very slowly walked away. His ego and quest for nicotine squashed.

Coach turned his attention back to the clerk. She had recovered quickly and flashed a toothy smile. "You ok?" he said in a controlled voice.

"Thank you, I really appreciate you helping me out."

His attention turned toward his purchase. "How much I owe you?"

She had not entered the beer or chips into the register. "On the house, I would be very upset if you didn't let me buy these for you."

He thought for a second to disagree. The kid did not have the right to take money out of her pocket. He looked at a cheap cigar behind the register. "At least let me pay you for one of those," he said. She handed him the cigar and allowed him to give her three dollars. He thanked her and left the store.

Morgan and Ponder sat in stunned silence. They watched the Coach get into his truck and slowly made their way to the register. Ponder laid the beer and the chips down. He eyeballed a starched piece of currency next to the register. He picked up the crisp twenty-dollar bill and handed it to the clerk. "I believe this is yours." She was stunned. The money not only covered the beer and chips but her next hour of work.

Ponder played dumb. "That man left the money for you," he told the clerk.

A little overwhelmed with the developments, the clerk gave a cursory glance to the fake license Morgan presented. Ponder scooped up the chips and Morgan carried the box of beer under his arm bouncing gingerly from his hip. They jumped in the QB's sports car and began to talk about the intensity of the events that had transpired.

"Did you see Coach?" Ponder said.

"He's definitely not one you want to make angry," added Morgan.

"We need to keep this one between us," the QB added.

Ponder nodded in agreement.

Morgan had tucked the beer under his gym bag behind the driver's seat. He placed the car in reverse and turned his body toward the road to back the vehicle up. Ponder was playing with the satellite radio looking for a rap station. Ponder noticed a delay in the shift to reverse and Morgan not backing the car up. He stared at his QB. "What's wrong?"

Morgan was frozen. He had shifted his body from looking behind the car to now using the rear-view mirror. The car was still in reverse. Ponder couldn't stand the suspense. He turned around and saw the truck that had been in the parking lot earlier lined up right behind the star player's car. "Shoot," Morgan said in a muffled tone.

Coach walked slowly along the driver's side much like a cop before he explodes into a stern lecture and rewards the unlucky sole with an expensive speeding ticket. There had only been one practice under the new leadership. And with that, there was no undefeated season and flawless execution on the table. Morgan and Ponder knew the man before them had them by the short hairs.

Coach looked at the gym bag then lowered his body so that he was eyeball to eyeball with Morgan. "You boys stopping for a Gatorade?"

Morgan decided to go with it. "Yes sir," he said.

Coach never took his eyes off Morgan. He reached with his right hand behind the driver's seat and pushed the gym bag aside. "You boys picking that up for your Daddy at home?" Coach pulled the beer up from behind the seat.

Morgan knew playing along was not working. Ponder was speechless. He started counting the stadium steps in his mind and how many would he run after practice for this little stunt. "No sir," said Morgan.

"Well Gentlemen, I am going to make you a deal, you take that pack and pour it out on the grass over there and I will do the same. We both need to be at our best and this ain't gonna help anybody." Morgan looked hard at the coach. No one had ever called him out like this but more importantly he had not seen this type of accountability being held by an adult either.

Morgan nodded in agreement. He grabbed the beer and proceeded to pop the top and commence to pouring the amber liquid on the grassy patch adjoining the store. Not to be outdone, Ponder grabbed an aluminum can and popped the top to begin as well. Coach grabbed his six pack from his truck and walked over and began pouring.

"Gentlemen, we don't need this." That was the last remark as he threw the empty cans in the trash can by the gas pump and headed toward his truck.

CHAPTER 37

The school bell rang and the kids trudged their ways to their respective classrooms. The sluggishness being exhibited screamed Monday all over again, but it was Tuesday and the countdown to the Patriots next home game was at three days. Nate sat at his desk. He massaged his temples thinking about what was next on the list. He had managed three hours sleep. His Coaches had arrived promptly that morning at six am with a pretty good handle on their next opponent from their film study.

Coach had found some areas that he hoped to exploit with the Clayton defense. It would be an uphill challenge all night. They had so much depth and when a kid needed a rest, a big bodied relief player was seconds from the field. Their backups could start at most schools. The thought process was going negative for Jackson and he knew he better clear the mind quick.

He looked at his watch, thankful for the early meeting with the coaching staff. He remembered Watters placing a thick file folder on his desk. There was a mischievous smile to his face as he handed it to him. "Your morning and afternoon PE class teaching plans," he said. Jackson thumbed through the paperwork. Teaching the PE classes was part of the job. He looked at the prescribed workouts then laid the papers back on his desk. He stood and made his way to the work out room.

His first class of the morning had most if not all his skill players. He recognized Kyle Morgan and his top receiver Chris Ponder immediately. There were a couple of receivers that saw a decent amount of time on the field and his starting running back and a left tackle. He gave the kids a minute to get settled and went to work.

"All right, folks, I am not going to stand over you and play babysitter today. Each of you has had this class now for a several weeks and you know what needs to get done. This is an opportunity to get better. It does not matter if you are playing one of the sports or have signed up because you needed a credit to graduate. Let's make the most of the opportunity and maximize our time in here." He called out each kid's name and handed them their workout plan.

When he got to the sheet for Quincy Davis he did a double take. The kids had already changed into the normal PE attire of navy shorts and white t shirt. It didn't matter if the kid was in PE attire or the same jeans falling off his waistline. He recognized him immediately from the previous evening and the confrontation at the convenience store.

He held the paper inches from the kids outstretched hands. "Have we given any thought to quitting smoking?" The kid gave him a stunned look. Coach didn't let it fester. He handed the kid the paperwork and called out the next name.

When Coach had delivered all the workout plans, he gave one last set of instruction. "All right, let's hit it." The kids formed groups of three and made their way to an open weight set. The prescribed plan today was upper body and there would be a cycle of chest presses, pull downs, dips, and extensions they would need to complete. Confident the kids knew what to do, Coach slid back into his office to continue his game planning for Friday night.

Kyle Morgan had no problems pushing 300 pounds in his first set on the bench press. Chris Ponder stood behind the weight as Ponder bounced up from the bench after completing. He eyeballed the kid from the store waiting in line at the parallel bars. Kyle walked over to him. "Did you ever get your cigarettes, you idiot?" The kid looked at QB 1. He didn't want a confrontation nor was he scared of one. He was oblivious to the amount of weight that the star player for the Patriots had just lifted effortlessly.

Quincy Davis said nothing. The endorphins were singing with QB 1. His breakfast had been a 50 gram protein shake coupled with a monster energy drink. He now stood inches from the kids face. "Why don't you get your shit and get the hell out of my weight room." The other kids were now catching on to the conversation. They began to circle the Davis and Morgan. Chris Ponder thought for a second about rescuing Davis. He knew that would be a lost cause and elected to stay quiet.

Davis was not rattled. The only thing constant in his life was misfortune and pain. He was a product of broken family and public housing. He had witnessed shootings where lives had been lost right outside his bedroom. A kid with a seemingly perfect life, perfect family, and any and everything he wanted was sure as hell not going to intimidate him.

He looked Morgan in the eyes. Outweighed by at least seventy-five pounds did not stop his enthusiasm.

"Screw you," Davis said. Morgan reached for the kid's chest. He was going to grab the kid by the shirt and sling him across the room. Morgan was a half a second too slow. The kid lowered his body and shot his arm forward and caught Morgan square in the midsection. Morgan doubled at the ricocheting pain through his groin. He caught his breath and stood upright with fire in his eyes.

Morgan came at Davis again and this time the kid head faked and jerked his body left. Morgan had pulled his arm back to deliver a knock-out punch but only connected with the air. His momentum carried him past the kid into a weight bench that now came crashing to the floor.

Morgan rose slowly from the floor. Coach Nate Jackson was now blowing the whistle. He got into the face of his top quarterback. He pointed toward the empty bench press turned over on its side. "Does this look like focus, Morgan?"

The quarterback was embarrassed and tried to catch his breath. "All right, gentlemen, since we can't do what we are supposed to do, we are going to run. On the track, now!"

When they got outside, Coach lined them up in three groups of ten. He blew the whistle and the first group started around the track. He made sure Morgan and Davis were not in the same group. Ponder ended up in the third and final group with Davis. The whistle blew and now all three groups were making their ways around the track.

Ponder decided to try to talk to Davis during the jog. "Pretty impressive moves inside, Dude," he said.

Davis remained quiet with his eyes forward. "Where do you live?"

Davis mumbled something about an apartment on tenth street. Ponder knew the area. There was government housing on that side of town. He and his mother had spent several years there

He thought he should give Davis some advice. "Just stay clear of Morgan, he will let this go with time." Davis didn't buy any of it. He just kept his pace with the group.

"Dude, you look like you can run as well, you want to take a shot at the fastest person in the school?" Ponder was confident. He had track scholarship offers to the Division 1 school of his choice. He threw out the challenge to Davis more as a peace offering for Morgan's behavior.

Davis looked at him. The other groups had finished and were now waiting on the grass for Coach to let them go back into the building. "Sure, where you want to start?"

They finished the lap and came to the line. "One lap around, you beat me, and I make sure Morgan stays off your ass." They crouched into a starting stance. Morgan was talking to Coach when his eyes noticed what was transpiring on the track. Coach Jackson saw Morgan look away and turned toward the two students who were now racing toward the first turn. The other kids were now lining the track. The two were neck in neck as they made the second left and were running down the back side straight away.

Nate was impressed with the speed of both kids. He had watched a lot of film on Ponder and knew he had a deep threat receiver and perfect complement for Morgan's rifle arm. The kid from the convenience store, he knew nothing about, and from the episode the day before didn't have high expectations.

At the back stretch, Davis inched ahead. A surge of sudden fear shot through Ponder. His show of good will toward Davis was backfiring. He had never lost a race to any of the kids in Dance County. Everything was now on the line in a stupid impromptu challenge, and the kid was winning.

They hit the backstretch. Ponder kicked in the afterburners. He was not going to leave anything to rest. He gave it everything he had as the dirt flew and the lungs tightened.

Davis beat him by a foot. Morgan shook his head. Coach went through the rolodex in his mind trying to place all the rosters he had looked at for the name Quincy Davis. Ponder grabbed his knees. Both looked as if they were trying to take in air through a plastic straw. They had expounded every bit on the last forty yards. Ponder acknowledged Davis effort. He gave him a fist bump and made his way toward the school gym.

Coach Nate Jackson stared at Quincy Davis walking off the field through his mirrored Ray Ban glasses, the Georgia sun beaming down across the now empty track. He would talk to him before school would end that day.

He was confident another Laney Jefferson had just come into his life.

CHAPTER 38

Donnie Tillman had been teaching US History at Dance County High School for the last four years. He was a graduate of the Georgia Institute of Technology and had gone with the minority pursuing a career outside of engineering and management. He was a passionate reader and always added more to his daily lectures through his expansive knowledge.

Tillman was lecturing his third period class on Franklin Roosevelt and his ties with the Great State of Georgia when there was a slight knock on the door. He looked over to see the face of the new Football coach through the tiny window. "Everyone, turn to page 121 and read the next two chapters. Excuse me for just a moment, I will be right back."

He made his way from the chalkboard toward the only exit to the classroom. When he opened the door, he greeted by Coach Nate Jackson. "Good morning, Mr. Tillman," he said. "I am sorry to interrupt your class, but I wanted to see if I could speak to one of your students for just a moment, Quincy Davis?"

Tillman had a somewhat startled look on his face. "Sure, is everything ok? Jackson looked into the classroom hoping to make eye contact with Davis.

"Absolutely, I wanted to follow up with him from an incident in PE this morning."

Tillman looked squarely at the Coach. "He's not in any trouble, is he?"

Coach Nate smiled. "Absolutely not, he actually outran one of the fastest kids on the team. I just wanted to see if there is any interest in him joining our football team."

That was enough for Tillman. "Give me a second." He walked back into the room. "Quincy, would you come here for a minute?"

Davis looked at both men like he did with all authority. Skeptical, distrustful, and apprehensive. "Do I need my books?" he said.

Tillman looked at the student, trying to deflect any awkwardness or embarrassment for the call out during class. "No, Coach Jackson had a question for you and needed a few minutes of your time?"

Tillman wanted to give Coach one more thing to think about before talking to Davis. He looked back at Coach and said, "I don't think this kid has had a lot of positive things happen in his life, sports, even at this stage may be a catalyst for something good for this young man."

Davis rose from the chair and made his way to the door. Tillman told them to take as much time as they needed.

Coach Nate put his arm on Davis shoulder and they walked toward the hallway. They walked past two classrooms in silence then Jackson led him out the door into a small courtyard just across from the lunchroom.

"You want to tell me what happened in PE this morning?"

Davis looked at Coach, very suspicious of where the line of questioning was headed. "That quarterback was pissed off about something; he took a shot at me."

Jackson listened, David added. "I didn't do anything to those players. I have to take the class;

I don't have a choice," Jackson said. "I don't think you will have to worry about anyone messing with you anymore. Not after that performance on the track."

Coach decided it was time to move the conversation.

"How long have you been running?" he said.

Davis was slow to respond, carefully considering how much he wanted to share with the Coach. "Not something I practice," he said.

Coach paused for a second and continued the conversation. "I know you don't know me, and I don't know you, but I saw athletic talent this morning that does not come around very often. You have a God given gift, what you do with that gift is up to you."

Coach let the words sink in.

"I reached out to the Georgia High School Association today with a special request to allow you to join the football team. I know that is a lot to swallow in just a few hours, but great opportunities don't always park outside our front door and sit and wait. I would like to start working with you Son, and help you get where you want to be in life."

"I haven't played since I was a little kid," he said.

"We can work through that," Coach said.

Davis considered his options. Life outside of school was a few troublemaking friends and boredom. He had not been a part of a team since early grade school. He was excited and scared at the same time. Those were two emotions that had only been raised in his formative years from police lights and gunfire.

He didn't stew on his decision and with the fact that he couldn't remember the last time he touched a football did not feel there was anything to leverage for his gain with the new Coach.

"Ok, I'll be there."

Nate smiled placed his arm back over the kids shoulder and walked him back to class. He once again applied a small knock to the door. Tillman paused in his lecture and made his way back to the door. He waived his hand toward Quincy and motioned him toward his seat. Coach remained just outside in the hallway.

"Coach, it was nice to meet you, hopefully, it was a good conversation," Coach Nate said.

"Yes, it was, it looks like Mr. Davis will be joining our team."

Tillman smiled. "That is great news," he said.

"Clayton graduated their secondary last year." The statement caught Coach's attention. "They are thin in their defensive backfield and susceptible to the deep ball with the right receiver. Mercy Academy had them on the ropes until the end by connecting with a couple of long passes and some well-timed out routes to their running backs."

Nate smiled. He was impressed with the young man before him and his earlier demonstration of rapport with his students and expansive breadth of knowledge.

"You watch a lot of games, Mr. Tillman?"

"I played corner in high school and try to make as many games as I can on the weekends. I guess once the game is in your blood, it never leaves."

Coach smiled. "We could use the extra help, you interested in adding coaching football to your resume?"

Tillman smiled. "What time you want me on the field, Coach?"

CHAPTER 39

Nate Jackson couldn't bring himself to eat another protein bar. He stared at the silver package sitting on his desk. Principal Lee knocked on his door. "Got plans for lunch?"

Nate smiled. "Good timing."

They headed toward the parking lot. "I know we have only a half hour, I have the perfect place."

Six minutes later they were in one of the booths at the Waffle Stop. Rose Wilkes warmly greeted Principal Lee. "Rose, I would like for you to meet our new Head Football Coach, Nate Jackson."

Nate smiled and stood. "Mrs. Wilkes, it is a pleasure to meet you."

"It is very nice to meet you, Coach Jackson, can I bring you some sweet iced tea."

Both nodded. Nate usually tried to cut calories on his fluid intake but a sweet tea sounded very good at the moment.

"I asked Donnie Tillman to help us out with the coaching; I hope that is not a problem."

Lee smiled. "As long as it doesn't hit this year's budget, I am good with it."

Jackson smiled, having suddenly remembered budget discussions and arguments over head counts in his previous life. That could wait. He was more concerned with a defensive front that weighed over 300 pounds that would be in his stadium on Friday.

Rose returned with the tea and lunch suggestions for the men on the tight schedule. "We have meatloaf on special today with mashed potatoes and green beans, I had some earlier, very good." Rose smiled first at the elder of the two. Principal Lee quickly accepted the offer. Jackson asked for a BLT on wheat.

Lee changed the subject. "How is the transition from South to North Georgia? Everything ok with your living arrangements?"

Nate said, "Yes, good, slowly getting settled. I am appreciative of Mr. Green and all of his assistance."

Lee was glad that Nate brought up the name of the largest booster and one of the counties wealthiest citizens. "He hasn't placed any unrealistic demands or expectations on you."

Nate smiled. He wanted a little extra time before he responded but didn't leave the principal hanging.

"No, not at all." He paused then continued. "My expectations for this program are championships, we are not there yet, but we can get there. I am not going to go into Friday night with unrealistic thoughts or beliefs. The region schedule ahead of us with our current injuries is a four-hour flight across the water and we are down to one engine, but I can promise you this, I didn't take the job to turn the plane around."

Lee liked the enthusiasm. The food arrived and they dug into their meals. It was still only Tuesday but both of them knew without saying, there were three practices left before game night.

Tuesday's practice came on quick. It was unseasonably cool with a stout wind. The coaches huddled at the fifty-yard line and discussed the key goals of the afternoon. All had different types of pull overs with Patriot logos and more sports than just Football. All but one, Coach Nate Jackson. He had went with the generic sweatshirt pull over. Not by choice. He had remarked to the staff how nice the school apparel looked. He made a mental note to follow up on coaching attire before Friday.

One of the school's marquee players and best shot for a division one scholarship, Kyle Morgan, stood on the sideline. His mind was elsewhere. He had learned that his girlfriend Stephanie had not traveled to Atlanta as originally planned the previous weekend. Her parents were considering a move out of state and had traveled to Tennessee to look at Knoxville and Nashville. Morgan had been courted by several schools, but the University of Tennessee and Vanderbilt were not courting the young gunslinger. He thought his relationship with the family was tighter. They had kept the travels from him and he was hurt. Stephanie's mom was not looking at their relationship as the storybook high school cheerleader marries the star quarterback. It was bothering him, and he was having trouble compartmentalizing it.

Chris Ponder stood twenty yards away. Morgan's throw zipped through the air with a whistling sound. There was brute arm strength on display and the pop of the ball against Ponder's gloved hands screamed a stinging sensation was being felt with each catch.

All the players were on the field awaiting Coach's whistle. All but one. He ran under the goal post a minute later. His jersey hung off his body at least one size to big. His helmet seemed to slide as he jogged on the field. His chin strap dangled unfastened. The players turned wondering who was joining their team at this point in the season.

Dante Alexander jogged over to Quincy Davis. "Sup, man, I am Dante. Are you Davis?"

Quincy nodded, suspicious on the friendliness.

Dante reached over and snapped the one loose strap to his helmet, he was ready to go. "You play receiver?" Davis considered the question. He didn't want to show his cards and lack of football acumen this early.

"Yeah." Alexander slapped him on his back and led him to the sideline. "Stand down by 83, that's Ponder, and get some catches in to warm up."

Davis obliged and jogged down to Ponder. Ponder acknowledged him with only eye contact. Morgan looked at the new receiver and couldn't believe his eyes. This was the kid from the gas station and the kid from the locker room. "Un fucking believable," he mumbled under his breath.

Morgan squeezed the ball tight around the laces. He gritted his teeth and stepped toward Davis. The football sailed through the October air with no arch and no hang time. It flew toward Davis as if it was a slug leaving a rifled barrel. Davis was not fazed. He threw up his hands like he had watched the NFL receivers on the small flat screen in his apartment. His fingers were outstretched with his thumbs pointing inward. He caught the ball like he had done it a hundred times.

The coaches were all watching. Nate said nothing until Davis threw the ball back to Morgan. It fluttered through the air like a shot duck crashing toward the water. The ball had nothing on it and barely made it back to Morgan. Nate spoke up. "Well we won't be running any pass option plays with the new guy." The coaches chuckled. The whistle blew. Practice 2 was under way.

Nate introduced Donnie Tillman to the Dance County Patriot football team first. He talked about his high-level of playing experience and extraordinary skills as a teacher. "The take home here, gentlemen, is simple, listen to what Coach Tillman and all of your Coaches say to you and you will get better."

His next introduction was dicey. Bringing in a player mid-season would be a distraction if not handled properly, especially one that had not sacrificed through the summer workouts and preseason practices. It was a risk for the new guy with the team and the school. Jackson was willing to take them, and it was always a gut decision and usually worked out.

Quincy had just not had a lot of experience with high-level organized sports. He was already showing a step behind in just huddling up for the start of practice. Coach thought about assigning a veteran to him, but Dante Alexander was already on it. He had slapped the player on the pads when it was time to sit.

"Gentlemen, we have a new man joining the team today as well. Some of you may know him from our morning PE classes." Nate paused and looked at Chris Ponder then moved his eyes toward Kyle Morgan. There was a slight smile delivered from the Coach to both players. "It is not common for a player to join midseason, but Gentlemen, I think we can all agree this is not a normal season for any of us. Quincy Davis has demonstrated some outstanding speed on the track and I have asked him to bring that ability to our football team. He is new to the game and he has the ability to contribute to our goals."

The whistle was raised, and the kids knew what was happening next. After two short bursts, Watters delivered the next set of instructions. "Alexander and Morgan, lead us in stretching, then everyone report to their respective stations."

CHAPTER 40

The normal contingent of Dads had arrived and had taken up most of the first row of metal bleachers with a handful them standing along the fence. They were excited to see the changes in practice and flow. For the first one on Monday, they had witnessed choreography on the field with seamless transitions between stations and rest breaks that were filled with coaching instruction. The kids kept moving and they had looked like they had been doing the drills in that format all season.

Today would be different. Time was not a commodity or an allied team member. There would have to be serious game planning for the visiting opponent, Clayton, and the dads in the stands knew it.

William Alexander had visited Rose at the Waffle Stop a couple of hours after Principal Lee's and Coach Jackson's impromptu lunch. She had quizzed him on the new leader for the high school team. She wanted to hear about the man that he had shared a sideline and college playing experience with many years earlier. William was very positive in his response.

Internally, he was relieved that it had all worked out. He couldn't believe that less than a few weeks earlier, the team was coming off the first win of the year and Parks and Davis were alive and well and leading this team. He was reminded again of the fragile nature of life and not taking anything for granted.

He left the Waffle Stop after consuming his customary eggs and sliced tomatoes. Rose had made him a large iced tea in a Styrofoam cup with two sugar-free sweeteners and extra lemon. She passed it to him on his way to his patrol car. He was scheduled to start work at eight and had already donned his uniform. He was excited to spend some time at practice before starting his evening shift.

When he arrived, he saw Dan Green standing next to the fence gate on the twenty-yard line of the practice field. He was alone which was not surprising. Dan's physical and community stature was intimidating and many of the townspeople were comfortable in giving him plenty of space in public.

He found a spot a few feet from Green and placed one hand on the fence with a slight lean against it. The players were huddled at midfield. Practice had been underway for just over a half an hour. The team had stretched then moved to various stations with their position coaches for drills designed to strengthen individual skill sets and provide further warm up and conditioning in anticipation for the meat of the practice.

Coach Nate called for first team offense and second team defense to take the field. The remaining twenty players headed toward the sideline. The bulk of the work for today's session was now underway. Some of the dads in the stands put down their phones trying to keep up with work and family duties via text and email. Conversations suddenly wrapped up and the dads in attendance turned their attention to the new Coach and the players.

"All right, Gentlemen, we are going to put in our plan for Friday night. As I have told you this week, they are a big team and they are going to crowd the line and come after us. We have to be quick and decisive. No hesitation with our style of play. We have to run through people then get our asses back up and do it again."

Dante Alexander listened to the Coach bark instructions from his place in the defensive huddle. The new coach looked toward his side of the ball. "Alexander, you're on 1st team offense." Dante moved across the line of scrimmage. Kyle Morgan extended a fist bump to the fellow senior.

"Line up at tight end!" Coach yelled.

"Ponder and Davis!" Coach screamed. "Both of you line up in the wide out position. Ponder, I want you spending every available moment from now to Friday working with Davis on his routes. We got to cram a lot of information in the next three days into this young man's head. You up for the challenge?"

Ponder nodded. "Yes, sir."

The move of Dante Alexander to offense gave Dan Green the green light to walk over to the uniformed Trooper leaning against the metal railing. "You expect this?"

Alexander's first reaction was to say no, but he remembered from their college days Nate's affinity for shaking things up and keeping opponents guessing. He was using every available asset in the best way possible. Any remote hint of traditional game planning had been thrown out the window.

The first few plays were a mix of runs and short passes to Alexander. He caught the first one but dropped the second one. There was energy on the defensive side. The second team players were trying to get the attention of the Coaches and potential playing time for Friday night. Coach liked the enthusiasm but knew if his top athletes were not on the same page, it would be a long night for the Patriots come Friday.

Jackson and Watters stood in the backfield well behind the offensive huddle. They had made very few changes to the plays and system that had been in place. Morgan moved the team down the field settling into a rhythm. The second team defense had made some nice plays, but the athleticism of the offense was starting to shine.

Quincy Davis had been relegated to running empty patterns. His head was spinning. A couple of days ago he was a lost soul in a small town. Now he was at a large public high school donned in helmet and shoulder pads running down a field with the first team offense for the Dance County Patriots. Coach Nate had kept his eye on him wary of not allowing himself too much focus on the new player. He was cognitive of the potential of a one and done with the young man and he wanted the experience to bring him back for the next practice.

The offense had moved the ball from their twenty-five-yard line to the twenty yard line on the defensive side of the field. Coach knew they would need to eat play clock along with moving the ball to level the playing field against Clayton. They had run ten plays to get to this point in the field in a balance of run and short throws from the senior QB.

Morgan was now zipping the ball with authority and the receivers were doing their part in catching the pigskin. Morgan's dad had arrived at Practice and was now standing a few feet from Green and Alexander.

Coach Jackson was now ready to give Davis a shot with the offense. He told Watters to try a throw to Davis in the end zone. Watters delivered the play through a rotating running back. Ben Young raised his hands and the offensive line filled in the huddle behind the line of scrimmage. The skill players followed. Morgan looked Davis in the eye. It was now time to bury the bad blood between the two players. He barked the play to the offense and then added additional direction. "Quincy I am going to hit you on a post, be ready." Davis stared at the QB. His eyes were wide. He bit down hard on the mouthpiece and moved his head up and down toward Morgan. The offense broke the huddle.

Ponder was the wideout on the left side of the field with Davis lined up on the right. New Coach Donnie Tillman was simulating game conditions by having double coverage on the talented receiver. The move was not lost on Coach Jackson and he told himself to make sure he recognized the effort with the newest member of his staff.

Davis was alone along the right sideline. A deep back on the defensive side acknowledged his presence and slowly jogged toward him. The defense did not consider him a threat at this stage of his football career.

Morgan hit the second cadence and Young snapped him the ball. He graciously moved backwards and allowed the receivers to make their way down the short field. The second team line was not getting any penetration through his offensive line. Morgan's arm was cocked, and he didn't telegraph his intentions. The ball sailed from the backfield in a perfect spiral aimed for the right corner of the end zone.

Davis had shot off the line with the first move of football from the hands of Ben Young. He looked at the goal line and moved his arms up and down gaining tremendous speed with each firing of his legs. The backs had ignored him for a second until two had seen the trajectory of the pigskin. They were woefully behind and tried to make up impossible ground. They had been burned, bad, by the newest member of the team.

The football seemed to float at the last second. Davis suddenly remembered being eight years old again and catching the ball in a pickup game in a park near his home. His hands had been around his chest and the ball seemed to hit him without any movement. This catch would be no different. He opened his hands just at his jersey numbers. He squeezed the ball and pulled it tight to his chest. He kept running, even after the Coach's whistle. He found himself ten yards outside of the end zone before pulling to a stop.

A couple of dads yelled their approval from the sidelines. The school band had been practicing on a hill adjoining the practice field and had finished. A kid carrying a tuba acknowledged Davis. "Nice catch."

"Good job," said Nate Jackson. He waited a second for the teams to assemble. "Ok, start again back on the twenty-five. Run it again."

CHAPTER 41

The birds sang at the highest of pitch perched atop the dew stained oaks. Slivers of bright sunshine angled through the cheap plastic blinds. The coach opened his eyes slowly then instinctively flung himself upwards from the mattress. His pulse raced, heart thumped. He looked around the room praying the clock would read six but the light piercing through the blinds said eight am or later.

He reached for the iPhone on the night stand. 7:27 it displayed. First bell was less than 20 minutes away. He jumped to his feet and ran toward the small bathroom, grabbed a toothbrush and went at his gum line. With the other hand he started the shower. Within seven minutes, he was backing the F 150 out of the apartment space and headed toward the high school. He chose not to digress on the bottle of Jack Daniels appearing statuesque on the coffee table.

Sergeant William Alexander was trying to remember the last time he had slept. He had completed his regular shift, but he was not going home now. The favor had been requested two hours before his night shift had ended. A senior officer had a school program he wanted to attend for a young child. He asked if Alexander could cover two hours after his workday was scheduled to end. Favors were not taken lightly at the patrol and Alexander knew the father's attendance at his daughter's program was very important. He graciously committed and didn't ask anything in return. He nursed a black coffee from the Waffle Stop. A new shift of employees had been busily taking care of customers. Rose Wilkes was back at her acreage still enjoying some well-deserved rest.

He had not had any calls. He decided to remain in town and provide some additional support for the Greenwood PD during the busy school rush. Traffic seemed lighter than normal on the main thoroughfare. He pulled the cruiser out of the gas station across the southbound lanes and headed north. The south bound lanes would have taking him past the high school and into rural country. He made his way toward the county seat.

Coach was still getting used to his new community. His apartment was near a shopping mall and a couple of fast food restaurants. He was a little further from work than he ordinarily would like but in the grand scheme of things a ten-minute commute seemed easy, but not today.

He pushed the Ford to 60 mph in the 45 mph. He was gambling, and he knew it. He was hoping the local PD was in a shift change or at the donut shop. Anywhere, but running radar on this four-mile stretch of highway he was now on. He zipped around two old ladies in a ten-year old Buick. He knew it was errand time and probably the first stop was the hair salon. He looked at his watch. The school bell was four minutes away.

The blue lights came on at the last curve before the high school. He was hoping he was the only one tardy this morning. This one would not be fun to explain, not to his boss, his peers, or one of the thousand students with the audacity to ask him about the traffic stop now taking place.

He dug into his glove box. He then fished his registration and insurance card out hoping to expedite the process. He looked into his rear-view mirror. This was not a local police car. The vehicle in his mirror represented a Georgia State Trooper. "Son of a gun," he whispered under his breath.

The bottle of Jack Daniels he had looked at on his way out the door of his apartment was a gift left for him when he moved in. There was no gift card or reference on who had purchased the liter size bottle. He knew it was from the Dan Green led boosters. Bottles had been purchased during his coaching time in Savannah. There was never a direct thank you for the gift, but they always showed up after a big win.

This bottle was left unopened on his coffee table. He had moved it from the coffee table to under the kitchen sink when he moved in. After reading a text from William Alexander just after practice on Tuesday, the bottle had moved back to the coffee table.

He had stared at it in between game preparation and distracting thoughts about what Alexander had shared with him via a text.

He had debated most of the night in between film study whether or not to bust the cap on the bottle. A couple of beers and he had a chance of staying on the right side of normal, liquor on the other hand was prison in his world. He tried to avoid it at all cost. Deep down inside he struggled with his thoughts. It would be denial to blame the cat and mouse with the bottle on the received text message. No doubt, it had thrown him for a loop. Things were moving fast. Much more so than he had ever anticipated the day he made the decision to be the next Head Coach.

William Alexander looked at the truck. He realized who he had stopped when he saw the Chatham County plates. He let his dispatcher know his present position and checked the traffic to make sure it was safe for him to exit the vehicle.

Alexander rose from the Charger. He adjusted his wide brimmed hat, did a quick glance at the approaching traffic, and made his way toward the pickup.

"Good morning," he said.

Coach looked at him through squinted eyes. His sunglasses had been left on the kitchen bar in his rush to get out the door. "Good morning, William, I guess I am not going to make that first bell after all."

"Now you know that doesn't set the best example as a leader, you getting pulled over in front of all those young men and women across the street."

Coach kept the eyes locked on the veteran officer. He knew he deserved the lecture. It was the first week and he blew it. Can't coach the kids on accountability if you're not willing to pay the freight, he thought to himself.

"I can promise, William, this will not happen again." That was good enough for Alexander. He changed the subject mindful of the approaching school bell. "Did you get my text?"

Nate responded with a yes. "Stacy is driving into town late Friday. Pam is coming in Friday as well. The plan is for the girls to meet at the hotel and drive over to the game. They were hoping you could join us after the game for a late meal over at Chilis."

Nate had struggled with how he was going to handle the pending invitation. It would be easy to walk away. There was his new job and a ton of time between them. But he took the job for a reason and whether he was ready to admit it, Stacy was part of the equation. He wasn't going to hem and haw with his old friend now, not with a ticket looming and a school bell less than a minute away.

"I am looking forward to it, William, it will be great to see both of them."

Alexander nodded. He looked back at his car then looked across the street at the school. "Can you slow it down?"

"Yes sir, William." He put the truck in drive and headed for the high school. Two practices remained before game night.

CHAPTER 42

He sat in his pickup truck eleven hours after he had pulled in to the school parking lot and after his run in with Sergeant Alexander. He stared at the pack of chewing tobacco that was smashed in the side panel of the door. He contemplated removing it for only a second. It was the same pack he had bought in San Francisco and he had been pretty good about not going down another dark road with a dangerous habit. But it was Wednesday and there was one more practice left. He was on edge and needed to decompress. It was always an option in his younger years but he was older, supposedly wiser he told himself, and elected to leave the pack where it was.

He cranked the truck and backed out of the parking space. The coaches would be meeting again first thing Thursday morning for final preparations. He had sent them home after a practice with mixed results. He had seen some good play from both sides of the ball. The kids were executing the plays and were buying into the new process and hurried up sessions. They had moved from full pads to shoulder pads and shorts. There was less contact and a lot of emphasis on the formations they could expect from Clayton. The kids and Coaches were impressed with Nate Jackson's preparation and knowledge of the team coming to town on Friday night. He had done his homework. Kyle Morgan had quipped during a mid-scrimmage lecture from the head coach, "Does this guy even sleep?"

He should be headed home he thought. A quick sandwich and then start with the film study. But he had other plans. He looked at his watch hoping that his timing would be ok. The drive from the school would take about ten minutes.

He pulled into the yard and saw the Cadillac parked under a carport. He exited the vehicle and made his way to the front door. He waited a second then gently knocked on the thick wood.

She opened the door and smiled at the young Coach. He was wearing a plain white sweatshirt and grey khaki pants. There was no reference on his clothing to the school or team he would lead Friday night.

"Mrs. Davis, my name is Nate Jackson, I am the new coach over at the high school. I wanted to introduce myself and see if we could talk for a few minutes."

She never lost the smile. She opened the door as wide as it would go. "Yes, I know who you are, would you please come in."

Nate made his way into the neatly furnished brick one story home. He said thank you as he was greeted by the smell of a recently prepared dinner.

"I was just about to fix me a plate. If you have time, would you join me for dinner?"

Nate was immediately apologetic. "I'm sorry, Mrs. Davis, I didn't mean to interrupt dinner, I can come back."

"Nonsense, you will do no such thing, please." She touched his shoulder and directed him to a dining room to his left.

He passed a worn leather recliner. He visualized Coach Matt Davis stretching out on that recliner and how hard it must be now for Mrs. Davis being there alone each day and night. He turned toward her. "Thank you, I would love to join you for dinner." She motioned him toward a chair. She left the room and returned with a second plate and a glass of sweetened iced team. They sat down to a table adorned with bowls of collard greens, creamed corn, and a tossed salad. There was a small platter with a baked chicken and corn bread. It was a lot of food for two people, even more so for one. Nate was so appreciative of the generosity. He filled his plate and thanked her again.

"Doctor says I have to get my weight up, I lost quite a bit with the cancer."

Nate paused in his response. He wanted to make sure he said the right things.

She continued. "My last scan was very good. My doctor says I can beat this."

Nate smiled. He knew what he did was important. He knew there would be a lot of pressure less than forty-eight hours from now on his coaching staff and players.

None of it mattered compared to real life and what Mrs. Davis was now going through.

"That is great news, Mrs. Davis." She looked at him. It reminded him of his mother and how she always seemed to care about everyone before herself. "Now enough about me. What can I do for you?"

"Well, Mrs. Davis, we have a big game against Clayton Friday night. I wanted to see if you would be able to attend."

Her smile was infectious. "I would like that. My daughter and her family are driving in for the weekend. I will make sure she knows so we can head over."

The response was uplifting. Nate was looking for that good news and he got some. "Did you know my husband?"

Nate was thankful she had broached the subject. "Yes, Ma'am, I had the opportunity to attend several coaching camps that your husband led. As a new Coach in South Georgia, he was the one that all of us gravitated toward during the clinic sessions and breaks. He was such a mentor and friend to so many. I learned a great deal from your husband."

"Thank you for the kind words, I miss him dearly."

They finished their meals. Mrs. Davis rose and disappeared in the kitchen with both of their dinner plates. Nate tried to rise and assist her with the clean-up. Her hand touched his shoulder. "You will do no such thing. You are my guest, please stay seated."

She disappeared for a moment into the kitchen. A minute later she returned with a steaming cup of coffee and a slice of pie. She placed it before Nate. He wasn't sure what kind of pie it was until he took his first bite. He quickly tasted peanut butter with chocolate and graham crust. It was incredibly sweet and the perfect match for the dark roasted coffee. He savored each bite with a sip of the hot brew.

"This is so good, Mrs. Davis, I can't thank you enough for the invitation."

Mrs. Davis skipped the coffee but had a slice uncut before her. She was ready to talk football.

"I read in the paper Clayton is going to have north of seventy players Friday night," she said.

"Yes, ma'am, the paper is correct. They have a big strong team and they have a lot of depth. We have our hands full."

Mrs. Davis cradled her coffee cup with two hands taking a small sip of the hot beverage. "Matt was worried about Clayton before the season started. He had remarked after a bad scrimmage this past summer that it would take an Act of God for us to beat them."

Coach chuckled. He could envision Coach Davis saying that to his team or staff or both.

"You have had less than a week with the boys, how do you feel about Friday night."

Coach didn't want to sound like a guy standing in front of a bunch of reporters. He always tried to be as transparent as possible. "Well, we are going to try to do opposite of what they expect. We are going to run a lot of no huddle and pass when they think run and opposite when they think pass."

She sat her coffee down. "That Kyle Morgan has an arm, he is going to always give you a chance. Matt felt confident we would watch him play on Saturdays with a chance he might one day play on Sundays."

Coach nodded in agreement. The pie was the perfect touch, the caffeine from the coffee would help with the film study.

He rose from the table. He offered again to help her with the clean-up. She led him to the living room. A family picture caught his stare.

"I love those boys just like Matt did. We would do anything for those kids. They meant everything to him like I know they will mean everything to you." She extended her hand. "Thank you so much for stopping by and best of luck Friday night.

He said goodbye and made his way to his truck enjoying the coolness of a fall night in Georgia. He made a note to send her some flowers with a card of encouragement from the team.

He was glad he had made the decision to visit. He was hopeful she would make the game Friday night.

CHAPTER 43

Nate was back in his office before sunrise. The meeting with the coaches had gone well. Coach Griffin had brought donut holes and a large cardboard container of coffee to the meeting. "Where did you get that?" Nate asked.

"Waffle Stop, while I there, Rose Wilkes volunteered her land for a team BBQ when we are ready."

Nate smiled and told him to remind him of that once they had a couple of games under their belt. "Her husband has two-barrel shaped smokers and can put out a beef brisket and pork shoulder that puts ninety nine percent of the BBQ restaurants in the state to shame."

The donut holes were not on the nutrition radar, but Nate knew another 18-hour day was under way and grabbed two from the box. There was enough coffee in the box to fill several cups and the coaches were appreciative to have with the early hour.

They settled on their practice plan. It would be shorts and helmets only. The squads would be split with final preparation on play selection and defensive sets. There would be a light run through and expectation was the practice to be less than two hours. The weather man had said expect cold-weather for game time. Nate made it a point to emphasize the new playing conditions during their drills.

The men wrapped up their planning as the first bell sounded. Nate directed his first PE class to the weight room and handed out their workout plans. He asked if there were any questions and went back to his office to make a note. He had picked up a flaw in the Clayton defense from the previous night's film study and wanted to make a note for the afternoon practice.

The morning clock was moving now. Class changes were occurring and Nate found himself back at his desk sorting through a large stack of print outs. He stared did not leave his desk as the slight knock came from the office door. "Coach, you got a second?" The voice was deeper than the average student.

Nate recognized it before raising his head. He looked up and smiled without hesitation. "For you guys, absolutely," he said.

Standing before him was the Offensive Coordinator along with the Defensive Backs Coach for the States Flagship University. Nate jumped from his chair and came around the desk with an energized step and outstretched hand. "Brice, John, how are you my friends."

Brice responded with a hard handshake and quick shoulder hug. John slapped him on his back and told him how good it was to see him. Nate shook his head trying to remember how long it had been.

Brice spoke up. "One of our recruiting trips to Savannah. We stayed overnight and closed down one your local watering holes."

Nate remembered. "I was a much younger man then."

"So, what can I do for you fine gentlemen?" Coach said.

"Well, if it is ok with you, we would like to speak with Kyle Morgan and Dante Alexander."

Coach motioned for everyone to take a seat around his desk. He had added a few personal items to his office during the short week. One of them was a team picture from his college years.

Brice saw it and picked it up. "Now why in the hell did you get to keep that thick head of hair and mine has been missing since graduation?"

Coach chuckled. "Well at least you don't have to pack a hair dryer with all that travel."

Brice smiled. "Good point."

"Kyle and Dante are in the weight room now next door. I can get them, and you can use my office. How do the opportunities for them look for next year look?"

Coach knew both men would be straight up with him. He had always enjoyed a very good relationship throughout their careers. Several of his players had been signed by the state's largest and oldest University.

"There has been some staff shake ups at other schools and the kids are all connected through social media. We have picked up some key commitments, but we are not where we need to be in some areas," said Brice.

"Dante's willingness to work on both sides of the ball is seen as a real plus. Morgan is a gunslinger and there is a little weaker field for his position this year. There are some really strong players in the class behind him but as you know, you got to win now," added John.

"So, what are their chances you sign them?"

The question did not hang in the air long. "Both players have spots at the University if they want it," said Brice.

Nate flashed a wide smile. He looked at both men. He had missed the interaction with his former teammates. There had been a lot of blood, sweat, and sacrifice between them on the practice field. But with hard work and timing, there was reward. The career path had been fast and lucrative for both of them ascending to prominent coaching roles at a young age. He was very proud for them and their families.

"Anything else you need before I go get Morgan and Alexander?" Brice turned toward John. There was a hesitation and Nate caught it. Something else was about to be revealed. He had been in this situation several times and knew the best thing to do was to sit tight and listen.

Brice decided to be the one that shared what was coming next.

"The head ball coach has dropped your name a few times, to both of us. If I'm reading the tea leaves right he is testing the waters on your interest to head our way."

Nate looked at both men. He paused for only a second. "Gentlemen, I am flattered, but you know what this town and school has been through and I have been here less than a week." He paused again then continued. "This team needs everything I got right now. I'll go get Morgan and Alexander for you."

When Nate left the room, Brice turned toward John. "I told you he was old school; you won't find a more loyal guy in our profession."

CHAPTER 44

The alarm clock was still an hour before sounding. Nate stared at it before turning his head and returning his glare toward the ceiling. He had fallen asleep just after midnight. Four and a half hours passed quickly, and he awoke to the realization game day was here.

He knew lying in bed would not accomplish anything productive. His body turned, and the legs hit the floor. He skipped the usual walk toward the kitchen and the starting of the coffee pot. It could wait he told himself. No need for caffeine on game day.

A quick shower and he was dressed an out the door a little after five. He made his way to the school and his office. His team was ready. The preparation had been sound. He liked the crispness of the workouts on Thursday and the attitude of the players. They were not too high but not low. Very even keel is how he would describe it. He expected Clayton to hit hard and fast. It was not the beginning of the game that concerned him but if they got down 14 or 21 points. Coaches worry. It always was there.

He went through the agreed upon plays and schemes on the laminated sheets. He saw everything was in order and ready to go. He checked his notes to make sure everything was a go for the pregame meal. His preparation was on the money and he couldn't find anything that needed his attention.

A little after six he made his way from his office back to the parking lot. The darkness was still there. A slight light over a hilltop whispered sun rise was on the way. He looked across the back -parking lot, at the stadium. So peaceful, tonight there would be a full house. It was a beautiful sight this morning and would be a beautiful sight tonight. Nothing beat the pageantry of playing under the lights of Friday night where football is everything. There was excitement to come and a wave of adrenaline surged through his body.

He was back in the truck and left the empty parking lot. He turned west and headed to a place he had spotted a few days ago shortly after he moved in. It would take only a few minutes to get there and he would be back in plenty of time and in no risk of triggering William Alexander's radar gun.

The building sat on a fifteen acre plot next to the two lane highway. Wide and expansive farms as far as the eye could see surrounded the back and right side of the property. The building was over one hundred years old. It was just like he had remembered from his youth.

The building was small white church and it seemed to have sat almost frozen in time.

The sun started to peek through the towering pines that lined the acreage to the left. It brought light to a cemetery about seventy-five yards from the church. It provided a memory for the coach as he recollected on lost loved ones and funerals from what seemed like another lifetime.

A separate wing had been added on the other side that housed the Sunday school classes and Wednesday night supper. More memories flowed of when he was a small child. Being with aged loved ones, running with your buddies through the freshly cut grass, asking for an extra slice of cake made by one of the church members or your own grandmother. Nothing store bought seemed as good as what the ladies could create in their kitchens.

He got out of his truck and made his way toward the church. It was all white in color with a narrow steeple that reached high into the sky. He stepped on the porch. The wood creaked as he made his way from the last step to the door. He didn't know what to expect at this hour. He reached toward the metal handle and turned. The door opened.

There were 15 rows of wooden pews in the center. To the left and right side of the church another 10 rows. Not all of the lights were in use, but it was plenty. A small sign hung on the side wall. It gave attendance numbers and weekly offerings. The totals were small but consistent. He hoped he would find himself back and counted one day.

He walked toward the front and settled on the second row of pews. He stared at the cross, buried his face into his hands, and let it all out.

He thanked God for his opportunity in front of him and a second chance at his profession. He asked for strength praying for a team that had been through so much and to be able to help them through a very difficult time. He thanked God for his coaches and their leadership. He even threw a mention in for Dan Green and the boosters. He still didn't know what to expect but he had learned with age it is always best to take the high road.

He then turned everything toward him. The demons that pulled at him and now were hitting him on a daily basis. He knew there was a problem in San Francisco with his behavior and more importantly his lack of control with his drinking. There was only one way to move forward. Now was the time to admit it. Now was the time to ask for help.

He prayed hard. He surrendered to God and pleaded for His intervention. He never wanted to go down those dark roads again. Tears welled in his eyes. He had never been this emotional at any stage in his life. He didn't fight it, just continued to ask God for understanding and assistance.

He turned his thoughts toward Stacy. He would see her tonight. There were years between them. He was excited, terrified, and very wary of being broken again. He continued to pray.

He dried his eyes with his sleeve. He looked at the cross again. He felt a sudden wave of inner strength and peace in the confession and thanked God. He pulled himself up from the pew, a new man, and walked toward the door and his truck.

CHAPTER 45

School ended, and the players made their way to the locker room. From there, they would store their books and backpacks and head toward the cafeteria for the pregame meal. Meanwhile in the coach's office, Nate Jackson was meeting with his staff. He pulled a large cardboard box from under his desk. He opened it and began handing out just delivered athletic pull over jackets to each of his coaches. "A little something for the cold air tonight," he said. The jackets were red with the Dance County Patriot logo on the sleeve. On the left side each read 'Dance County Football Coaching Staff." Donnie Tillman immediately tore off his windbreaker and put the jacket on. The other coaches quickly followed. Nate Jackson smiled. "Looking good, Gentlemen," he said.

Dan Green had a contingent of Dad's working grills that had been transported from homes in pickup trucks hours earlier. Grilled chicken breast with a light BBQ sauce was the meat of choice. The players walked by the men and their grills anxious to see what was being served in the cafeteria. The ladies from the school lunch line warmly greeted the players as they entered the serving line. There was a buffet line set up with the dad prepared chicken, large baked sweet potatoes, green beans, and fresh garden salad. A large basket of just baked dinner rolls completed the pregame meal.

The parking lot was down to just a few cars. That would all change in a couple of hours. It would be packed with many vehicles having to park along the grass and state highway.

The coaches entered as the players finished lining up for their food. The new attire was not missed by the players. "Sharp jacket, Coach," said Chris Ponder. What they didn't notice was two large boxes strategically hidden by Nate Jackson in a storage room adjoining the cafeteria. The players would be receiving one of the pullovers after the pregame meal.

The players enjoyed the meal. The sweet potato had a small serving of cinnamon and butter that was a big hit and just enough to keep a few of the lineman from asking about dessert. Coach remarked to Coach Jackson how was impressed with the amount of greens consumed by his new team. Many of Savannah players mostly avoided the vegetables and pleaded for seconds on the meat. Not with this group.

As some of the players were refilling their cups of iced tea, Coach Jackson asked for everyone's attention. "Welcome to game day, Gentlemen. We are going to stay in here a little longer before we head back to the locker room. I first want to thank all of you for a good week of practice. There was a tremendous amount of effort on display. I saw it, and your coaches saw it." I also want to thank the coaches tonight. These men work long and hard hours to prepare you for your battle with Clayton. That effort is greatly appreciated." He paused for just a second and continued. "I would like for each of you to introduce yourself tonight and state your position, then I would like for each of you to share with the team two pieces of information. One, what did you improve on this week, and two, what did you learn about your opponent."

Coach looked toward the first table of players to his left. "Dante Alexander. Let's start with you."

Dante rose from his seat. "Dante, tight end and Linebacker, I got better this week catching the ball and I learned Clayton is going to bring a lot of players up the middle on defense."

Coach nodded toward Dante then looked directly at Quincy Davis sitting next to him. He rose from the table. He was nervous. He had never been asked to speak in front of a large group. He looked around the room then looked down at the table. "Davis, Receiver," he said. He looked at the coach then looked back down at the table.

Nate shot him a reassuring look. "When the ball is thrown to me, I gotta catch it." There was a chuckle from a couple of players. "Clayton is gonna be fast, I gotta be faster." Nate Jackson gave the kid a smile. The encouragement was not lost on Ponder and Morgan as they both remembered the scene from the convenience store.

Coach Watters looked at Davis, smiled and said, "You will be."

The remaining team members finished thirty minutes later. Nate was appreciative of the thought that went into the responses. Kyle Morgan stood up. "Everyone, I would like to say something." A hush fell over the room. "Last time we took the field, I made some decisions and some plays that were not too smart and not in the best interest of this team." Morgan paused and looked back and forth across the room.

He had debated on whether or not to address the team, but after the offer to play at the next level this past week felt it was his duty as a leader and QB 1. "I just want to everyone to know, that tonight through the rest of this season everything I got will be given on the field and for this team." The room was quiet at first. Some of the players looked around wondering who was going to say something next.

Dante Alexander took the lead. "Let's get out there and kick some ass tonight."

The coaches remained quiet. Nate Jackson left the room unnoticed and returned with the two boxes from the storage room.

"Ok, Gentlemen, I have here a little something for each of you to wear. This will be our travel attire and worn for school events that we are together as a team. Take care of them. Get with your position groups and your coaches will call you forward to receive. Before I hand these out, I want to recognize Mr. Dan Green and all the dad's that manned the grills tonight for your pregame meals and those special ladies that delivered all the fixings for your meal. Let's make sure we thank them for their commitment to Patriot football."

Suddenly it was Christmas in the Dance County High School Cafeteria. The kids immediately pulled the bright red cover ups over their shirts. The team looked good. There was laughter, joking, and good-natured ribbing with teammates. There was also a pep in the step like Nate knew there would be.

The mood was quickly challenged. Three hundred yards from the cafeteria building two executive chartered busses rumbled into the beaten asphalt parking lot from the highway. A county sheriff's car escorted the busses to the rear of the stadium. The lone blue light atop the patrol vehicle was turned on. The players saw the activity from an open door leading to the parking lot. Nate Jackson looked at his watch then at his players. It was time to shift gears. "All right, Gentlemen, it's all business from here, no talking during dress, focus is on what you need to do tonight. Everyone to the house, backs and receivers full gear and on the field in 30 minutes."

CHAPTER 46

The stands were almost eighty percent full. The sun had disappeared just after the players had begun their pregame stretching. The weather was cold for early October after a freakish front had moved through the East Coast dumping several inches of snow on the states to the north.

Many of the parents were bundled up in large down jackets and had brought blankets to cover their legs. A hot chocolate stand that was normally reserved for the last couple of games in the season was operating with a line of twenty or so fans in front of it. The band was getting ready to take their seats in the upper level of the home end zone section.

Coach Nate had stayed on the field well after the players had jogged back to their locker room. He trotted over to shake hands with the Clayton staff huddled in the center field near the twenty-yard line. "Coach Jackson, welcome to North Georgia," said their head football coach Paul Eames as Nate walked toward them. "Thank you, Coach, good to see everyone tonight," he said.

There was small talk on the weather. Each coach was thankful for the cool air and dry conditions. Coach asked if their team needed anything. "All good, Coach, you all have a very nice facility, thank you for the hospitality."

Nate looked at the seventy plus players lining up to return to their locker room. "Coach you all didn't leave anyone back-home did you? he said jokingly. The coaches just nodded. The tension was starting to rise. There was no more warm and fuzzy feelings coming from this group tonight.

Nate returned from the field to the underbelly of the stadium. He paused outside of the door. He embarked on a ritual that had been with him throughout his career. He closed his eyes, touched the locker room door. He thanked God again for the opportunity. He looked to the sky, thought of Coach Davis and Parks, prayed for them and their families, and prayed for his team.

He waited a minute, collected his thoughts and entered the locker room with a force and swagger seen by all in the room. The clock read ten minutes before kick.

There was no music, no joking around. Phones had been placed securely in lockers. It was all business and Nate's first worry of the night was resolved.

He stood before the players, looked each of them with an emotional fire brewing directly into their eyes. The assistants were standing along the locker room wall to his left. This was game 1 of the Coach Nate Jackson tenure and everyone was watching. A few of the Dad's had snuck their way into the back of the locker room. Any other game, this would not be tolerated by the head coach. That would be for any other game, but not tonight.

Coach cleared his throat. A half smile formed across his face. He once again scanned the room looking at each of the players before him. His heart was racing, and he could feel the adrenaline again surge through his body. It now seemed like an eternity had passed since being let go of his coaching duties in Savannah on a hell hot stagnant day in September. An eternity since he stood on the riverbank, with the old man and the fishing pole. Tonight, he was back, Coach Nate Jackson, back in his office.

"Well, Gentlemen, it is Friday night and here we go. There are no warm up games tonight. No chance to line up against an inferior opponent." He let the words settle with his team then pointed toward the door. "Sitting in that visitors' locker room is a regional playoff team that is a heavy favorite to win the State Championship," he paused, "and they are a heavy favorite to win tonight."

"Some of you may have wondered what I was doing earlier this evening walking the stadium. Well, men, I wanted to see our opponent up front and up close. Not on some highlight film or on television. I wanted to see them in person, standing on our field in our house." He paused again. "Because that is, Gentlemen, where this game is going to be played tonight on your grass, in your stadium." He paused again wanting the words to sink in. He caught a glimpse of a couple of dad's buying into the words, ignored them, and continued. "This will not be played out on some social media platform. Not on twitter, snapchat, or whatever is the flavor of the day. All the talk and naysayers lose their stake in this one when the whistle blows. It will all come down to each you, the men in this room. Each of you has an assignment. An assignment we have asked each of you to think about all week. With each of you executing the assignment, we walk off our field tonight in victory."

"Clayton brought two big busses. There are a lot of players on that sideline. When one gets tired a new body is waiting to come in. We might not have that luxury tonight. But I can assure you we don't need it. Because when it is all said and done, I take the men in this room and just as the sun is going to rise tomorrow and I will always go to battle with you."

Nate moved a step toward his players. "Kyle Morgan, are you ready to lead this offense?"

Morgan looked at the veteran coach with eyes aglow. "Yes, Sir! Dante Alexander."

"Are you ready to lead this defense and help us out on offense?" Alexander screamed, "Yes, Coach!"

"Gentlemen, you don't know me yet. But you know Coaches Watters, Griffin, Williams, and Tillman. I have seen first-hand how much these coaches care about you and how hard they have, and you have worked under enormous challenges." He paused. "This team has been knocked down and kicked unlike any other team in the Nation right now. The circumstances under which your season has gone would derail even the biggest of men and best of the best teams. But we are not talking about circumstances tonight and we are not talking about just anyone." Nate paused. He smiled. His eyes showed that connection point with each player.

"Tonight, I am talking about each of you."

Nate's eyes watered slightly. The smile formed at the corner of his mouth. His players and coaches looked at him with a buy in there was no challenge that couldn't be overcome.

Coach continued.

"What I see tonight is a group of young men that are going to go out on that field and dig deep in their hearts and play their absolute best, one play at a time."

"That will be all that anyone will ask, and I promise you that will be all it will take to win."

"It's time, Ben Young, lead us in prayer, then, Gentlemen, buckle up."

CHAPTER 46

When the Patriots took the field, the Greenwood Trojans football team was sitting on the home side of the stadium. They had a bye week and were not scheduled to play. Earlier that day the head football coach had called Principal Lee and asked if they could attend to show their support. Lee was overwhelmed with the gesture and had two teachers reserve the space in the stands prior to their arrival. Nate Jackson had no clue of their intentions. The coaches for Greenwood thought it would be a good community gesture to support their county team as they were the last team to play against the Davis and Parks led Patriots.

The Greenwood Head coach along with his assistants were wearing their school colors as they jogged toward the gate to meet Coach Nate Jackson and his three assistants at the fence before they took the field. "You and your team have been through a lot this year, Coach Jackson. On behalf of our team and staff, I wanted to let you know, that we will be your 12th man in the stands tonight. Good luck tonight and the rest of the season."

The assistants for both schools, exchanged fist pumps and handshakes as if they were fraternity brothers at a ten-year reunion. The moment was spotted by Dante Alexander who motioned for his teammates to look toward the gate. The players were gathered behind the goal post waiting to run through the large banner being held by the Patriot Cheerleaders.

Nate looked at the opposing team in the stands, then turned back toward the Greenwood Coach. The emotions were running at a fevered pitch. The assistants turned their attention toward him. "Coach, in all my years it would be tough to remember a classier act."

A tear formed in the corner of his eye. "Thank you."

The players were all aware of the presence of their rival team in the stands. Morgan took advantage of the gesture. "Greenwood didn't come here to see us lose, let's win this thing."

The enormity of the game rose even more.

The Dance County Band is drowning out the stadium noise with bellowing tubas and deep beats of several drum sounds. The cheerleaders had taken position with the banner that simply read, "Beat Clayton." The opposition had run through the south end zone and were ready to take the field from the visitor's sideline. Three Clayton captains made their way to the midpoint of the field.

The Dance County Patriots burst through the banner to the fevered screams of the home crowd. Two cheerleaders were comfortably ahead of the mass of players running under the goal post and doing cart wheels toward the home team sideline. Nate Jackson stood on the sideline getting outfitted with the headset to communicate with Coach Watters and Coach Tillman standing in a metal enclosed space atop the press box.

Kyle Morgan, Chris Ponder, Ben Young, and Dante Alexander were the Patriot Captains and took the field. The officials greeted the players. They reminded them of the importance of keeping their heads up to prevent injury, they also warn against any unsportsmanlike play. The coin was shown, and it flew into the air. Kyle Morgan waited for instruction as the Clayton linebacker called tails and the coin landed on heads. The official turned toward Morgan.

"We will take the ball on offense." The official turned back to the Clayton player and asked about field preference. He then turned toward the home crowd and let them know Dance County will start the game on offense.

A roar rumbled through the stadium. The excitement level from the stands was reverberating through the players and the coaches. A nervous energy sent Nate pacing up and down the sideline.

Dan Morgan smiled and looked at the packed stadium from his perch along the fence line. With the exception of a few rogue students, everyone else was in the stands, including William Alexander and his two female guests.

The Clayton kicker sent the ball from the tee sideways toward the end zone. The act set off a thunderous clap through the stadium when foot catches leather. The ball never rotated in a typical end over end. It stayed flat like a shoe box and hung in the air. Chris Ponder caught it on the fly at the ten-yard line. He easily passed the first wave of defenders. The crowd roared thinking a run back on the opening kick was in the mix. He made it to the forty and a defensive back stood him up and stopped him in his tracks.

Kyle Morgan took the last-minute instruction straight from the head ball coach. He leaned in close. Both sides of the stadium had raised the decibel level. Nate screamed into the QB's ear. "Just Like we practiced, keep the pace moving, let's wear their big asses out."

Ben Young cleared the huddle and trotted to the line. Chris Ponder looked at the official, check his alignment and waited for the snap. Morgan took the ball from Young and shot toward Ponder and the sideline. The tailback was trailing just behind him. He flipped the ball as a Clayton defender came around the end. The running back caught the ball and headed for the sideline. Brute Athleticism got him to the end of the line of scrimmage. Pure speed got him to the corner. The first offensive play was good for 12 yards and the Dance County Patriots were in Clayton territory.

The second play was not on a game film studied by the Clayton coaches. Morgan took the ball and this time took a stutter step and followed the path cut in the middle by his veteran center Ben Young. The interior line couldn't get enough helmets on Morgan and he was suddenly in the secondary with his quarterback keep. A safety had to make the tackle. The Patriots were very close to being inside the twenty.

They ran one more play, this time a toss sweep to the short side of the field. It was good for six yards. "You feeling a pass, Coach Watters?" said Nate.

"Let's do it," Jackson screamed out for Dante Alexander. He carried the play into the huddle. He was not only the messenger but the first target for QB 1.

Morgan smiled. "Already, Dante, get us first blood."

Morgan took the snap from the shotgun. Clayton sent the house with eight players rushing the line of scrimmage. Morgan was ready as two mammoth defensive line-man grabbed at his jersey. The spiral was perfect. The ball slapped Alexander in the hands on the two-yard line with one defender a step behind. He crossed the goal line to the screams from the student section. He flipped the ball to the official and prepared for the onslaught of offensive players toward the end zone. Morgan jumped three feet into the air and into the arms of the new star receiver. The point after kick followed two minutes later. Dance County led Clayton 7-0. There was only four minutes elapsed on the clock.

The Patriot kick was taken by the Clayton back on the seven-yard line. He was able to push through three defenders and group tackled on the twenty. DeAngelo Baker took the field as the starting QB for Clayton. He was big and strong and had the internal confidence of twenty all-stars. He was sitting on three in-state scholarship offers but many predicted he would sign with his Father's alma mater, NC State. He huddled with his team on the visitor 13-yard line.

Dante Alexander was leading his defense after his offensive score. He looked across the line at Baker scream the cadence. The ball was snapped, and Dante sensed a tailback dive headed his way. He shook off a guard trying to open a hole on the left side. He drove his helmet into the backs chest and tried to slow the momentum. The play was positive, and Clayton picked up four yards. The next play was a dive play as well. This time it worked the other side of the line. Clayton's big boys up front were getting a big push and moving the smaller Dance County players. Two plays produced sixteen yards and Clayton was first and ten and moving the ball toward the midfield stripe.

"We have to get pressure up front. They are getting way too much push up front." Donnie Tillman heard Coach Jackson's screams through the headset. He knew heat would need to come from the secondary. He suggested to Griffin bringing in a couple of his deep backs. The Clayton offense was content on running the ball until they had passed the end zone and into the parking lot. Baker took the snap and went to hand again to the tailback this time looking to sweep around the end. A defensive back had made his way toward the line and had anticipated the handoff beautifully. He cracked the back behind the line of scrimmage for Clayton's first negative yards of the night.

"Good call, men."

Clayton bit off another first down through two more run plays. On first and ten just shy of the fifty, the home crowd and defense was given the first look of the opposing QBs arm strength. He lifted a spiral that hung in the air for just under forty yards. A hush fell over the crowd as they waited for the conclusion. A spectacular play by the Dance County Free safety prevented a long touch-down and caused an exasperated sigh from the crowd then another thunderous explosion of cheers.

Clayton went back to the run game and proved quite successful. The Dance County linemen continued to get pushed off the ball. Dante and his linebacker corps were making the tackles, but the positive yards continued the drive. Clayton tied the score with a three-yard run. The execution of the runs and with only one pass play brought no stoppage to the game clock. Clayton kicked the ball back to the Patriots with only six seconds left in the first quarter.

This time the Patriots found themselves in their own territory at the twenty-five. Two run plays and a short pass to Alexander failed to move the ball past the needed ten for a first down. Nate crouched low on the sideline. He pulled a handful of grass from the sideline and mashed it in his hands. He turned toward the sideline as he rose from the ground. "Punt team, Let's go!" he screamed.

The Clayton deep back caught the kick in stride and went untouched down the sideline for the quick touchdown and a thirteen to seven lead. The extra point followed and the Patriots were down by 7. The game clock read eight thirty-seven remaining in the first half. Disaster followed for the Patriot special teams when a long kickoff run was negated by a fumble in Clayton territory. The Clayton offense and their all region quarterback were suddenly back on the field. Nate found it somewhat amusing with such a big quarterback with a high-powered arm, there would be content with running the ball. The Dance County Defense was crowding the line and executing way more blitzes than Nate and his staff would ever be comfortable with. It made the night challenging for the Clayton offense. With just under seven minutes on the clock Clayton stared at a third and three.

Griffin and Parks barked orders for their defense. The film study said on third and short Clayton went with a sweep or short throw to the end. One of the targets went in motion from right to left on the bark from their quarterback. Dante Alexander had him in his sights and the Clayton QB dropped two steps back to pass. The throw was a perfect spiral and Dante hit him with everything as the receiver pulled it to his chest. He held on and Clayton had a fresh set of downs to work with.

The Patriot defense lost momentum and began to tire. The mammoth lineman up front continued to push the defense down the field. Clock was now evaporating before the sold-out crowd. Dan Green looked at it hard sensing the Patriots would not see the ball until the second half. With one-minute left before halftime, a toss sweep was called by Clayton from the seven. The back had the angle and the speed. He went untouched into the end zone for a 20 to 7 lead. Clayton's fans in the small bleachers on the other side of the field screamed with excitement. A couple of small kids could be heard talking under the stands. It was that quiet on the home side of the field.

Nate moved down the sideline. He grabbed Chris Ponder and

pulled him up close, face to facemask. "Line up at end, whatever it takes, get your hand on that damn ball when he kicks." Ponder affirmed the order with an up down motion of his helmet. He ran toward the huddle centered near the end-zone. The snap to the holder was poor. The ball dug into the dirt before the place holder could get a hand on it. Ponder raised his arm and pushed himself around a large end trying to hold him back. He ran toward the holder as the kicker approached the ball. He extended himself as if he was doing a belly flop into a neighborhood pool. The outstretched fingers were just enough to catch the tip of the ball and move it off course. The ball had no shot of splitting the post and the kick was no good.

Clayton tried to get revenge for the defensive play with the ensuing kick. In addition, they showed no respect for the tiring Patriot Defense. An onside kick went high in the air to the gasping sounds of the Patriot fans. Watters had coached the kids hard on the possibility at practice. Watters still burned from the embarrassment of the successful kick from Liberty. The skill hands players were on the line with a mix of receivers and deep backs. Chris Ponder had no problems with another standout play and cradled the ball on the Clayton thirty-seven.

Morgan had two maybe three plays at best with 41 seconds on the clock. Ponder and Quincy Davis were the deep threats and they headed toward the end zone for the first two. Ponder had a ball broken away by a Clayton defender. The second and ten-throw was well over the head of Quincy Davis. Nate didn't hesitate with the call of his next play. He ran a QB sneak with Morgan that caught the defense off guard. It was good for fifteen yards and brought new life into the stadium. A timeout was quickly called with two seconds left in the half.

"Kicking team!" Nate screamed. The line remained on the field. Kyle took his place at holder. Tray Goldman was the place kicker and was seventy-five percent from this distance. Ben Young got off a good snap, but Clayton had loaded the line with their skill people hoping to match the Patriots earlier performance. They were not successful, but neither was the kick. It missed the upright by inches on the left and the horn sounded. Some of the Patriots standing on the field looked at the ground and exuded defeat. 20-7 at half.

Nate and the coaches screamed for the players to hit the house. Nate screamed for a couple of players to get their heads up. He then looked into the stands for just a moment. He saw her sitting on the second row on the twenty-yard line. Nate broke coaching protocol and crossed the sideline benches and the track to get to the wall surrounding the home stands. He looked up at Mary Davis seated next to her daughter. "Mrs. Davis, would you join me for a moment during half time."

"Yes sir. Please, give me a minute to get down to the field."

CHAPTER 47

Nate was approached by a young man he did not recognize as he walked the locker room. "Coach Jackson, Clint Black, Patriot News Today."

Nate made the connection with the school paper and stops and allows the kid to catch up. They stood a few feet from the gate separating the field from the stands. A couple of dads lining the fence tried to eavesdrop and catch the interaction between the two.

"Coach, I have a couple of questions from the first half of play?" Nate waited for the question. "What does the team need to improve on to start the second half?"

Nate allowed a second for the junior reporter to move his iPhone up from his pocket to record the coach's words. "Clint, we have to make adjustments on our offensive and defensive lines. Clayton is controlling the line of scrimmage right now and is in control of this game."

Black moved his head up and down. He decided to push his luck with one more question. "Will you be making any personnel changes for the second half?"

Nate smiled and turned toward the locker room. "Not planning on it," he said.

He got to the locker room and walked inside. Many of the players huddled in the center of the room balancing their large bodies on one knee. Trainers moved between them with water bottles and sliced oranges. Kyle Morgan was closest to the door. His hair was matted in sweat despite the cold temperatures. Ben Young sat at a bench behind Morgan. He was taking in deep breaths. Nate sensed the anger and frustration in the room. He looked at each player throughout the cramped space then lowered his voice and said: "Gentlemen, when you get into the ring with a heavyweight, you are going to take some hits and sometimes you are going to get knocked down." He paused and continued. "We are in that battle now. We are in a heavyweight fight that is going to go the distance. We have been knocked down and the scorer's table is not in our favor. Now we will have to deliver a knock-out to get back in this thing. Let me make this clear we can win this thing. It will take everything in the tank, our absolute best effort. But I can assure you I have never been more confident in a group of players that can stand up to that challenge than the ones I am standing before tonight."

"Offense, we are going to a quick strike game plan. Defense, we are going to bring the house and force them to throw it deep if they want to move the ball. Get with your position coaches, we will circle back up in five minutes."

Watters and the assistants moved quickly with rectangular white boards detailing the changes. The players were engaged. Morgan asked for clarification on a route and Watters dug in with the black sharpie outlining the play. There was chemistry in the locker room and a sense of belief. Nate moved toward the door. He looked back at the team then walked over and cracked it. He looked at Mrs. Davis standing just outside. "One second," he said to her.

He turned around. "Gentlemen, may I have your attention. We have a very special guest that will be sharing a few words with you tonight. Please give her your undivided attention." Nate turned back around and held the door wide. Mrs. Davis entered the locker room. She moved toward the players with a confident look, a swagger that they had seen countless times in her late husband. A hush fell over the room. She had the undivided attention and then some of every player and every coach. Kyle Morgan looked at Mrs. Davis then shot a quick glance at Coach Nate. His impression of his new Coach had been high, now it just went through the stratosphere.

Mary Davis began to speak. Her voice was strong and easily carried through the locker room. With a big smile on her face she began to speak. "It is so good to see you boys. When Matt and I talked this summer about his feelings toward this team he told me simply, Mary, this group is special. He was so excited about this season. And when you have been doing something as long as Coach Davis, well, as all of you know, it takes a lot for him to get excited about."

She paused, looked across at Nate making sure she still had time to continue. His look and smile said take as much time as you need. "Coach Davis, Matt mentioned Clayton quite a bit. He would look at me over dinner and say how much this game worried him. He would say, 'Mary, they are going to bring kids that have the size to be playing in the NFL.'" She paused, chuckled at the memory, and continued.

"I always said to Matt, they may be big, but your team will be better prepared, and they will find a way." She paused again and realized the time to return to the field was nearing. "You have great coaches, you have worked hard, find a way tonight, and let's beat these guys like I told Matt in July you would."

The emotion hit hard when she mentioned her husband the last time. Her eyes misted. She swallowed and moved away from the locker room entrance to allow a pathway to exit. Coach Nate Jackson approached her. He gave her a big hug and thanked her for addressing the team. He turned toward his players. This time the voice was raised. "You heard Mrs. Davis, second half we find a way. Buckle up, Gentlemen and let's get out there and win this thing."

The players filed out of the locker room single file. Each player extended their hand to Mrs. Davis and she shook it warmly. When they exited the locker room they circled at the gate leading to the field. Kyle Morgan screamed, "Second half we find a way, Patriots on three!"

CHAPTER 48

The temperature had seemed to drop even more. Blankets of all shapes and colors were draped over the legs of most of the fans in the stands. The hot chocolate and coffee inventory that had been sold through halftime had been depleted. Everyone had made their way back to their seats when the second half kick sailed toward the Clayton deep backs.

They weren't ready. The ball sliced through the middle of the field and bounced and turned then rolled through the back of the end zone. Like a couple of stunned little leaguers watching a baseball roll toward the fence, the Clayton deep backs stared at each other eager to assign blame for the lack of movement on the other player. The Clayton coaches screamed for the offense. The two backs trotted back to the sideline. It was first and 10 for Clayton to start the half.

Dante Alexander led an invigorated defense to the line. Baker screamed the cadence. He was not ready to call an audible. The linebackers for the Patriots were crowding the line. It would not stop there. Their defensive backs were moving up dramatically. There would be no audible. A handoff to the first back running behind the right guard produced a negative gain. The defense popped to their feet after the whistle. Clayton brushed it off and returned for second and 11 after a quick offensive huddle. They went to the same back with the handoff and tried to work the left side. Alexander met him after a one-yard gain and drove him to the ground.

Coach Tillman pushed Coach Griffin for an all-out blitz on third and ten. Griffin agreed and threw in a surprise that caught everyone off guard. Dance Counties newest player, Quincy Davis, and star receiver Chris Ponder made their way on the field. Nate Jackson turned his attention from the field and looked briefly at the coaches' box with a devious smile. His Coaches were pulling out all the stops. It was the dealer showing a 5 in blackjack and the player doubling the bet.

Ponder took the right side and Davis the left. Davis still weighed a buck sixty at best. He came across the line untouched. He was a small kid again. Flashback ten years earlier and he was playing on an empty school lot with kids ranging in age from 6 to 20 without any equipment and any rules. Baker took the snap and was going to get it all back and then some with one throw. He looked at a lone receiver beating the defensive back by a solid stride down the near sideline. He cocked his arm ready to fire.

Quincy Davis had other plans. He left his feet in a perfect dive toward the massive QB. He knew he couldn't get him down with a high hit. He flew through the air arms extended with his shoulder pad aimed right below the knee. The force was too much and the big star QB was knocked helplessly to the ground.

There was new life on the Patriot sideline. Clayton's kick was field-ed at the thirty- five and advanced just short of mid field. Nate looked at this sideline. "Ponder and Davis, you are in." Morgan was already on the field. There were a lot of people in the stands including the of-fensive coordinator for the flagship university. The play came from the running back. Nate wasn't holding anything back, much like his defen-sive coaches. First and 10 and he wanted it all in one play.

Morgan took the snap and immediately trotted right toward the visitor sideline and the long side of the field. Ponder and Davis had lined up on the left. With the snap of the ball, both were now flying down the field exposing a secondary not in position. Ponder stayed the course and hugged the sideline making his way toward the end zone. Davis ran fifteen yards then cut across the middle of the field toward the visitor sideline in concert with Morgan. QB 1 loved the separation his newest offensive target was achieving on the Clayton defensive backs. He cut loose with a spiraled throw that flew effortless through the cold crisp air. Davis outstretched hands caught the ball on the Clayton twenty. He turned and ran untouched through the end zone. The extra point was good and the gap on the score board became smaller. Clayton 20 Dance County 14.

The teams exchanged three plays and out for the next possession. Clayton was still trying to find a way to move the ball on the ground. The only movement came with the game clock. Dante Alexander was continuing to encourage the players on and off the sideline. The third quarter suddenly ended, and the teams flipped the field. Clayton was back in Dance County territory with a first and ten from the Patriot 45. The alignment screamed pass all the way. The Clayton coaches fi-nally decided they were going to let loose with their D 1 QB prospect.

Baker took the snap and let go a perfect spiral that headed toward two players at the Patriot ten. One of the players was Chris Ponder. The coaches had left him in the game as a safety. He was stuck to the big Clayton receiver like Dan Green would later describe to a buddy at the Waffle Stop as "white on rice." Ponder easily made the catch for the interception. The momentum was turning. The high school reporter covering the game made a note on the play. He would later describe it as the wind seemed to die under the sail of the Clayton offense.

Kyle Morgan brought his team to the field. Nate knew they needed a good drive at least but a score would be a game changer. He told Morgan before he left the sideline that the plan was to throw it. Morgan lit up at the news of the strategy; the enthusiasm was evident when he addressed the players in the huddle.

Alexander, Ponder, and Davis were the targeted receivers. Ben Young looked up and down the line at his offensive lineman. Any success would start with his group. He told the guys to stay with their blocks and give Morgan time. The broke the huddle and lined up. This time it was Ponder that had the jump on his defensive back. He raced in a post route down the sideline. Morgan hit him just short of the fifty with a beautifully thrown pass that Ponder pulled in with zero adjustment to his speed. The afterburners were on and he beat the closest defender by three yards.

The stands erupted in cheers and screams. With the extra point Dance County led 21 to 20.

The train of momentum that the Patriots were on now would not be slowed. An average kick-off return had the Clayton team starting first and ten from the twenty-seven. The clock was moving and there was less than seven minutes left in the game.

Clayton's Baker tried a mix of short passes to the tight end on the first two plays. They were moderately successful with a short third and one needed for the first down. Decision time came again for the Clayton coaches. Do they continue to pound the ball and pick up the first down or do they turn it over to their highly touted quarterback and let him work his magic through the air?

The crowd roared. The college coaches in attendance had been through a long week themselves. They had not looked forward to a recruiting trip during their season. The pageantry of Friday night football had changed that. They were now taken back fifteen years ago and personal memories to the excitement and suspense of a couple of regional heavyweights trading punches in the ring.

Baker barked the signals. Alexander brought his linebackers up. His instinct told him of a possible QB sneak. Clayton had been getting a pretty good push off the nose guard. Baker tried to get the defense to jump with a long count. The Patriots remained frozen on the line. The clock was not in their favor and seemed to be moving with accelerated speed to the Clayton staff. Baker took the snap and dove right of his center. Alexander saw the footwork and met him at the line. Dante's form was textbook. He was under the pads and thrust his legs upward as if he was doing a squat in the weight room. The momentum picked up Baker's feet from the ground and allowed Dante to drive the big QB backwards. When it was over, the ball laid two feet behind the line of scrimmage. Fourth down.

The clock was under three minutes. Clayton called a timeout. The ball was just shy of their 35 -yard line. There was no turning back. Clayton had to go for it.

This time there was no QB keeper. Clayton did not try to pull the line off-sides. Baker took the snap and rolled to his right looking for his good-hands tight end. The receiver was four feet from the sideline and safely in first down territory. He looked at the QB awaiting the throw. It was perfect slapping him on his outstretched hands. He didn't pull it in. The receiver turned to get his precious yards after the catch. The split second was just enough to allow the ball to fall from his hands. It bounced innocently on the stadium turf. The crowd gasped then let out a collective roar.

Nate Jackson looked at the sky and smiled. He knew any shot at a victory tonight would require not only the absolute best effort from his team but also a gift. He just got it.

The offense took the field. The clock read 2:37 to go in the fourth quarter. Kyle Morgan was buckling the chin strap and had taken one step on to the field. Nate grabbed his arm. "Protect the football, after each play, you remind them, we have to hold on to the ball."

Morgan smiled. "Yes sir," he said.

The first play was a dive off tackle. It was good for four yard and ate ten seconds of clock before Clayton called timeout. The second play was a toss sweep, this time good for three yards and fifteen seconds. The final timeout came from the sideline. 2:12 on the clock and a third down and three. Nate crouched down. He pulled a large piece of turf from the ground and rubbed it in a ball. He looked at the clock, then the huddle. He grabbed Quincy Davis, called the play, and watched the receiver run toward the huddle.

The players were surprised with the call. They had only run the play a few times during Thursday's practice. It was not a customary play for the Patriots and the circumstances screamed risk outweighed the benefits. But Nate Jackson had proved he was not a Coach that played the customary or the recommended averages. He gritted his teeth and waited for the play.

Ponder was the wideout to the left and Davis was split wide to the right. Morgan barked a long cadence that sent Ponder in motion left to right. He was just short of Morgan when the ball slapped the QB's hands. Morgan turned and flipped it to Ponder who remained on course running toward the sideline.

The Clayton defense shifted and prepared to shut the play down with no gain. Quincy Davis, the new human rocket, had begun a slow trot toward the Patriot backfield. Ponder had the ball with Kyle Morgan cutting a path for him toward the right sidelined. The Clayton backers rushed in. When the first wave of defenders got close to Ponder he flipped the ball to Davis. The speed went from a trot to a sprint. There was plenty of green space along the opposite sideline. He carried the ball as tight as he had ever held one. He had heard the warnings. Knew Clayton would pull out all the stops. He was not dropping this football.

Of course, for him to drop it meant someone would have to hit him. And that was still a few yards off. Clayton had been caught off guard again. The momentum had swung, and it was affecting the defense. Ponder raced across the line of scrimmage. He wanted the firsdown but protection of the ball came first. He knew he needed to milk clock but a first down would take care of that as well. He had open space for ten yards. At the twenty- five a DB tripped him up with a nice open field tackle. The ball remained cradled in his arms. It was first and ten Dance County and barring a sudden offensive catastrophe, a tremendous upset and win for their newest head coach.

Kyle Morgan took the snap on three plays from Ben Young to roll the remaining seconds off the clock. The remaining players from the sideline rushed the field. The coaches had come down from above the press box. After the initial celebratory hugs and fist pumps, the players and coaches lined up to shake hands with the opponent.

"That was a fine job of coaching, young man," the Clayton head coach said to Nate as he squeezed his hand. "Welcome to the Region, we will see you next year."

Nate smiled. He was used to the tone from his time in South Georgia and responded with his usual phrase. "Thank you. Looking forward to it, Coach."

The players and coaches' attention was immediately diverted by two large explosions from the sky. A multitude of colors rained down well above the outstretched stadium lights. Commercial grade fireworks had lit up the sky. There was a second risk taken tonight, a gamble by local businessman Dan Green on a Patriot win. Jackson and Green were two for two in that department.

The players interacted with each other, students, and band members that were now on the field. Kyle Morgan was trotting toward the goal post when his name rang out. He turned to see Stephanie standing at the twenty-yard line. "You played great."

He stopped and looked at someone he had greatly missed. "Some us are heading over to Chilis, would you join us?"

Kyle didn't dwell on his response. "Sure, I'll be there."

The congratulatory handshakes for the new Coach continued. Principal Lee was the first and flashed a big smile when he got to Coach Nate. Dan Green was a couple of steps behind as trotted across the field to greet the Coach and staff. "So, my goal is to have you run up a big bill with the firework distributor for this area?"

Green looked at his Coach, impressed with the made connection, and said, "You don't worry about that, great job, Coach."

Ten minutes later the players and coaches were all circled under the goal post. There were smiles and laughter. It was a feeling that seemed so elusive only two weeks ago in the same stadium location.

Nate Jackson addressed the team. "Gentlemen, you did it. You found a way." He paused then continued. "I could hand out a game ball tonight, be justified handing out 50 of them, everyone on this team deserves one. Trust me, I think you know me well enough to know I don't reward participation, I reward accomplishment. Tonight, you all achieved. Tonight our coaches achieved and you as players achieved.

"You went up against one of the best teams in the Southeast US, and my apologies for my lack of political correctness, you whipped their ass."

The players chuckled at the colorful language. The coaches smiled. "You bust your tail in the unforsaken heat of July for this moment.

Take that extra rep in the weight room for this moment. Tonight, is your reward." He paused. They knew what was coming next. The great coaches always differentiate themselves.

"Enjoy it, Gentlemen, because Monday, we are buckled up and back on the practice field getting ready for Friday night."

CHAPTER 49

He had left the locker room about an hour after the clock horn had sounded. The assistants remained taking care of the post-game requirements. He apologized telling them that he had a personal matter he needed to take care of. There was no explanation needed. The assistants were ecstatic over the win and the positive attention victory had brought. Two weeks earlier had seen a whirlwind of emotion and grief following the loss to Liberty. All was now right in Dance County.

As he made his way to the door, Coach Watters' voice was heard behind him. "Hey, Coach, got a second?"

Nate turned around. "Absolutely, what can I do for you, Coach?" Watters stumbled with his words.

"What you did for me this week, the push, the encouragement. Thank you."

Nate put a hand on his shoulder. "Thank you, Coach, we will see you Monday."

The parking lot was almost empty. Much like it was when he pulled in during the predawn hours. He turned the ignition and made the decision to drive to the little white church he had stepped in only 17 hours earlier. This time he got out of his truck but stopped in front of his vehicle. He looked at the steeple reaching high into the air. He took a deep breath and slowly exhaled. He went to his knees in the dewy grass. He placed his elbows on his truck bumper and thanked God again for the day's events. He prayed for Mary Davis, and the families of Davis and Parks. He prayed for his teams both in Dance County and Savannah. He asked God for strength in the days ahead. He knew with what went through his mind each day it would never get easier. He thought about Stacy. The restaurant was just a few miles away.

He rose to his feet and took one last look at the steeple and climbed back into his truck.

The restaurant parking lot was overflowing with cars and people. Nate shook his head. He suddenly craved a BLT from the Waffle Stop.

It would be easier taking up a booth with Dan Green. He was running in his mind and knew that was never a good place to be. He circled the truck twice. An elderly couple in a Honda backed out of a space and he took it. He turned off the ignition and looked at the rear- view mirror.

His face was clean. He ditched the hat and looked at his hair. He smiled making sure his teeth also passed inspection. "Well this is about as good as it gets," he mumbled to himself.

He walked toward the door. Students milling around near the entrance suddenly recognized him. One said, "Great game, Coach."

He looked at the group. "Thank you, the team appreciated all of your support tonight."

He was now at the entrance. His heart suddenly raced. He scanned the glass windows from the outside. William Alexander was easy to find. His large muscular frame seemed to take up a lot of space in a six-person booth. Sitting beside him was Pam. Nate froze. He took a breath and looked across their table.

Stacy's dark hair fell to her shoulders. Her smile was white and radiant. She was laughing, having a great time. Nate could not believe all of this was now happening. She was more beautiful than the memory he played out in his mind from San Francisco. He shook his head, smiled to himself, telling the anxiety and nervousness he was feeling to hit the road as he was done with it.

He moved toward the door, pulled the heavy glass toward him and walked into the restaurant.

OTHER ANAPHORA LITERARY PRESS TITLES

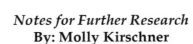

The History of British and American Author-Publishers
By: Anna Faktorovich

Notes for Further Research
By: Molly Kirschner

The Encyclopedic Philosophy of Michel Serres
By: Keith Moser

The Visit
By: Michael G. Casey

How to Be Happy
By: C. J. Jos

A Dying Breed
By: Scott Duff

Love in the Cretaceous
By: Howard W. Robertson

The Second of Seven
By: Jeremie Guy